LESLIE

A Novel by

GARY ROHR

Leslie
Copyright © 2022 by Gary Rohr

Disclaimer

Some sections of this work are erotic in nature. If you are a minor (in the US, this means if you are under eighteen (18) years of age; other countries may enforce their own definitions of "minor"), or if pornographic content is offensive, do not continue. The opinions expressed in this publication are those of the authors. They do not purport to reflect the opinions or views of BluePrint Press, its members, or its affiliates. The presentation of material therein does not imply the expression of any opinion whatsoever on the part of BluePrint Press.

ISBN
978-1-957895-95-6 (Hardcover)
978-1-957895-96-3 (Paperback)
978-1-957895-97-0 (eBook)

Dedication

*I dedicate this book to the women who will always
hold a special place in my heart. In the order they
appeared in my life, I would like to thank Nancy, Leslie,
Debbie, and Patty for all they have given me.*

Preface

This is a story based on real events in my life. The facts are as I remember them. This does not necessarily make them true or accurate. Other people may remember these events differently. That does not make their memories more right or wrong. Time has a funny way of distorting our perceptions concerning past events. I feel the story is a good one, which needed to be told. I hope you enjoy reading about it as much as I enjoyed living it.

Acknowledgements

Precious And Few
Words and Music by Walter D. Nims
Copyright ©1970, 1972 (Renewed 1998, 2000) by Famous Music
Corporation and Emerald City Music
All Rights for the World Controlled and Administered by Famous
Music Corporation
International Copyright Secured All Rights Reserved

How Can I Tell Her
Words and Music by Kent Lavoie
Copyright ©1973 (Renewed 2001) by Famous Music Corporation
International Copyright Secured All Rights Reserved

I'LL BE AROUND (Whenever You Want Me)
by Thomas Bell and Philip Hurtt
© 1973 (Renewed) Warner-Tamerlane Publishing Corp.
All Rights Reserved   Used by Permission
WARNER BROS. PUBLICATIONS U.S. INC., Miami, FL. 33014

WHEN WILL I SEE YOU AGAIN
by Kenneth Gamble and Leon Huff
© 1974 Warner-Tamerlane Publishing Corp.
All Rights Reserved   Used by Permission
WARNER BROS. PUBLICATIONS U.S. INC., Miami, FL. 33014

Table of Contents

Dedication iii

Preface iv

Acknowledgements...v

Chapter 1   Love At First Sight 1

Chapter 2   Lunch With Leslie 6

Chapter 3   Best Friends 9

Chapter 4   Nancy 12

Chapter 5   The Kiss 25

Chapter 6   Reconciliation 29

Chapter 7   Unbridled Passion 32

Chapter 8   Our First Time 35

Chapter 9   Moving On 37

Chapter 10   Still Friends 41

Chapter 11   Debbie 43

Chapter 12   First Contact... 46

Chapter 13   Gone, Not Forgotten 51

Chapter 14   The Wedding..56

Chapter 15   Christmas 1975.......................................61

Chapter 16   Leslie's First Letter 63

Chapter 17   Early Marital Problems 69

Chapter 18   Good Times..72

Chapter 19   Leslie's Second Letter 75

Chapter 20 Having Fun 79

Chapter 21 Leslie's Third Letter 82

Chapter 22 Home Sweet Home 86

Chapter 23 The Phone Call... 90

Chapter 24 Worth The Wait 92

Chapter 25 Too Late To Turn Back 97

Chapter 26 Swing Shift 107

Chapter 27 Still On Days 119

Chapter 28 Marriage Vows 126

Chapter 29 Pregnant? 130

Chapter 30 The Journal 132

Chapter 31 Love Is Blind.. 142

Chapter 32 Our Anniversary...156

Chapter 33 Sleep Over 162

Chapter 34 The Water Pump 175

Chapter 35 Debbie Suspects 180

Chapter 36 Vacation... 190

Chapter 37 For All Eternity... 200

Chapter 38 Lost Ring Found 203

Chapter 39 Out Damn Spot.. 207

Chapter 40 Playboy 211

Chapter 41 Daring Rendezvous....................................217

Chapter 42 Kiss You All Over 222

Chapter 43 Shit Hits The Fan 233

Chapter 44 Now What? 243

Chapter 45 Patty...253

Chapter 46 When Will I See You Again?....................... 270

Chapter 1

LOVE AT FIRST SIGHT

I'm no longer sure exactly when it was, but as they say in "Star Wars," it was long, long ago and far, far away. I was working the graveyard shift in Toledo, Ohio. I had arrived for work early so I could relax in the break room before my shift started. That was when I first saw her.

What first caught my eye was her face. She was exquisite. Perfect in every way. Her long blackish brown hair flowed down her smooth white neck over her shoulders and rested on ample mounds bursting forth from her tight pink sweater. I felt myself staring, but I couldn't help it. I have never believed in love at first sight, but the throbbing in my chest told me I might have been wrong. I guessed her to be five foot four and weigh a hundred and five.

I was having trouble tearing my gaze away from her face, but I desperately wanted to check out the rest of her. She was wearing pink slacks that matched her sweater and showed every curve. Women wearing dresses or skirts have always been my preference but it was hard to find fault with the way the fabric caressed her lovely derriere.

I knew in an instant that this was the vision I had carried with me my whole life. The vision of the perfect woman. I had to know who this woman was. Was she a new employee? A visitor?

I first saw her just 30 seconds ago, and I already panicked that I would never see her again. I wished that I could walk up to her and introduce myself, but I knew that was impossible. I have tried that in the past with girls that were not half as attractive as her, and the words wouldn't leave my throat. I would speak, but nothing would come out. No, that wouldn't do. There had to be a better way.

I asked various persons and found she was a new employee in the keypunch department, but nobody knew any more. I was a friend to a few of the ladies in the keypunch department, so I decided to inquire about her on my break.

However, before my break, the new woman was brought around and introduced to everyone. Her name was Leslie. I had never known a Leslie, and I had never seen a woman as attractive as her before.

Through the years, I have noticed that people with the same name tend to have similar traits. It is as though a person shapes themselves around their name. Learning what a Leslie was like was something I wanted very much.

Her eyes were the same color as mine. People say my eyes are blue, but they are a mixture of blue, green, and gray. The makeup around her eyes was perfect, creating a contrast that made them sparkle.

I was terrible at remembering names, but this was one name I wanted to remember. I repeated her name in my head: Leslie, Leslie, Leslie. The name had a sweet ring to it, like chapel bells. My mind raced. I visualized Leslie and me in a chapel, getting married. I wanted this woman. Suddenly, something brought me to my senses. Did somebody say something? I looked around. Everyone stared at me. How long had I been daydreaming? I have no idea.

I quickly faked a cough, cleared my throat, mumbled something like, "Nice meeting you," and went back to my desk. As she walked away, I checked her left hand. A small diamond glistened on her ring finger.

I was trembling. Life is so unfair. The woman I had waited for my whole life was married. I collapsed into a nearby chair, as my knees became too wobbly to support me. Logic was fighting for control. My emotions were running away with me, and I couldn't allow that. Maybe she wasn't married yet. I had noticed only the diamond. Maybe she was only engaged. Or maybe she was in an unhappy marriage. I had to learn more about her.

As the weeks went by, one thing was evident. There was a lot of jealousy in the keypunch department. When the department went on break, guys would come in and join the women. While the guys used to spend time with certain ladies, now they all swarmed to Leslie. I knew I couldn't compete, so I didn't even try. The other women started treating Leslie as though she had leprosy, and they made it clear that she was no longer welcome at breaks. Attractive women are often unpopular with women who are not as pretty.

When she followed them anyway, they would ignore her, and make her feel unwanted. As a result, she would frequently stop by my department for visits, seeking a companion to spend time with. Unfortunately, it wasn't me she sought out. No, Dave was the lucky guy.

Dave was about 6'2" tall, blond hair, dark blue eyes, athletically built, and unquestionably a lady's man. I couldn't fault her taste. He was an attractive guy, and really nice, too. Dave and I had first met at work a few years ago, and grew to be pretty good friends.

We also did a lot of things together when we were away from work. We both had motorcycles and frequently rode together. I had been to his parents' house to go swimming once or twice. I visited him in the hospital after he was injured playing baseball. And, I had attended his wedding.

Dave introduced me to professional football. He was originally from Pittsburgh and loved the Pittsburgh Steelers. After watching this scrappy team play, I became a Pittsburgh Steelers fan for life.

Like me, Dave started in the mailroom. I liked Dave a lot, and helped him learn the ropes, so he could progress quickly through the ranks. Dave was a great guy, and I was happy for both him and Leslie. I truly loved Leslie, and I wanted her to be happy, even if it was with somebody else.

Dave and Leslie began spending more and more time together. It wasn't long before they were spending every break and lunch together. It was through Dave that I first learned about Leslie.

She was my age, she was married, and she had two sons. Her husband, Joe, was abusive, and sometimes hit her. She genuinely enjoyed the time she spent with Dave, and it appeared as though they were falling in love.

At least it would look that way to the casual observer. However, I was privy to inside information.

Dave often confided in me, and told me how close he was to "getting lucky." As the months wore on, they appeared to be having trouble keeping their hands off one another. I frequently saw them touching each other at work when they thought nobody was watching.

Dave let me know that he was finally going to get what he wanted, sex with Leslie, but they couldn't find a safe place to do it. I offered them my apartment. We all got off work at 8:00 am, and I usually went out to play tennis, or stop at a bar, before heading home. I told him they could have two hours every morning to do whatever they wanted. They grabbed the opportunity to be alone together.

Every weekday morning, I would arrive home to the smell of Leslie. God, I loved her. I imagined what it would be like if she loved me, the way she loved Dave. I would frequently fall asleep crying - praying that someday Leslie would be mine.

This went on for months. I might not be able to have Leslie, but she somehow felt a lot closer, with her sweet smell in my apartment.

One day Dave came up to me all panicky. Leslie had told him that she was going to get a divorce so they could get married. He said he was already "happily" married, and didn't want her to get a divorce. He just wanted to get what he could, when he could. I guess I was naive, as I hadn't expected this.

I asked if he had told Leslie, and he said he had. He had broken off their whirlwind romance. Later, on break, Leslie came over to talk with Dave, but he brushed her off. He told her in no uncertain terms that he didn't want to have anything more to do with her. She collapsed into a nearby chair, sobbing.

For about a week, Leslie would come over to our department on every break. Obviously, she wanted to talk with Dave, but he would quickly disappear whenever she showed up. I watched as the days took their toll. Leslie was crumbling before my eyes, and it was tearing me apart.

I felt she needed someone to talk to, but she had nobody. The women in keypunch thought she got what she deserved. All of the guys that used to flock around her now avoided her, because she had chosen someone other than them to be with. And she certainly couldn't discuss it with her husband.

I felt like crying myself. Here was the woman I loved, crushed. I wanted to take her in my arms and comfort her, tell her everything was going to be OK. My heart ached for her. I could feel tears forming in my eyes. I didn't know what I should do, but I felt I had to do something for the woman I loved so much. I walked up to her and said softly, "I'm a friend to whoever needs one." She glanced up to see who was there, and tried to smile.

"Thank you," she said, "but I'd like to be alone."

I started to say something else, but changed my mind, turned and walked away.

Leslie quit coming over to our department after that, and I didn't see her for several weeks.

Then one day, out of the blue, she came over and said, "I need someone to talk to. Will you have lunch with me?"

WOULD I? WOW!!!!!!

"Sure," was all I managed say.

"See you at four," she said as she turned and headed back to her department.

I stared after her, my heart starting to pound in my chest.

Chapter 2

LUNCH WITH LESLIE

It was after four o'clock and I was a nervous wreck. Had I imagined the whole thing? Did she decide she didn't want to go to lunch with me? Had she forgotten we made plans, and left without me? Should I go looking for her? Probably not, since appearing too eager may scare her off. It was now four-ten, and Leslie hadn't shown up yet. Was she waiting somewhere for me? I was scared. This was my big opportunity, and I didn't want to blow it. I decided to peek into the keypunch department, to see if Leslie was still there. The women were just getting up from their keypunch machines for lunch break. I rushed back to my desk and pretended to be working hard. Leslie breezed through the door, and started walking toward my desk. I pretended not to notice, although I was sure she could hear my heart pounding in my chest. Every beat sounded like sledgehammers to my ears.

I was somewhat surprised that I could actually hear Leslie when she asked, "Are you ready?"

"Am I ready?" I thought, "Hell, yes, I'm ready. I've prayed that we'd be alone together since the day I first saw you."

"Just let me grab my coat," was what I told her.

###

I don't know what I expected, but whatever it was, this wasn't it. I thought I would learn more about Leslie. About how she felt, but all she talked about was Dave. Leslie would say, "Dave this" and "Dave that." I wanted to say, yes, I know Dave is a jerk, but she still had feelings for him and I didn't want to risk upsetting her. She told me all about their affair. I had to pretend that everything she told me was news to me. I knew most of it, but Dave had left out a few details. I gazed deep into her beautiful eyes, and hung on every word. Her luscious lips tempted me. Her fragrance filled my senses. I was with the woman I longed for, and I couldn't let her know.

I had been dumped before, several times in fact. The first time I groveled, begged, and pleaded for the relationship to continue, but it ended anyway and I felt like a jackass for having embarrassed myself. All I have is my pride, and I won't sacrifice it so quickly in the future. After being dumped the first time, I came to realize that if you truly love a woman, you'd let her have what she wants, even though it hurts terribly.

Leslie was obviously not used to getting dumped. At the time, I assumed it was because she usually did the dumping, but I would find out later that I was wrong. Anyway, I tried to give her the benefit of my experience. Make sure she saw the positive side - like having lunch with me. I said that jokingly, but I was dead serious. I was better for her than Dave ever could be. I would love her for all eternity, but I couldn't let her know. If I told her I loved her, she wouldn't believe me. She would think I was just like Dave. That all I was after was sex, and I didn't ever want her to think that.

It seemed as though our lunch had just started, when she said, "We better be heading back."

I glanced at my watch and saw we had been gone nearly an hour. I couldn't believe how quickly the time had passed. I looked at my plate. I hadn't eaten a bite. I had been too busy listening to Leslie. Oh well, I wasn't that hungry anyway. Something about your stomach doing flip-flops that causes you to lose your appetite.

She asked, "You want to take that with you?"

I replied, "No, I guess I wasn't all that hungry."

Which was a lie. I was starved, but it wasn't food that I wanted - it was Leslie. I didn't know how to describe the feeling at the time, but a song released years later said it perfectly: I had "Hungry Eyes."

Leslie had driven us to the restaurant. The drive there was quiet, with neither of us knowing exactly what to say. The drive back; however, was quite different. We chatted the whole time, which is very unusual for me. I'm normally a very quiet, and shy, person. I longed to hear her voice, so I kept her talking. I was quickly becoming more comfortable with her than I think I've ever been around any other woman. It felt as though she was becoming more relaxed around me, too. She even laughed at some of my dumb jokes. Hearing her laugh was infinitely more pleasurable than hearing her sob. If I have my way, she will never be sad again.

When we got back to work, she said, "Thank you. I had a really nice time."

I replied, "Me, too. I hope we can do it again."

"Tomorrow?" she asked.

"Sounds great."

And so, it started...

Chapter 3

BEST FRIENDS

We continued going out to lunch together. It may just be wishful thinking, but I was starting to think she enjoyed being with me, as much as I loved being with her. After a few weeks, I began to realize how important her friendship was to me. Sure, I loved her, and wanted to make love to her, but I didn't want to risk losing her friendship, so I realized that we could never be more than just friends. And that was fine. I figure that everybody has a "dream person." The perfect soul mate they spend their whole life searching for and never find. I figured, what the heck, I was further along than most people were. I may not be able to spend the rest of my life with Leslie, and make love to her, but at least she was no longer just a dream. I knew who, and where, she was - and I was able to spend some time with her, nearly every day.

When we were apart, I spent every minute wishing I could be with her. I dreamt of holding her in my arms, tasting her sweet lips, and feeling the fire in her body. But when we were together, just being with her was enough. We were very good friends, nothing more, and nothing would ever change that.

The time we spent together continued to grow. We were soon worse than she and Dave ever were. We found time to be together before work, we spent our breaks together, we lunched together, and we got together after work. I found out her house was only a few blocks from my apartment, easily within walking distance. Leslie suggested that we carpool to work. Her husband didn't think much of the idea, but they only had one car, so when he worked second shift, she needed a way into work. Every night I stopped by her house and picked her up.

Some nights, when I knew she was going to be home alone, I stopped by her house early, so we could spend more time together. Some nights we just sat and talked, other nights we watched programs on TV. At least I pretended to be watching TV while I was actually watching her. As it got later, she excused herself, so she could get ready for work. I often watched her, after she had changed clothes, and was putting on her makeup. The transformation transfixed me. In my eyes, she went from a beauty to a Goddess. She left me absolutely breathless. Painful thoughts sometimes snuck into my head. Thoughts of her loving me, and us being together forever. Thoughts of things that could never be. One night, as I was watching Leslie apply her makeup, and I was having one of these depressing thoughts, she cheered me up by asking, "Like what you see?"

Without thinking, I replied, "Oh, yeah."

It was an innocent question, and an honest answer. At least that was what I thought at the time. However, on our way to work that night, I was hoping there was more to her words. Did Leslie want me to like what I saw? Was she interested in looking her best, to please me? Did she want to become more than just best friends? My heart raced, as I thought about the possibilities. My heart was once again pounding in my chest, and I was getting butterflies in my stomach. I wanted her so badly. Did she want me, too?

Suddenly, I realized we were already at work, and pulling into the parking lot. I was so preoccupied with my thoughts; I didn't even remember the drive.

"You were kind of quiet tonight. Is everything OK?" Leslie wondered.

I longed to tell her my thoughts, my hopes, my dreams - but I knew I couldn't. I didn't like lying to her, but I couldn't tell her the truth.

I replied, "I'm sorry. No, everything is OK. I have a problem at work, and I've been trying to think of ways to resolve it. I promise I'll be better company on break."

And I was. Being away from her for a while allowed me time to collect my thoughts, and think things out logically. Logic told me that if she meant anything by her words, I would find out eventually. Until that time, things had to remain as they were. I'm her friend, and she is the woman I long for.

As time went on, you would have to say we had become almost inseparable. We knew we weren't doing anything wrong, so we really didn't care whether or not anybody saw us together. If her husband had their car, and she had an errand to run during the day, I was only too happy to take her.

I took her to my parents' house one time, and she met my mother. That could have been considered a mistake. Right away, my mother noticed that she was a married woman. I think she was polite to Leslie, but she sure let me have it later. I had no business being alone with a married woman.

I shot back some snide remark, then turned around and walked out of the house.

I suspected my mother was beginning to think I had a thing for married women. Leslie was the second one I had brought to her house. Nancy was the first.

Chapter 4

NANCY

A few years before I had first seen Leslie, I was working the four to midnight shift. After work, I'd stop in at the cocktail lounge of a bowling alley that was nearby. I sat at the bar, so I could be close to Tina, the barmaid. She was a babe - about 5'6" and 115 lb. She had long brown hair that went clear to her tiny waist. Her tiny waist made her breasts and hips appear larger than they actually were, giving her that hourglass figure most women dream of having. She always wore teeny, tiny hot pants with stockings and stiletto heels. I was a regular there, and she knew me by name. I'd leave her good size tips, and she frequently treated me to free drinks. One night, I had my camera in there, and took some pictures of her. From what I could see of Tina, she probably could have been in Playboy if she had wanted to.

One night after work, I was heading to the lounge as I normally did, when a few friends decided to join me. There were too many of us to sit at the bar, so we grabbed a table. A pretty cocktail waitress, whom I had never seen before, came up and took our drink order. While she was gone, we were normal guys, and talked about how hot she was.

She was really short, maybe 5'2" tall and a little on the heavy side. The sturdy frame was required to support her ample bosom. I guessed that she was a 38-D, or larger. She wasn't fat by any stretch of the imagination. You could just tell she was "all natural," and the rest of her body had to support the weight. Her plunging neckline revealed a lot of cleavage, and she sported high heels that showed off her curvy, well developed, leg muscles.

She came back with our drinks, and while she was setting them down, I asked, "What's your name?"

She replied, "Nancy."

I'm terrible with names, but that shouldn't be too difficult to remember, since it was my sister's name.

She finished delivering the drinks, and then asked, "Would you like anything else?"

The words were out of my mouth before I knew it.

"Just your phone number," I said.

My request caused laughter to erupt around the table. Nancy smiled and walked away. A few minutes later, she came back and set a small folded piece of paper in front of me.

"What's this?" I asked as I picked it up and unfolded it.

"My phone number," she answered, and then inquired, "Now what are you going to do with it?"

Duh!!

"I'm going to call and ask you out."

"OK," she said as she walked away.

"OK," I'm thinking, "this has got to be a joke."

Out loud, I said, "Must be dial-a-prayer," which got a good laugh.

I walked out of the lounge, to a pay phone, and called the number. It rang, and rang, and rang - no answer. Not dial-a-prayer? Not a joke? Come on. This has got to be a joke. This kind of thing only happens in the movies.

I went back into the lounge, and sat down with my friends. They were all looking at me. Waiting to hear what I had to say.

"I think it's really her number."

This elicited a whole lot of congratulatory comments and offers of free drinks, which I accepted.

We stayed almost until the 2:00 a.m. closing time and then got up to leave. I glanced at Nancy, and saw her watching us leave.

I held the note up so she could see it, and said, "I'll call you tomorrow."

She just smiled back at me.

The next day, a few hours before I had to leave for work, I tried calling Nancy. I don't think I had ever heard "Hello" sound so sexy. Her voice was very deep - very sexy. I guess I hadn't noticed that last night, since she had to speak really loudly to be heard in the lounge.

"Nancy?" I inquired.

"Yes," she said in a cautionary tone.

"It's Gary; you gave me your phone number last night. I said I'd call you today, so I'm calling you."

"I remember."

"I was wondering if you were free Saturday night. I thought maybe we could go out to dinner, and perhaps a movie."

"What time?"

"Five O'clock?"

"Can we make it six?"

"Six is fine."

"Then it's a date."

"Are you working tonight?"

"Yes."

"Good, then I'll stop by after work, and you can give me directions to your place."

# # #

I stopped by the lounge after work. I was alone, so I sat at the bar.

Tina came up to me and said, "I hear you have a date."

News sure travels fast.

"Appears so," I said, as I glanced in Nancy's direction.

Nancy looked even better than I remembered. She's a very attractive woman. Any guy would be happy to have her at his side.

"What would you like?" Tina asked.

I grinned.

"To drink."

"I'll have my usual."

My usual was Chivas on the rocks.

Tina brought my drink. I took a sip, then walked over to the Juke Box. I plunked in some quarters, selected a few romantic songs, and then went back to my drink.

Tina came up and asked, "Do you know where you're taking her, yet?"

"No, not really, kind of depends on what she likes. I was thinking of maybe The Surf."

"I hear that's good."

"It is."

While we were talking, Nancy slid into the seat next to me. She crossed her lovely legs, hiking her skirt up almost to her panties. I longed to look, but wanted to be a gentleman.

She leaned close to me, and whispered, "Here are directions to my house."

Damn she smells good. I wonder what she's wearing. Suddenly, I realized, here I am with two beautiful women - and I'm the only guy they're paying any attention to. One of them practically has her cleavage in my lap, and her perfume is intoxicating. Then there was the fact that I was now on my second drink.

Anyway, I could feel a stirring between my thighs as I started to grow. My underwear was starting to cut into me and I had to grab at my crotch to straighten things out. Neither Tina nor Nancy seemed to notice. I suppose they're used to having that effect on men. I didn't want to dwell on what it might be like to make love to Nancy so I tried thinking about our date.

"Do you have any place special you'd like to go Saturday night?" I asked Nancy.

"No," she said.

"Will The Surf be, OK?" I asked.

She said, "That sounds good."

"Well, I better get going," I told Nancy, "I'll see you Saturday, at six."

Saturday was only two days away, but it seemed like it took forever to get here. I was a nervous wreck, all day Saturday. I had never been out with such a beautiful woman before, and I wanted to make sure I made a good impression. I was still living at home with my parents, and was only about ten minutes away from Nancy's place. I wished she had lived farther away, so I could be on my way to see her, rather than just pacing the floor.

Finally, it was time to go. I had no trouble finding her house. It was a cute little split-level. I'd taken four years of architectural drawing in high school, and this had always been my favorite style home. Not quite a ranch style, and not quite a two story, but the best features of both.

I nervously walked up to the door, and rang the bell. A few seconds later, Nancy answered the door. Oh my God!! She's incredibly gorgeous. It may be a cliché, but I think my heart actually skipped a beat.

"You look great!", I said.

She was wearing a low-cut black dress with spaghetti straps and a slit up the side that went high enough so you could tell she had nothing on underneath.

"Thank you."

"Are you ready to go?"

"I am."

We walked out to my car and I opened the passenger door, to let her in. Her slit parted as she sat down and I was treated to a delightful view. Nice! I walked around to the driver's side and got in. I started the car and we were off.

One thing was obvious to me, as I glanced at this incredibly gorgeous woman. She belonged in a much classier car than my 1971 Ford Pinto. This was the first chance I had to learn anything about Nancy, and I was eager to know everything about her.

Nancy was 28 years old - I was 22. She was married, but legally separated. Her husband was a policeman, which meant he had a gun, or two. I hoped he wasn't the jealous type. I was thankful that I had a few guns of my own, and was a pretty good with them. She had one son. She liked to drink scotch on the rocks, and she enjoyed playing chess. Her cup size was 40-DD. She had gone shooting with her husband and considered herself a pretty fair shot. She liked being a cocktail waitress, because she got very good tips, and enjoyed the attention.

Dinner was nice, but I thought it should feel more romantic than it did, considering how gorgeous my date was. We hadn't decided if we should see a movie, so we drove past Showcase Cinema to see what was playing. Nothing sounded of particular interest to either of us, so we headed back to her house.

Nancy fixed us both a scotch, then we sat down on her sofa to cuddle and talk. She moved fast. I mean, if I was interested in having sex with her, I might have been able to. As it was, she cuddled close, resting her head on my chest, and her hand resting on my thigh. She smelled great, and I could feel the desire pulsing through my groin. I held her close and kissed her inviting lips. She was the first woman I had kissed like that, so I thought her kisses were exquisite. I was getting dizzy, and didn't know if it was the drinks, or the passion taking control. I don't know if I was falling, or she was pushing, but I slid from a vertical, to a horizontal position.

I was getting hard now. Nancy was lying on top of me, smothering me with warm wet kisses. I thought I was falling in love with her. She started unbuttoning my shirt, and all I could think of was making love to her.

A voice in the back of my head screamed, "This is going much too fast."

I tried to ignore the voice, but it wouldn't go away.

I struggled to get up from under her weight. I think that surprised her. I know it did me. She let me up, and I sat there trembling. My breathing was strained. Not quite gasping, but definitely labored. I had never been so close to making love to a woman before. I felt weak, and my groin ached. My hands were shaking, and I had no idea what I was feeling.

"I'm not feeling very well," I told Nancy, "I think I better go home."

Before I left, I asked, "Could I see you again?"

"I'd like that," was her reply.

On the way home, I couldn't decide if walking away from what may have been my first sexual experience was a smart thing or a really dumb thing, but I was leaning toward the really dumb. I had only known Nancy a very short time, but I thought I was falling for her. She caused stirrings within me, like no other woman I had ever known. Not that I've known very many women. In fact, compared to Nancy, I guess you would have to call every other female that I've gone out with, a girl. No, Nancy couldn't be confused with a girl – she was all woman.

I got home and went promptly to bed. I was completely drained. As I lay in bed, I realized that Nancy's scent was all over me. I had to find out what that fragrance is. I fell asleep remembering how good it felt to have her lying on top of me, smothering me with her warm wet kisses.

I awoke in the morning to find myself wet and hard with images of Nancy spinning through my head. I longed to be with Nancy and hold her in my arms. I wanted to call Nancy. I wanted to hear her deep sexy voice. I knew if Nancy wanted me to make love to her, I wouldn't be able to resist a second time.

I reasoned, if she went to bed when I did, she should be up by now. Would she like it that I awoke thinking of her, and had to hear her voice first thing in the morning, or would she be upset? Sure, would be nice if I could read minds.

I've never had very good luck with letting females know that I care. They seem to prefer a challenge, so I decided to wait before I called her. I couldn't decide how long to wait, though. Hours? Days? It was hard to decide. By late afternoon, I couldn't wait any longer. I was dying to smell Nancy, to hold her in my arms again, and to taste her sweet lips. At the very least, I had to hear her voice. Finally, I broke down and called her.

"I'd like to see you again," I told her, "Would you like to go out later, for a bite to eat?"

She said, "Sure."

We decided where we were going to eat and I left the house to pick her up. After we had eaten, we drove past my house, actually my parents' house, so I could show her where I lived.

As we drove past, I saw that nobody was home, and asked, "Would you like to see my room?"

"I would," she said.

We pulled in the drive, entered the house, and went up to my bedroom. I turned on the TV, then we sat down to watch it, on the only place there was to sit in my bedroom – the bed.

I don't even know what happened. One minute we were watching TV, the next we were in each other's arms, and our lips were firmly locked together. Nancy was stroking me between the legs, and I was getting very excited. I had no experience in this area, so I just followed her lead.

My hand reached under her skirt, and I started massaging between her legs. I could tell she was wearing pantyhose, and nothing else. As I stroked her, I could feel her getting wet. Within a short time, she couldn't take it anymore, and ripped a hole in her pantyhose, to give me free access to her womanhood.

I'd never been this far with a woman, with any female, before – but I could tell she was ready for me. She wanted me. She had quit stroking me, and was undoing my slacks. Meanwhile, I was undoing her blouse. Her ample bosom looked magnificent. I was sure many women were very jealous of how well she was built.

My face was buried in her cleavage, when she reached up and freed one beautiful breast. She guided my mouth to her hard nipple. I gently licked it, then took it into my mouth and sucked hard. It must have something to do with being breast-fed as a baby because this seemed so good, so natural.

Nancy had quit undoing my slacks and was firmly holding my head to her breast. It must have felt as good to her, as it did to me. My head was spinning. I was dizzy, and totally under her control. I loved this woman. I wanted her so bad.

I managed to get my hand back between her thighs, and as I worked her, she released her grip on my head, and sunk back onto my pillow. My mouth sought out hers, and she parted her legs, to allow me in. While mostly undone, my slacks were still in place. I mounted her, and started rubbing our crotches together.

I was on the verge of having an orgasm, when she asked, "Are you still a virgin?"

I thought I was doing a pretty good job of pleasing her, but I admitted, "Yes, I'm still a virgin."

"We'll have to take care of that," Nancy said.

"Obviously not tonight," I thought, as I heard my parents' car pull into the driveway.

We fastened ourselves back up and then went downstairs so I could introduce my new love, to my parents. They weren't pleased that I had a woman in my room. I don't remember how badly they tried to embarrass me that night, but I do know I hustled Nancy out the door, and took her home.

"I'm sorry for the way my parents acted," I told her.

Thankfully, she said, "There's no need to apologize for your parents, they're just concerned about you."

At her house, she fixed me a scotch, and we played a game of chess, which I won. After I thought my parents were asleep, I headed home. No such luck. They were waiting up for me. They yelled, screamed, and called me names. When they started calling Nancy names, I drew the line. I wouldn't allow that. Now they were talking about the woman I loved.

The woman I loved. This brought it home to me. I had fallen in love with Nancy. Next step is to marry her, so I won't lose her. It was starting to get hard to imagine a life without Nancy. I wanted her so bad.

My dad argued that she wasn't the type you married; she was the type he would have an affair with. I told him I thought he was stupid. If you marry her, you wouldn't need to have an affair. Yes, Nancy could get a man to cheat on his wife. I was sure Nancy could get many men to do lots of things. I could hardly wait until she made me make love to her.

I called Nancy and made plans for the following weekend. Naturally, I managed to see her nearly every day, at the cocktail lounge. Saturday finally arrived, and Nancy wanted to cook me a homemade meal. She fixed spaghetti. It was just the way I liked it. Most places, when you go out, think the sauce is supposed to be thick. Hers was runny, like it should be. The noodles are supposed to stay moist, so they slide down your throat.

After dinner, we shot some pool in her game room. Sorry to say, she beat me. Considering she can practice every day, and I seldom get to play, it was very close. Nancy was very pleased with herself. I started to suspect that she enjoyed putting men in their place.

We sat on her sofa, and started to watch TV. I had decided that I wanted this woman to be my wife. I wanted to make love to her, every night of my life. I know I wanted to make love to her, but I'm not sure how we got to that point.

One minute we were on her sofa watching TV, the next minute we were all entwined. I wanted her, I had to have her, and I didn't care what the consequences were. I was pulling down her pantyhose, and she was pulling down my pants. She suggested we go into her bedroom, and I obediently followed.

Once in her bedroom, she excused herself, and went into the master bath. She was only gone a few minutes, and it was well worth the wait. She was wearing the sexiest whatever, I had ever seen.

She walked up to me, threw her arms around my neck, and gave me the longest, wettest, sexiest kiss I ever had. Her kiss made me dizzy, but I couldn't pull myself away. After what seemed to be a few minutes, she undid my pants, and let them slide to my ankles. My knees were starting to get weak, as she slid my underwear down around my ankles. I was on the verge of falling down, and I was dripping with desire. Nancy dropped to her knees so she could savor my desire.

My knees buckled as she took me into her mouth. Her hand gently massaged the family jewels, and I moaned in ecstasy. I had no control — she owned me. I was hers to do with as she saw fit. She lay on the bed, and pulled me on top of her. I wanted to make love to her. God, how I wanted her. I had never been throbbing so hard, or dripping so much.

Sliding deep inside of her was all I could think of. However, she wasn't ready for that.

She was gently pushing my head toward her womanhood. I allowed myself to be directed there, and took a soft lick. Nancy trembled under my tongue. As I tasted her sweetness, I gently stroked her with my finger. Her juices were flowing out of control. I loved the way she tasted. I was drinking in her essence. She was moaning, as she pulled my head from between her legs, and to her lips. I knew she could taste her womanhood on my lips. She seemed to enjoy the taste, so I dipped my fingers between her legs, then painted her lips with her sweetness. She moaned in delight, and reached between her legs, guiding me deep inside her.

Being that it was my first time, I exploded within seconds. I could feel my hot cum squirt deep inside her. Nancy kept going. I don't know exactly what she did, but she milked another orgasm from me. She tried to make me cum a third time, but I couldn't make it. I ran out of steam, and collapsed into her arms – spent. I vaguely remember thinking that I should get up and wipe off, as I drifted off to sleep.

In the morning, I woke up, but was afraid to open my eyes at first. Had that wonderful night been just a dream? As I was lying there wishing "please make it real," I realized that I could smell Nancy lying beside me. I opened my eyes, expecting to see Nancy with messed up hair, and smeared makeup. What I saw was incredible. She was beautiful beyond words. It was as if she had showered, put on her makeup, slipped back into her nightgown, and climbed back into bed to watch me sleep. She didn't have a hair out of place. I don't know which thought amazed me more. That she could sleep all night long and wake up looking that good, or that she would care enough to wake up early so she could get cleaned up and look her best - for me.

I glanced at my watch and saw it was after seven. I knew I should hurry home. Maybe, if I were lucky, I'd get there before my parents noticed I hadn't been home all night. They would be pissed.

I showered at Nancy's, and cleaned up as best I could. Without my own brush, comb, hair dryer, and hair spray, I couldn't look my best, but it was definitely an improvement. I said goodbye to Nancy, holding her in my arms. She gave me a slow gentle kiss, as her hand came up to caress my cheek. There was none of the hot passion as there was the night before, but

I enjoyed kissing her every bit as much. I hated to leave, but I tore myself away, and headed home.

I wasn't mistaken. My parents were waiting for me when I got home, and they gave "pissed off" an entirely new meaning. They ranted, they raved, and then they ranted some more. They demanded to know where I had been.

"Nancy's."

"That SLUT!!"

"Don't EVER call her that again!"

I turned and walked away. I'd heard enough.

"You come back here! I'm not done talking to you!"

"I'm done listening."

For the next several months, Nancy and I seemed to spend every moment we could with each other. We both worked evenings, so we would sleep late, and then meet each other for lunch. I was so happy.

I usually enjoyed being around her son, too. However, there were times when he would get too rowdy and she would get mad at me if I corrected him. I wondered if that would change, after we got married. Then I'd remember that we had never discussed marriage. In fact, she never said she loved me. While her actions said one thing, her words, by omission, said another. I'd often wonder where our relationship was heading. Was it all one sided? Was I just fooling myself into thinking this beauty could actually love me?

Then we were in bed, and our long-term relationship was the furthest thing from my mind. All I wanted to do was please her the way she pleased me.

She educated me in the ways of making love.

"Women prefer the top," she told me, "That way we can control where the stimulation is directed."

She would let me be on top until I was ready to pop, then roll me onto my back so she could take control. I actually preferred the bottom. On top, I'd climax too fast. On the bottom, I could let my mind drift from the genital stimulation, and admire her beauty. Her long blonde hair cascading over her shoulders. Her large voluptuous breasts bouncing, now with very hard nipples. Droplets of sweat would form in her cleavage, and run down to her stomach. Her lips would part, and she would moan as she started pumping faster. Nancy would climax, and I'd let myself be swept along for the ride, climaxing in harmony. She would collapse, onto me, and I'd hold her tight. We would often fall asleep like that, with me still hard in her, wanting to cum again.

Life was good. Then it all came apart. I was at Nancy's one night. We were downstairs in the family room, when she excused herself to go upstairs. While she was upstairs, the telephone started ringing. It rang and rang. I decided she wasn't going to be able to get it, so I picked it up for her. I was just about to say "Hello," when I heard Nancy on the extension. Before I could hang up, I heard a man's voice on the other end.

I didn't think anything about it, until she came downstairs, and I asked, "Who was on the phone?"

"My girlfriend," was her reply.

"She has a rather deep voice," I commented.

"You were listening?"

"I didn't think you were going to be able to get it, so I was going to take a message for you."

"How dare you!"

"Excuse me?"

"I can't believe you'd eavesdrop on a private conversation."

"Wait a minute. Don't be twisting this around, and making it about me. Why did you say that was your girlfriend, when it was obviously a guy?"

"I don't have to explain myself to you!"

"No, you don't."

I picked up my coat and walked out of her house. On the way home, I wondered, "What the heck just happened?"

For weeks, I hoped she would call and apologize, but she never did. My pride prevented me from calling her.

I saw Nancy one time after that fateful night. It was about six months later. I had moved out on my own, to the Alexa Roan apartments in Sylvania, OH. My birthday was approaching, and I didn't want to be alone. Nancy agreed to celebrate with me.

I picked her up at her house. She looked as stunning as always, but was attired in what was probably her least sexy outfit. The tan skirt nearly reached her knees and didn't have any slits. The white cotton blouse she wore didn't show any cleavage, and was heavy enough that I couldn't see through it. I think even my parents would have approved of how she was dressed.

We had dinner at Mancy's Restaurant. We had scotch on the rocks before dinner and a nice wine with our steak and lobster. Neither of us had room for dessert. Nancy didn't want to go to a movie, so we headed back to her house. She stopped at her door and turned around.

"I had a nice time," she told me.

I guess I wasn't going to be invited in.

"I did, too," I told her, "Thanks for going out with me. It meant a lot."

I went to kiss her on the lips but she turned her head and the kiss landed on her cheek. I guess there was no getting back what we once had.

"Take care of yourself," I told her.

I managed to turn away just before tears started flowing down my cheeks. I never saw Nancy after that, but I often think about her, and wonder how she's doing. I wish her all the best.

Chapter 5

THE KISS

Leslie and I were practically inseparable. If we couldn't see each other, we talked to each other on the phone. She had a family to take care of, so it was usually easier for her to call me when she had some free time. I'd often hang around my apartment, praying that she would call. I'd think about how much I loved this woman and how I wished she loved me. When the telephone finally rang, I'd rush to answer it.

"Please, let it be Leslie," I'd pray.

If it weren't Leslie, I felt as though my heart sank to the floor, but when it was, my spirits would soar. It was unbelievable how happy the sound of her voice made me feel.

The nights were starting to get warmer, so some nights I'd pick Leslie up for work on my motorcycle. The route we took was unlit, and extremely dark, with large trees blocking the little light from the moon and stars. As we zipped along at a high rate of speed, Leslie would hold on tight. I knew it was for safety, and because I blocked the wind, but it felt great to have her arms around me anyway.

Yes, it felt great to have her arms around me, but my arms ached to hold her. I loved her so much. I wondered how long I could go on having her so close, wanting her so bad, and knowing that I can never have her. Sometimes the ache in my heart is more than I think I can bear.

We continued to share breaks and lunches together when at work. Sometimes, when we were both broke, we just drove around. The city looked so quiet and peaceful at four in the morning. Leslie liked to check out the expensive homes in the city, so we often drove through the more luxurious neighborhoods. She longed to have a large fancy house, and unbeknownst to her, I longed to give her one.

On one of these outings, we found a rather large estate with a mansion sitting about a half mile from the road. We didn't know there were such homes in Toledo. The estate was surrounded by a five-foot brick wall that went as far in both directions as we could see. I couldn't tell how many acres of land there was, but it was a lot. There were so many trees on the property, that you could barely see the home in the distance. You would think that a place like this would have a locked gate, but there was none.

"Let's drive up to the house," Leslie said, "I want a closer look."

I was nervous about going up somebody's driveway in the middle of the night. Especially since it was so dark that I'd have to keep my headlights on to see where I was going.

"Somebody will see us for sure," I told her, "I don't want to get shot. Why don't we park the car, and walk up to the house?"

I figured it would be harder for anybody to see us that way. I parked the car and we started walking up the long winding drive. Ten paces onto the property, and it was so dark that we couldn't see where we were walking. Instinctively, I checked my watch to see what time it was. I could barely see the illuminated numbers that indicated it was 4:30 a.m. I could sense Leslie next to me, so I reached over and took her hand in mine. I expected her to pull away at my touch, but she held my hand firmly.

We inched up the driveway, trying to follow the curve of the long road. Sometimes we wondered off the drive and crashed into nearby trees. It was so dark. I held my hand in front of my face and could see nothing. It seemed as though we had been inching along the drive for 20 minutes, but we couldn't tell how much further the house was, with the trees obstructing our view.

I doubt if we were more than one hundred feet onto the property, when we heard a dog howl somewhere on the grounds. Somewhere close. Leslie turned and bolted back down the driveway toward the car and safety, with me in hot pursuit. We reached the car at the same time. Once we were both safely inside, with the doors locked, we had a good laugh. It was the first wild and crazy thing that we did together, but it wasn't to be the last.

# # #

Leslie and I shared many days and nights together for over a year, becoming very good friends. Some evenings, her husband would be out of town, and I'd go out to dinner with Leslie and her two boys. Bryan and Joey were their names. They were good kids, and Leslie loved them a lot. The fear of losing them was the reason why she wouldn't divorce her abusive husband. It seemed like a silly concern to me, because in Ohio, the man got to keep very little in a divorce. Custody of children always went to the mother, and the father had to pay alimony and child support. But Leslie still thought the risk was too great.

I enjoyed being around Bryan and Joey, a lot more than I did around Nancy's son. If I corrected them, they would listen, and Leslie wouldn't get upset with me for doing it. I think she actually welcomed my help. Sometimes it felt like I was a part of their family. I often wondered what they thought about this man who was always showing up when their father wasn't around. One thing for sure, they knew I cared a great deal about their mother.

One day I even picked up Leslie, to take Bryan and Joey to the doctor for their routine checkups. Sitting in the waiting room, waiting for them to be seen, was just about the neatest feeling. Even though I knew I shouldn't be there, I felt like I belonged with them.

While Leslie thought of me as a good friend, I loved her so much that I would do anything to be with her. She didn't know how I felt about her, or at least she wouldn't admit it. She found out one night, during lunch, and it changed our lives forever. On that fateful night, we didn't have enough money for lunch, but with our combined resources, we managed to scrape together enough money for a single milkshake. We both liked vanilla milkshakes from Schmucker's Restaurant, so we went there and bought one to go.

We picked up a pair of straws, and then headed back towards work. When we were about a block away, we realized that we still had over twenty minutes before we had to be back at work, so Leslie drove us to a secluded side street and parked the car along the curb.

To me, this was the most romantic moment I'd ever experienced. Sitting there alone in the darkness with the woman I loved. The dashboard provided dim mood lighting. Quiet music played on the radio as we leaned close to share the milkshake. The sweet smell of her perfume made my head spin and my heart race. I was having a bit of trouble swallowing, as a lump formed in my throat.

I could hardly control myself. All I could think about was taking her in my arms and kissing her lips. I longed to savor the taste of a long, wet, passionate kiss. I was fighting the temptation so hard, I felt as though I was going to pass out. I suggested that we head back to work. I needed to get away from her, for a little while, and let my head clear.

When we got back to work, Leslie started to get out of the car. There was this voice in my head saying, "If you don't do it now, you'll never forgive yourself."

I said her name softly, "Leslie," as I put my hand on her arm, preventing her from leaving. She turned to see what I wanted, and I leaned over and kissed her luscious lips.

She pulled back quickly, and said, "I don't think we should go out to lunch anymore."

She jumped out of the car, and ran into work, leaving me sitting alone in her car.

What had I done? I cursed myself up one side, and down the other. I called myself every name I could think of. I felt sick. How could I be so dumb? She trusted me as a friend, and now she thought I was just like Dave. That the only reason I was nice to her, was so I could get in her pants.

I had to fix this, but how?

## Chapter 6

RECONCILIATION

After that night, Leslie avoided me completely. When I saw her in the halls at work, she glared at me with hate burning in her eyes. It was tearing me up inside. Every chance I got; I'd beg for her forgiveness. I promised to never do it again, if only we could remain friends. I groveled like I had never groveled before. To hell with pride. I loved Leslie so much; the thought of never being close to her again was killing me.

Weeks went by. I quit taking breaks, and going to lunch. I didn't know what Leslie had told people about me, if anything, but I imagined the worst and wanted to avoid all contact with everyone.

Then one day Leslie came up to me and asked, "Will you go out to lunch with me?"

Would I? YES - YES - YES!!!!!!!

"Of course. I'm so sorry for what I did. Please forgive me. I'll never do it again. Just please, be my friend."

When we left work, I began driving to Schmucker's Restaurant, where we would normally go for lunch. It was just a truck stop, but they had excellent food, and were open 24 hours a day. However, Leslie didn't want to eat. She wanted to stop and talk, so we did.

"Why did you kiss me?" she asked.

I guess it was a logical question, but it wasn't one I expected. What did she want to hear? Should I tell her the truth and risk everything? Or should I try to make up something in an attempt to save our friendship? My mind was racing, and not getting anywhere.

I decided to tell her everything, but not all at once. So much pent-up passion for her would scare her off. I'd feed her a little at a time, so she could picture, in her mind, just how much I cared for her. How my love burned for her. How my arms ached to hold her. How I thought about her all the time. I was scared of losing her, so I chose my words carefully.

"Why did I kiss you?" I started. "I guess I lost control. No, that's not right. Well, it is right, but it leaves out a few things."

"This is going smoothly," I thought.

I continued, "For you to truly understand why I kissed you; we have to go back to the first time I saw you. I've never believed in it, but it was love at first sight, that night you first started working at O-I. I've been in love before, several times, but just seeing you that first night grabbed my heart like it has never been grabbed before. I was so afraid that you would walk out of my life, without my ever getting a chance to know you. I love you so much; I can't even put the feelings into words. They just seem so inadequate. All I've ever wanted was for you to be happy. Whether that meant you being with me, or with somebody else. That was why I let you and Dave use my apartment."

It took days for me to tell the whole story. How she affected me from the first time I saw her, and how my love had continued to grow until that night I lost control. When I was done telling the story, I said, "I never want to lose your friendship, but it's a tremendous relief to get all of my feelings out in the open."

I looked into her eyes. They were moist and reflected the light from the dashboard. I could tell that she was deeply moved and felt something. I just wasn't sure what. Fondness? Affection? Love? Empathy? Pity? I had no idea what she was thinking. Only that she felt something towards me, and I certainly wasn't hated.

She said it softly. I almost missed it.

"Would you kiss me?"

Was she serious?

"Are you sure?"

She was sure.

I leaned over to kiss her, the way I had before. A light, friendly kiss. One of friendship. I don't know what happened. I don't know if she started it, or I lost control again, but it wasn't a kiss like I had intended. It was a burning, compassionate kiss that consumed both of us. I had never known such a kiss. Her touch, her smell, her taste drove me wild. My tongue explored her mouth, while my arms struggled to hold her ever tighter, never wanting to let go. The more I tasted her sweet lips, the more I wanted. I couldn't catch my breath. Her kiss was better than I could have ever imagined.

I don't know how long the kiss lasted. A minute? Five minutes? Fifteen? I had no idea. I didn't know a kiss could last so long and it wasn't long enough. Forever wouldn't have been long enough. I couldn't have felt better if we had made love. I was exhausted, but ecstatic. Ecstatic doesn't seem to come close to describing how I felt. I had found the most perfect treasure in the world. But, how did she feel?

"Wow," she said, "that was some kiss."

"Yeah," was all I could say.

The clock on the dashboard said it was time to get back to work. I reached up to put the car in gear, and didn't think I was going to make it. My arms were shaking, almost uncontrollably. It reminded me of a drug addict that was desperate for a fix. I just had my first fix of Leslie, and I was addicted. I needed more.

We drove back to work in silence. Each wrapped in our own private thoughts.

Chapter 7

UNBRIDLED PASSION

The next night, for lunch, we found another secluded spot where we could park and talk. Mostly about the kiss we had shared the night before. The passion behind the kiss had taken both of us by surprise. We both wanted more of that feeling. But, could it be repeated? Or was it a one-time thing? We had to find out.

I took her into my arms, and gently kissed her lips. Our lips touched, and I felt her body press against mine. Being this close to her, every breath I took was filled with the smell of her perfume. I knew this kiss was going to be every bit as good as the first, and I let myself go. Letting the kiss build in intensity until we were forced to separate, or be consumed by its fire.

As the months passed, I went into much more detail about how much I cared for her. About the struggle I had gone through to try and keep her from knowing my secret for fear that I'd lose her friendship. I loved her. I wanted her. And I was becoming dependent on her. I told her how I'd go to sleep at night, dreaming about making love to her, and waking up with wet sheets. How I needed to be close to her. To be one with her. That even making love with her wouldn't bring us close enough and that every day was getting worse.

One night, for lunch, Leslie suggested that we go to her house. She said nobody was home, and she would fix me something special. I don't remember what she fixed me, only what happened afterwards.

I was standing by the door, leaning against the wall, waiting for Leslie to finish putting things away so we could head back to work. Leslie came up to me, stood on her toes, threw her arms around my neck, and placed her lips on mine.

Her tongue started exploring my mouth, and my tongue searched hers. Having my feet planted firmly on the ground did nothing for my stability. As her kiss took control of me, the room began to spin, and my knees started to buckle. If I hadn't been against the wall, I'd have collapsed to the floor. As it was, I was sliding down the wall. Leslie helped hold me up, as her kiss consumed me. She pushed herself between my legs, and I became aware of the heat pouring from her body. I began to throb and grow. Her hand followed the contour of my body, until it stopped between my legs and she started rubbing me.

The pounding and throbbing in my loins was unbearable. I had no control. I was hers. My body ached. As she started to pull her hand away, my body tried to follow, begging for more. Then she stepped back away from me and without the support, my weak legs gave way and I slid to the floor.

I don't know how you'd describe me at this point. I guess "a puddle of happiness and desire" comes as close as anything. I felt as though I had been drugged. I had no control. No strength. Moans of pleasure escaped my lips. I could barely understand myself when I told her I needed her, and wanted to make love to her.

Her response started to bring me back to reality.

"I can't Gary," she told me.

I was fighting to gain control. My head was filled with cobwebs.

"Can't?" echoed in my head.

I tried to get up, but fell back to the floor.

"CAN'T?" I repeated to myself.

My brain screamed. I was getting mad at myself for allowing this to happen. Control. CONTROL! Fight! FIGHT FOR CONTROL!! Not too steady, but I managed to stand up. A few more minutes and I'd be OK.

Leslie said something. What was it? Didn't seem to make sense.

"I can't make love to you, but if you want, I'll kiss you."

I tried rearranging what she said, and it still didn't make any sense to my cloud-encased mind, so I asked, "Kiss me? What do you think we were doing?"

She laughed.

"No, silly, not a kiss, a KISS," and she lightly touched me between the legs to emphasize her intentions.

Well, that did it. Now I knew what she meant. But as long as I was in control again, I planned on staying that way.

"Thanks," I said, "but that's not necessary. I'll be fine."

"In a week or two," I thought.

We headed back to work, and I was thankful that I had worn dark jeans, because the baseball sized wet spot on the front of me was barely noticeable.

While things with Leslie weren't developing the way I would have liked, at least my career was on track. I was promoted to Junior Operator and transferred into the Computer Room to begin operator training.

As a Unit Records Clerk, I already had experience with an RCA 301 computer, using it to read in punch cards and create reports. Some programs were read in from punch cards, while others I had to manually enter via buttons on the console.

In the Computer Room, I was first going to be trained on an RCA 3301 and later on a Honeywell. I was still working midnight to eight, but now I was making more money, and felt I could support Leslie if she ever decided she wanted to marry me.

Chapter 8

OUR FIRST TIME

As time passed by, a wall started to come between us. Leslie wanted things to continue the way they had been, while my whole reason for waking up each day was the hope that this would be the day, I made love to her. I didn't want to kiss her; because I knew her kisses would just leave me wanting more. The more that she wouldn't let me have.

We continued to spend time together, and I made like a broken record, repeatedly telling her how I felt, and how much I desired to make love to her. Then one day it happened.

Leslie told me, "Joe won't be home this evening. If you come over after dinner, you'll get what you've been waiting for."

Sounded clear enough to me, but the way she said it made it sound like a chore she wasn't looking forward to. I guess I didn't know how to feel. I wanted her so bad, but I didn't want her to do anything she'd be sorry for, or regret later. One thing was certain. Whether or not anything happened, I'd be at Leslie's house after dinner, because I loved her and enjoyed being with her more than anything in this world.

After dinner, I drove to her house. She let me in, and we sat close together on her sofa, watching TV. Her sweet smell made me light headed, and her closeness made my heart pound, but I was intent on maintaining control of myself. I wasn't even going to take the initiative and kiss her. If she wanted to change her mind about making love to me that was fine. I wouldn't push her.

The evening just seemed to fly by, and before I knew it, we had only another hour before we would have to leave for work.

And then she kissed me. Every kiss has been as good, or better, than the first. I felt myself losing control. My head was spinning and my heart was pounding. I was all hers and it felt fantastic.

She pulled me down beside her and I was vaguely aware that she had already unfastened my pants, slid her hand down my stomach and was holding my privates. My pounding heart felt like it had dropped a foot, as the pounding was now between my legs.

Shudders began to sweep over my body, as she expertly stroked me. I knew I'd cum any second. Leslie knew it too. She quickly slipped off her panties, and guided me into the most warm, wet, and wonderful place I've ever been. I was barely inside her when I exploded.

Making love with Nancy had been wonderful; this was incredible. Nancy had taught me that pleasing your partner could be as big of a turn on as them pleasing you. Because of my experiences with her, I knew it was important to hold back and allow the woman to catch up, so the beauty of a mutual orgasm could be shared. However, with Leslie, I couldn't hold back. The pent-up desire and the expertly administered foreplay were more than I could handle. I promised myself, next time would be better for Leslie.

I felt myself shudder one last time, then collapsed next to the woman I loved so much. I felt happier than I had ever been in my entire life. If I could bottle this feeling, I'd make millions. I loved this woman more than anything, or anybody, in the whole world and I wanted her for all time.

I finally managed to open my eyes, expecting to see Leslie as happy as I was. What I saw crushed me. She was crying and it was getting worse. I tried to comfort her, but it only made her cry more.

When she said, "We never should have done that," the words sliced through me like a hot, twisting knife.

Seeing Leslie hurt so bad and knowing I was the cause of it made me sick to my stomach. Tears quickly formed and ran down my cheeks. What was briefly the happiest day in my life was now the saddest. I was disgusted with myself, and I knew in my heart that we would never make love again.

Chapter 9

MOVING ON

After making love to Leslie, I realized I couldn't continue living in this dream world, where she would one day be mine. I struggled to spend a little less time with her, and worked on developing new interests, and new friends. It hurt a lot. Actually, it hurt a lot more than a lot, but I had no choice. Leslie had made that very clear.

I had talked with the guy living in the apartment next to mine a few times before. Since I was no longer spending every waking moment with Leslie, or waiting for Leslie, or fantasizing about Leslie, we spent more time together and became good friends. His name was Rich. We started doing just about everything together. We went to bars to look for babes. We watched ball games in his apartment, or mine. And, we had parties in the hall.

There were two women living directly across the hall from me, but I never had an opportunity to talk with them. With Leslie occupying my thoughts twenty-four hours a day, I hadn't had time for much of anything. Karyn was really cute and looked outstanding in a bikini. I was hoping to get a chance to ask her out. However, as shy as I am around women, I needed to find a good reason to talk with her. For some reason, wanting to take a woman out just never seemed like a good enough reason.

One Saturday, I noticed that Karyn was moving things out of her apartment. I was afraid it was going to be the last chance I had to talk with her, so I asked her, "Are you moving out?"

"No," she replied, "My roommate is moving out and I have another friend moving in with me."

Karyn introduced me to her new roommate. Her name was Debbie. Debbie was a big woman, nearly six feet tall. With the clothes she had on, it was hard to tell what her figure looked like. She definitely didn't dress to impress guys. I didn't care for her hair either. I prefer long hair on a woman, and hers was chopped short, the way most older women wear their hair. Debbie didn't look old, but her hair sure did. It was gray. I assumed that it was frosted. I always thought that was kind of dumb, for a young person to want to look old and gray, but hey, that's just me.

Debbie had nice facial features, and could probably be a model, but her hair and clothes didn't do a thing to enhance her natural beauty. The short gray hair and the clothes she wore, made her look pretty old, but I doubted if she was any older than me.

About a week after Debbie moved in, Rich and I went to a Beach Boys' concert and he saw her there. After the concert, we went back to my apartment, and I left my door open, so I could hear when she got home. When I heard her come in, I went out and talked with her.

"Hi," I said.

Debbie jumped, a bit startled, then replied, "Hello."

"Did you enjoy the concert?" I inquired.

"Yes, I did. Were you there?"

"Yeah, Rich and I went together," I said, as I gestured toward Rich's apartment.

"I saw him there."

"Yes, I know. That's how I knew you were there. Is this the first time you've seen the Beach Boys in concert?"

"Yes, they were great. Have you seen them before?"

"No, I've seen a lot of other groups in concert, but this was the first time I've seen the Beach Boys."

We talked for about half an hour. I was surprised by how quickly the time passed. She was so easy to talk with. With most women, I'd run out of things to say after five minutes. With Debbie, it seemed like we could have talked all night. However, with it being the first time we talked with each other, I didn't want to wear out my welcome, so I said, "Good night. It was nice talking with you. I hope we can do it again sometime."

Debbie said, "Good night," then entered her apartment and quickly bolted the door. I hoped I hadn't scared her.

# # #

About a week later, I was leaving my apartment to go to the store, when I heard a Buddy Holly song playing in Karyn and Debbie's apartment. I was curious as to which of them liked "good music," so I knocked on their door.

Debbie answered the door, and I said, "Hi. I hear a Buddy Holly song."

"I'm sorry, I didn't mean to play it so loud," Debbie apologized.

"I'm not complaining. It's not too loud. I was just surprised to hear Buddy Holly. I thought I was the only one that listened to the good old-fashioned rock and roll. I was wondering what you're listening to. Do you have one of his albums?"

"I'm listening to the American Graffiti sound track. Would you like to come in and listen to it with me?"

"I'd like that."

Debbie and I listened to the album while we talked about the American Graffiti movie. I found that several of her other tastes were similar to mine, so I asked her, "Would you like to go out for a drink?"

"I'd like that."

"Great. I have to take a shower first. Is half an hour, OK?"

"Sure."

I left her apartment and headed back to mine. I showered and put on some clean clothes. Then I remembered that I had never made it to the store. "Have to remember to do that tomorrow," I told myself. I was out of dishwasher soap, and I was getting tired of washing dishes by hand.

When I got back to Debbie's, she had changed clothes, too. She was wearing slacks, a blouse, a sport coat, and had a scarf tied around her neck. I'm an old-fashioned kind of guy. Some people would call me a male chauvinist. I prefer women to dress like women, not wear slacks and sport coats, like guys, but I didn't say anything.

At the lounge, Debbie ordered a Coke and I requested a Budweiser draft. While we waited for our drinks, I asked Debbie, "Do you always wear a scarf?"

"I usually do. Do you like it?"

"No. Not particularly," I answered truthfully.

I thought it was so cute the way she quickly removed the scarf and stuffed it in her purse. At that moment, I decided I wanted to know Debbie a lot better.

We stayed a couple of hours, and then headed back to our apartment complex. At her door, I said, "I have a motorcycle," then asked, "Would you like to go for ride sometime?"

"I've never been on a motorcycle before, but sure. Why not?"

"I can't think of a single good reason," I said and then added, "Well, good night. I had a really nice evening."

Then I leaned over and gave her a quick kiss on the lips. She didn't object. That was a positive sign. But she didn't seem to return the kiss, either.

Debbie said, "Good night."

I headed back to my apartment, wondering what this new relationship would bring. Then I laughed at myself.

"Relationship?"

It has only been one date. That's if you can call sharing a couple of drinks a date.

## Chapter 10

STILL FRIENDS

Leslie and I continued to spend a lot of time together. We were still the best of friends. We told each other things we wouldn't dream of telling anyone else. While our one night of lovemaking was something we both regretted, it formed a bond between us. A bond of mutual trust and respect that no other act could have accomplished.

Our physical attraction for each other was now limited to holding hands and an occasional kiss. Our kisses, while long by other people's standards, were getting shorter all the time, usually lasting only a few minutes. It was always me that had to break off the kiss, before I lost all self-control. I suppose I still wanted to make love to Leslie, but now I wouldn't admit it, not even to myself.

I told Leslie all about Debbie. At least I told her as much as I knew. Debbie was twenty years old and she didn't have a boyfriend. She worked at the Hudson's Department Store selling cosmetics. She drove a fairly new Plymouth Duster and this is the first time that she has been out living on her own.

Leslie seemed a little bit jealous as I rattled on about Debbie, but she didn't say anything. Probably because she knew I'd say, "If you don't want me seeing other women, leave Joe, and come live with me."

Although I was starting to divide my time between Rich and Debbie, Leslie and I still spent a lot of time together. While Debbie was at work, I'd still occasionally meet Leslie for lunch, dinner, or just to do some shopping with her. I longed to be with Leslie every minute of every day, but that wasn't possible.

I looked forward to going to work because that was when I could spend the most time with Leslie. However, there were some nights Leslie wouldn't come to work, usually because of a sick child. On these nights I felt lost and alone. On these nights I dreaded breaks and lunch, because I longed to be with Leslie and missed her so much. I couldn't stand being without her. Without her I felt empty.

Chapter 11

DEBBIE

A few days after I had taken Debbie out for drinks, I was leaving my apartment to go out to dinner, when I saw her coming home from work.

I asked her, "Would you like to go for that motorcycle ride now?"

"Sure," she said, "Just give me a minute to change clothes."

True to her word, it didn't take her much more than a minute. She came out wearing jeans and a cute little top. She looked much better than the last time I was out with her.

Since Debbie had never been on a motorcycle before, I took her on a long ride to let her get used to how it felt. At first, she was very rigid, and I had to take corners slowly, but after a while she learned to lean into the curves and we were flying. After I thought, she had gotten used to it, we stopped at Jo-Jo's Pizzeria for a bite to eat. She liked her pizza with everything on it, the same way I do, so we split a pizza and we each had a beer.

During supper I learned a little more about Debbie. She was born in Kentucky, raised in San Diego, and her family moved back to Toledo after her father retired from the Navy. Her father was born and raised in Haskins, a little town near Toledo, and he wanted to raise his family in the same area where he grew up.

To me, it sounded like cruel and unusual punishment to move a family from the warmth of southern California to the frigid cold of northern

Ohio. I commented on this and Debbie mentioned that the first year they were in Ohio, she slipped on the ice and hit her face on the ground, biting through her lower lip.

"That's quite a coincidence," I said. "I have a scar on my lower lip, where I fell on the ice and bit through it."

Debbie wanted to know more about me.

"I'm twenty-four. I was born in Toledo, I was raised in Toledo, and I plan on dying in Toledo. I went to DeVeaux Grade School, DeVilbiss High School, and attended the University of Toledo for a couple of years. I work as a computer operator for Owens-Illinois, where I feed punch cards into a computer, process the data, and print out the resulting reports. I currently work midnight to eight, Sunday night through Friday morning."

We finished our pizza and beer and then headed back to our apartments. It was still early spring, so the temperature was dropping rapidly. It was a little cool riding back, but it got Debbie to snuggle close, and hold on tight.

When we got back to our apartments, Debbie said, "I had a really good time. I hope we can do it again."

"I had a good time too. I'm sure we'll be seeing a lot more of each other."

# # #

Within weeks, we were practically inseparable. If we didn't have any place to go, Debbie would spend the evening in my apartment. Many times, I'd cook and invite her over for dinner.

When I was with Debbie, I'd frequently talk about Leslie. I liked both of them. Well, I loved one very much, and I was starting to like the other an awful lot. So, I hoped they could become good friends.

I dated quite a few different women before I met Debbie. I fell in love with most of them, and made love to two, but I never really had what I'd call a girlfriend.

There was something special about Debbie that drew me close to her, and I was starting to think of her as "my girlfriend." I thought I should introduce her to my parents, but she beat me to it.

It was late spring. The days were warming up quickly and it was staying warm late into the evening. We decided to hop on the motorcycle, and ride out to Point Place one evening, so Debbie could introduce me to her parents.

They had a nice ranch style, single level, brick home. Their house was on a corner lot, so their yard was much larger than most of the neighbors.

I pulled into her parents' driveway and turned off the bike. There were several people sitting in chairs on the driveway and they stopped talking when they saw us arrive. I held the bike steady while Debbie got off, and then I followed her.

One person there caught my attention immediately. He was an older gentleman with silver hair wearing dark sunglasses. He reminded me of a Mafia Don. If he had been wearing a coat, I'd have been checking for a shoulder holster. He was the first to stand up and head toward us. I heard somebody call him Don.

"Is this a coincidence, or what?" I wondered.

The gentleman, and at this point I wasn't sure he was, walked up to me and said, "I don't like guys on motorcycles."

"OK," I thought, "This is a great way to make an impression. What do I say to that?"

My mind was racing, calculating odds on what would happen when I gave my response.

"Tough," I replied.

It was obviously the correct response, because everybody burst out laughing.

"I guess he told you, Don," a woman said, who was later introduced to me as Debbie's mother.

A tall, thin man came up and shook my hand. "I'm Bob," he said in a booming voice. Nice friendly guy. He was Debbie's father. Don turned out to be Debbie's Uncle Don. His wife was Tinker.

Other than that, they almost gave me a coronary when I first arrived, they were all very pleasant. I can't say I've ever met nicer people. We visited for a couple of hours, then I told Debbie we should start heading back before it got much cooler.

It was about a twenty-minute ride back to our apartments. It was still early when we got back, so Debbie came in my apartment to watch some TV, until it was time for me to get ready for work and go pick up Leslie.

## Chapter 12

FIRST CONTACT

From the first day I met Debbie, I was telling Leslie all about her. How I felt when I was with her. What we did. Where we went. What our plans were. Whenever Debbie and I had a fight, Leslie was able to help me see Debbie's point of view. Leslie thought Debbie sounded pretty special, was happy for me, and hoped her and Debbie could become good friends. I hoped so too.

On a warm Saturday afternoon, Debbie and I decided to take a motorcycle ride to my parents' house so I could introduce her to them. Since I drove past Leslie's house every chance I got, we rode in that direction. I was excited to see Leslie outside, tugging on a hose, getting ready to wash her car. She was wearing a sexy little bikini that showed off her flat stomach and well-endowed chest. It seemed like a great time for my two best friends to finally meet. I pulled up next to Leslie, and stopped the motorcycle.

Now Debbie would know who this mysterious Leslie was that I was always talking about when I said, "Leslie this, and Leslie that." I think Debbie preferred her to be a mystery. That way she could picture her as someone that's fat and ugly. Now she had to face the fact that when I was with her, I was thinking and talking about a beautiful woman.

Leslie was a little bit jealous of Debbie. I knew that. However, we both knew we could never have each other, so it was something she would have to live with. I introduced my two loves to each other. It seemed as though Debbie was a little upset with my stopping to see Leslie. Since Leslie was busy and Debbie didn't appear to want to be there, we didn't stay long. When we reached my parents' house nobody was home so Debbie and I talked.

She wanted to know, "Why did you stop at Leslie's?"

"Because I care about the two of you and would like you to become good friends," I told her.

Debbie said, "I don't want to be friends with Leslie. I don't want to see Leslie. I don't even want to hear her name."

Although I was disappointed in her reaction, I didn't press the issue. Obviously, I had been talking about Leslie more than I should and it had made Debbie a bit jealous. I decided to try keeping thoughts of Leslie to myself.

My parents came home a short time later and I introduced them to Debbie. We sat in the living room and talked for a while, then my mother went into the kitchen to get us something to drink. I went in to help her.

"I like her a lot better than that other woman you were seeing," my mother told me in a low voice.

Obviously, she was referring to Nancy.

Since Nancy didn't want to have anything to do with me, I said, "Me too."

We visited for about an hour then we took off and headed to Ottawa Park. I parked the bike and we took off on a stroll holding hands and talking.

My relationship with Debbie was progressing at warp speed, leaving most memories nothing more than a blur. I first met Debbie in April 1974 and by November we were engaged. I didn't plan to ask her; it just kind of slipped out. We had gone to the wedding and reception of a mutual friend on a Saturday evening. After we left there, we swung by my parents' place. Nobody was home, so we let ourselves in, turned on the television, and sat on the sofa next to each other. Both of us were somewhat quiet, and then I asked, "You want to get married?"

Debbie said, "Sure, why not?"

My first thought was, "That's not the way this is supposed to happen." My second thought was, "I wonder what Leslie is going to think."

Then I said, "I guess we have to pick a date."

"And tell people," Debbie said.

My parents were the first to find out. We told them as soon as they got home. It was late, so we decided to wait until Sunday to go out and break the news to her parents.

We drove back to our apartments, I took her in my arms, kissed her goodnight, and we slept in our own beds. I didn't sleep well that night. I was excited about the prospect of marrying Debbie, and saddened by what it meant to my chances of ever having a romantic relationship with Leslie.

Early Sunday morning, I took a chance and called Leslie. I was happy she answered the telephone. It was the biggest event of my life, and I wanted to share it with the other woman I loved.

Some people think you can't be in love with more than one person. I was starting to wish that were true. Loving two women, when you can only have one of them hurts something terrible.

Leslie congratulated me, and said she was very happy for us. We talked for a while about what each other's plans were for the day, and then we said our good-byes.

I got cleaned up, then went and knocked on Debbie's door, to see if she wanted to go to breakfast. We had breakfast at the Bob Evans Restaurant, and then headed out to her parents' house. They hadn't been up long when we got out there. We told them our news, and they were excited. Their daughter was getting married. We stayed and had coffee, and visited for a while. Then we left so we could be alone.

The days and weeks went by fast as we made our wedding plans and started to set them into motion.

The day before Thanksgiving, Debbie and I had a fight. About Leslie - what else. Debbie said, "You love Leslie, not me. Why don't you marry her?"

I thought, "Because Leslie doesn't want me."

Then I said, "If I don't love you, why did I buy you this?"

I handed her a small gift-wrapped box. She felt like a jerk when she opened the box to find a half-carat diamond engagement ring. It was a solitaire cut on a white gold band.

"I hadn't planned on giving this to you until tomorrow," I told her.

"Oh, Gary, I love you so much," Debbie said, as she threw her arms around me and gave me a nice tender kiss.

After that, things went a lot smoother. Debbie was convinced that I actually loved and wanted to marry her. We had a nice Christmas. I spent more money on Christmas than I ever had before and both of our parents' bought gifts for their sons and daughters-in-law.

A few days later, Debbie and I decided to take a walk to Churchill's Grocery Store. It was only five to ten minutes away by car, so we thought we could make it there in twenty to twenty-five minutes. We just had to cross one busy street, a couple of not so busy streets, cross a field, and we were there. By the time we left the store, it started snowing hard. When we got to the field we had to cross, we could barely see two feet in front of us. We had no way to get our bearings; all we could do was creep forward on instinct, hoping we didn't run into anything.

We had been walking across the field for a longer time than it had taken us to get to the store. I was starting to fear we were lost, and it was a real possibility that we could freeze out there before we found shelter. Even if we could find it, crossing the busy street would be extremely dangerous. We wouldn't be able to see the cars, and they wouldn't be able to see us. Leslie's house was close by. If she were home, she would give us shelter until the snow let up.

"We're going to Leslie's," I informed Debbie.

Debbie didn't argue; she knew it was the smart thing to do. As close as her house was, it still took nearly fifteen minutes to get there. We were freezing by the time we got to her door. Leslie answered the door, and I explained what had happened. She was glad we had stopped by. Leslie ran and got us some towels to dry off with, then went and made some fresh coffee. We stayed and visited for nearly an hour, and then the weather finely broke.

I really enjoyed being together with the two women I cared so much about, but most of all, I liked that Debbie seemed to be getting along with Leslie. Maybe they could become close friends, like Leslie and I were. I'd really like that. Debbie and I left after thanking Leslie, then completed our journey home. Once we were safe and warm, we joked about our near-death experience.

Before I knew it, it was New Year's Eve. We had planned a nice night out, but I spent most of the night crying. I couldn't help it.

"What's wrong?" Debbie wanted to know. "Have I done something to upset you?"

She was so concerned, and so sweet, until I told her why I was hurting so badly. Then she was pissed.

Leslie had informed me that her husband had been transferred. They would be moving out of town in three weeks.

## Chapter 13

GONE, NOT FORGOTTEN

The three weeks that remained before Leslie would be gone went by faster than any I had ever experienced. I begged her not to go. "Please don't leave me." I was so scared I'd never see her again.

"I have to go. Joe and I have to sell our house so we can buy another place in Ironton. If I don't go, I'll have no place to stay."

"You could live with me."

"Debbie would love that!"

I was desperate. Scared out of my mind.

"I don't care how Deb would feel about it. Please don't go!" I pleaded.

Now I was whining. I didn't like that at all. Not only was I losing the woman I love, but I was also making a fool of myself.

"I have to run out to my mother's. Would you like to come along?" Leslie asked.

"Sure," I replied.

I knew I was choosing to spend more time with Leslie than Debbie, and I felt bad about it, but I had the rest of my life to be with Debbie, and less than a month to be with Leslie. I sat on the passenger side, and twisted in my seat, so I could gaze upon her beauty. I wanted to memorize every feature. I was quiet, listening to the tunes on the radio, and wondering how I was going to live without her.

"Will you write me?" I asked.

"Of course."

"Every day?" I pressed.

"At least once a week."

I guess that will have to do.

"And call me as often as you can?"

"Certainly."

"And you promise to come to our wedding?"

"I promise to try."

"It won't be the same without you. You have to come."

"I'll try."

I hadn't been paying attention to where she was taking me. I looked out the window and didn't recognize this part of town. I quickly checked the position of the late afternoon sun, and surmised we were in South Toledo. She stopped in front of a large house and parked.

"Wait here," she said.

I wanted to meet the mother of this woman I loved so much, but I did as she asked. If her mom was anything like my parents... I let the thought trail off as I watched her walk up to the house. Watching her walk away from me for a few minutes started to bring tears to my eyes.

"How was I ever going to manage without her," I wondered.

I sat in the car deep in thought, as tears started to well up in my eyes, and run down my cheeks. There had to be a way to stop her from leaving. I silently prayed for God's help.

Leslie startled me as she opened the car door and slid into her seat. I quickly brushed my cheeks and blinked rapidly, hoping to stop the embarrassing tears. As she started heading back home, I tried to get my bearings, in case I ever had to come out here on my own.

I sat quietly, not knowing what to say. Leslie knew how I felt, and it didn't seem to make any difference. Was there anything I could say to change her mind? Please God. Help me.

My thoughts started to drift, remembering the first time I started believing in God. My parents would drag me to church every Sunday. I hated it. Going to school five days a week was bad enough. Weekends were for recovery. I didn't like my childhood. Actually, I hated it. I figured there couldn't possibly be a God or I wouldn't be so unhappy all the time. I thought of myself as an atheist. There was no proof a God existed, so there couldn't possibly be one. Still, when I had no place else to turn, I'd say a prayer. I figured it couldn't hurt. Not that it ever helped, or so I thought at the time.

Then one day it just hit me. God had answered every one of my prayers. But he seemed to have a warped sense of humor. God would give me what I asked for, just not when I asked for it, and not in the way I expected.

Here is how God answered one of my prayers. I've always hated the smell of gum. I thought chewing gum was a nasty disgusting habit. So of course, I got a job at a discount store, and one of my chores was to go around scrapping gum off the floor. Naturally I hated this. The smell often gagged me. I prayed I wouldn't have to do this very long. I didn't. I was fired four months later. The reason? I didn't seem to be enthusiastic enough about my job. Like - duh! What low life would enjoy doing that?

I was just starting to wonder what funny way God was going to answer this prayer, when Leslie said, "You're awfully quiet. Are you OK?"

"Oh sure. The woman I love more than life itself is leaving town forever. Why wouldn't I be, OK?"

"We don't know that it's forever."

"We don't?"

"No."

Now I didn't feel so depressed.

"I love you," I said softly.

"I know you do."

I cracked a smile as I thought, "She needs more training in the proper way to respond. Hasn't she seen any movies, or read any books. She was supposed to say, 'I love you, too'."

We got back to Leslie's house, and I told her goodbye, and headed back to my apartment. I could hardly wait to tell Debbie the good news. Leslie might not be gone for good! The thought that Leslie might not be out of my life forever, brought a smile to my face, and lifted a crushing burden from my heart. However, the more I thought about telling Debbie "The good news," the more I thought that she might not like it as much as I did. I decided not to say anything.

Leslie quit her job so she could get things ready for the move, and I saw much less of her. Before I knew it, she was gone.

For months, I'd go past her house, wishing she were still there and remember the times we had spent there together. The pain was almost too much to live with. Breathing became difficult as sobs wracked my body and I'd ride away, trying to think of more pleasant things. As if there could be anything that was more pleasant than the time we had spent together.

A few weeks later, Debbie and I were out visiting her parents, and her sister Valerie invited us to her boyfriend's parents' house to play cards. Debbie sat across the table from me as my partner, Valerie to my left, and Jeff to my right. We were playing euchre and Debbie and I were winning.

I'm not sure how the subject came up, but Valerie said something about never getting a kiss from me. She said it like a challenge, as if I wouldn't dare kiss her with Debbie and Jeff sitting right there. Valerie was very pretty, and I've always been a sucker for a challenge, so I leaned over to give her a quick kiss on the lips. Our lips touched, and I thought "nice soft lips," then her lips parted and her tongue slipped into my mouth. Before I knew it, I was kissing her the way Leslie and I used to kiss.

Her lovely smell was invading my nostrils and I was melting. My arms were reaching to embrace her. I don't know how long that kiss lasted, but it wasn't long enough. Debbie started making some strangling sounds across the table and we tore ourselves apart. Simultaneously, we said "WOW." Since Debbie didn't know how to kiss, I was surprised that her younger sister could kiss so well. Valerie kissed even better than Nancy.

Valerie was only seventeen, and she kissed like a woman. I couldn't help but wonder what else she was good at. The kiss scared me. If we had been alone, I don't know how far we would have gone. I had assumed that Valerie, like Debbie, was a virgin. After that kiss, I wasn't so sure. She could easily get a guy to bed.

I didn't even like Valerie. She always wanted to be the center of attention. She would put other people down to make herself feel more important. And, she lied so often, I had no idea when she was telling the truth. All the things I disliked about her, and with that one kiss, she could have had me. I never felt anything consume me so quickly - so completely. I told myself it was because I missed Leslie. That had to be it. To be on the safe side, though, I had to make sure I was never alone with Valerie.

I didn't know what to say. Debbie hadn't said anything. I looked in her direction. She had a look I had never seen before. I wasn't sure what it was. There was definitely some hurt, and some jealousy. I had seen those before when I had talked about Leslie, but there was something else. Hate? I didn't know. We finished the card game and I said it was time for us to leave. Debbie and I drove back to our apartments in silence.

By the following day, Debbie seemed to have gotten over the incident. She never mentioned it, nor did I, but the memory of that kiss will last a lifetime.

## Chapter 14

THE WEDDING

I was so glad that I had fallen in love with Debbie. Without her to love, I doubt if I could have continued living. While the thought that I might see Leslie again someday helped a little, I don't know if it would have been enough by itself.

I struggled to get on with my life. Debbie and I were finalizing the details for our wedding. We would be getting married on September 20, 1975. From the time I had been a little boy, being dragged to church by my parents, I always felt like I'd get married in my church. It wasn't until I was much older that I realized couples got married in the woman's church. As luck would have it, Debbie didn't belong to a church. She had never been baptized, so that was done in my church. She became a member and we made plans to be married in our church.

Frequently, I'd wonder what ever became of Leslie. It had been months since she and Joe moved away, and I hadn't heard a word from her. I prayed she was OK, asking God to look after the woman I loved so much.

Debbie enjoyed not having Leslie around. It used to be that if we had a fight, I'd turn to Leslie. Debbie knew this and would make a conscious effort not to drive me into her arms. Without Leslie around, she felt she could push me a little bit harder, and often did. Debbie and her mother were deciding how I was going to spend my money, after we got married, while I thought that was something Debbie and I should decide. I was starting to have doubts as to whether or not this marriage was a good idea, but I was in love with Debbie, and couldn't stand the thought of losing her along with Leslie.

I was still working midnight to eight, so I was sleeping during the day, when the phone rang. Tele-marketers often woke me up, so the telephone was next to the bed. That way I wouldn't have to wake up all the way to answer the telephone and hang up on them. I groggily picked up the phone and said, "Hello."

"Hi Buddy!" said the sweet sexy voice that often invaded my dreams.

"Leslie!" I was instantly wide-awake.

"Did I wake you?"

"You can wake me anytime. It's so good to hear your voice. I've missed you so much."

"I miss you, too. I can't talk long. I'm on a payphone. We've been so busy getting settled I haven't had time to write. I just wanted to give you my address and phone number, and let you know everything was OK."

I grabbed a pen and paper. "OK - shoot."

I wrote down the information, and then she said, "Got to go. Bye."

I said "Bye," and she was gone. If I didn't have the paper in my hand, I'd think it was a dream, it happened so fast. Now I could at least contact her if I wanted. I got out of bed, found some paper, and started writing her a letter to let her know everything that has been happening. I wanted to tell her how much I longed to hold her in my arms and savor her kisses, but I was afraid Joe may get to the mail before she did, so I kept the tone light and conversational so I didn't betray my true feelings. I told her when our wedding was going to be and what things were like at work without her. I got cleaned up, then rushed to the post office to mail the letter.

Again, months went by without my hearing from Leslie. So much was going on that I wanted her to know about. Debbie and I decided to move back home with our parents so we could save more money before the wedding. I wanted Leslie to have my parents' telephone number in case she needed to reach me, so I called her. One of her sons answered the telephone, so I asked to speak to his mother. Leslie came on the line and we chatted briefly. She seemed to be busy, so I just told her why I had called and then let her go. It saddened me to think how far apart we seem to have drifted in such a short time.

# # #

I had several thousand dollars saved in a 401K retirement plan that I told Debbie we could either use for a honeymoon in Hawaii, or to buy furniture. She chose the furniture. Since she could get a 20-percent employee discount at Hudson's, we started watching for items to go on sale. We then put them on layaway until we decided on where we were going to live. Then we started searching for an apartment that we could call home. We must have checked out ten to fifteen different complexes before we decided on the Pine Tree Apartments in South Toledo. There we found what they called an Executive Apartment that was spacious and had a great view. From our front door, we overlooked a small ravine with a clearing, which led into a wooded area. In the clearing was a small playground for children.

We signed a lease for the apartment, then started getting it furnished. As long as I didn't think about Leslie, I was very happy. Preparing for a future with the woman I loved was so - NEAT - COOL – I'm not sure how to describe it, but I enjoyed it a lot.

The summer just flew by and before I knew it, September had arrived. I called Leslie to make sure she was going to be at our wedding. She didn't think so. I begged. I pleaded. I tried everything I could think of, but she didn't see any way they could make it up for the wedding. I gave Leslie our new address and telephone number so she could reach me after Debbie and I were married. Although based on the number of times she has contacted me since moving away - once – I really didn't expect to hear from her.

We had a rehearsal dinner the week before the wedding. The next day, Debbie and I had sex for the first time. Up until then, she had let me touch her private places, and she would let me get as horny as I wanted, but she would do nothing to give me relief. This time she didn't stop me. I was as gentle as I could be, knowing this was her first time, and that could sometimes be painful. I was afraid I'd hurt her as I came, so I withdrew at the moment of climax, and shot my load onto her stomach. While I didn't enjoy the sex as much as I had with Nancy, it was infinitely better than my only time with Leslie, which I still hated myself for. I collapsed into her arms on the floor of our apartment.

My friends threw a bachelor party for me the night before the wedding. It amounted to bar hopping and my getting increasingly smashed at each one. At every bar, the guys tried to fix me up with a girl to celebrate my last night of freedom. A couple of them were pretty hot, and if I was only in love with Debbie, I may have been tempted. As it was, I'd feel like I was cheating on both Debbie and Leslie, and that I couldn't do. I don't know what time they dropped me off at the apartment, but it was either very late, or very early. I passed out on the living room floor, not making it as far as the bedroom. Debbie says she called me, we talked for a while, and then I hung up on her. I don't remember a thing.

The morning of our wedding brought rain. However, by early afternoon, it was clearing and the sun was drying everything up. We had a late afternoon wedding. It was a beautiful ceremony, just the way I always imagined it would be. Family and friends filled the entire lower half and it's a large church. Debbie and I memorized our vows, and recited them to each other. Mine went like this:

> "I Gary, take thee Debbie, to be my wedded wife. To have and to hold from this day forward. For better, for worse, for richer, for poorer, in sickness and in health, to love and to cherish till death do us part."

When I placed the ring on her finger, I said, "With this ring I thee wed, and all my worldly goods I thee endow."

We were pronounced husband and wife and we left the church to a shower of rice. We drove away to give everyone a chance to leave, then we returned to have the wedding pictures taken. After that, we went to the reception. It was the neatest reception that anyone had ever been to. People would still be talking about it ten years later. Everybody had a blast. An open bar with just about every kind of booze imaginable helped to relieve any inhibitions. Dave and Karyn were both in our wedding, and they were paired together. Dave spent the night hitting on her, ignoring his wife. Another good friend of mine, Chuck, was on the dance floor ripping off his suit coat and spinning it over his head. I hate dancing, but that night I danced several dances with Debbie. I danced with my mother, Debbie's mother, Debbie's sisters, and I'm not sure who else. The only person missing was Leslie.

We left the reception early – about 11:30 p.m. and headed to our apartment. We didn't want to be disturbed, so we didn't tell anyone where we were spending the night. We hid our car and walked to the apartment. We kept the interior lights turned off so nobody would suspect we were inside. We sat in our bathroom, drinking wine, and opening the cards we received. When we were done, we went to bed to consummate our marriage. It was much nicer than our first time. More like making love, than just having sex.

## Chapter 15

CHRISTMAS 1975

When I saw Leslie again, it was just before Christmas. She was in town through the Christmas holiday and called to see if we could get together. She had to ask?

"I need to get some shopping done for Debbie. Would you like to come along and help?" I inquired.

"Sure," she replied.

Debbie was at work, and I was supposed to be sleeping. Leslie stopped by the apartment, and I gave her a quick kiss on the lips, and a tight squeeze. I didn't want to let go. She felt so good and her familiar scent started breaking down my resistance.

I took a deep breath and pulled myself away from this woman I loved so much.

"You ready to go?" I asked.

"Ready."

We left in my car and headed to Southwick Mall, the nearest shopping center. I had a great time that day. It was half of the way I had always hoped it would be. One of the women I loved helping me shop for the other. If only Debbie wasn't so selfish. She hated the mere mention of Leslie's name. I couldn't tell her that Leslie was in town, for fear of setting her off.

Leslie helped me pick out some cute outfits for Debbie. While I'd just think of buying separate items, she would think "outfits". She taught me about color coordinated tops and bottoms, and accessorizing. Not just buying tops and bottoms that go together, but getting a purse, shoes, jewelry, etc. to match. What would have taken me several torturous weeks, Leslie helped me complete in a single afternoon. Every time I'm with her, I find another reason for loving her.

While shopping, we stopped and relaxed, having a bite to eat. It felt so good to be with her again. Leslie reminded me that we needed wrapping paper, bows, ribbon, and tissue paper. I wasn't sure what we needed all that stuff for, but I bought it because Leslie said we should.

We headed back to the apartment, and Leslie helped me wrap the presents. I never knew you should line boxes with tissue paper when you are wrapping clothes until Leslie taught me. Ever since that day, when I wrap clothes for Debbie, I think of Leslie.

I was so intent on the task at hand that I hadn't thought about the fact we were sitting on the floor in the bedroom. I'm in a bedroom, with the woman I love, a Queen-sized bed, and I'm not thinking about making love to her. I'm thinking about how much Debbie will like the presents I bought her. Of course, that was partly because our only sexual encounter left both of us feeling terrible. Definitely not something I wanted to repeat.

It started getting late and Debbie was due home in about a half-hour, so Leslie thought she should leave. I walked her to the door and gave her a tender goodbye kiss.

"Thank you for going shopping with me," I said.

"I had a good time."

"Will I be able to see you again before you head back home?"

"I don't know. I doubt it, but I'll try. Take care."

"You too."

I watched as she walked out of my life one more time.

Chapter 16

LESLIE'S FIRST LETTER

Christmas was good. Debbie liked everything that Leslie and I had picked out for her, and she was surprised at how well I did shop for her. I liked the presents Debbie bought for me, too. We had to sit through two Christmas dinners, so neither set of parents would feel slighted. It was one of the most enjoyable Christmases I ever had.

We celebrated New Years' Eve with some close friends by going out to dinner and a movie, then heading back to their place to play euchre. We stayed until well after midnight then went home to usher in the New Year with a bang. On New Years' Day we again sat through two dinners so we could spend part of the day with our own parents.

As always, the New Year started out as kind of a letdown after the big holiday season. I entertained myself by watching the football playoffs, and then I heard from Leslie. In mid-February, I received a letter she had written dated February 12, 1976.

It was an eleven-page letter that she started out with, "Hi Lovebirds!" She then congratulated us on our marriage and apologized for not making it to our wedding. I'm sure Debbie was glad Leslie hadn't made it to our wedding. I also felt that if Leslie was really concerned about having missed my wedding that she would have written a lot sooner. I mean five months after the wedding is kind of a long time to finally get around to congratulating me and say she was sorry for missing the most important day of my life. Some friend.

She went on to say that we had a beautiful apartment, and great looking furniture, and thanked us for sending the pictures of it. I couldn't remember sending her any pictures of the apartment, so I guess she made that up to hide that she had actually been to our apartment. I can't imagine Debbie sending her pictures.

She said it sounded like Debbie and I had a great Christmas and then went on to say that their big Christmas present was a chest freezer full of meat. That husband of hers is such a romantic. What a jerk. Leslie should be living in a fabulous home, driving a fancy car, wearing the finest clothes, and be getting diamonds for Christmas and her husband is buying her a chest freezer full of meat. What an ass.

I may buy Debbie something to make her life a little easier, like an electric mixer or a food processor, but that's after I've bought her more personal things and I can't think of anything else to get her. Joe goes and blows their entire Christmas on a chest freezer. Leslie didn't seem to be upset at all, which made me even madder. She doesn't even realize that Joe treats her like crap. I'd love to be the one to show her how a lady is supposed to be treated.

She did say that Bryan and Joey got lots of toys, which made me wonder if that was because of her, or there was something that Joe could actually do right. She said that the nicest part of Christmas was that they were all together. She does love her family.

Their New Years' Eve consisted of entertainment provided by Bryan and Joey banging wooden spoons on pots and pans. The way she described it, I could almost picture the smile on her sweet lips. I wished that it could have been me there with her rather than Joe.

She went on to say that it was hard getting settled in down there and initially she wanted to run up to Toledo every chance she got, but now she doesn't miss the people like she thought she would.

A tear fell onto the page as I read that she no longer missed seeing me. Sure, she was talking in generalities, but I took it personally. I had to get a tissue to dry my eyes so I could finish reading the letter. She continued, saying that she and Joe were closer than ever, and I couldn't read any more. I threw the letter down, fell onto the sofa, and started crying like a baby. I was so glad that Debbie wasn't around to see me like this since I knew she would just get mad.

I'm not sure how long it took me to regain my composure, but I finally picked up the letter and tried to continue reading it. I got as far as Leslie saying they might make it up in March but she didn't care whether or not they did. More tears; more sobs. I ached to see her, I missed her so much, and she didn't care whether she ever saw me again.

"Why did she even write this letter?" I wondered, "Just to make me feel miserable?"

It was better not hearing from her for months on end. At least then I could imagine that she was thinking about me and dreaming about holding me in her arms.

I had asked her about where she was living in one of the letters, I had sent her. I was concerned that Joe had her living in some dump, as their house in Sylvania was quite modest. She went on to tell me about her house and where they were living.

She said they were living in the country and she loved it. She said she had grown up in the country, missed it, and was glad to be back. Since her mom lived in South Toledo, and she attended school in South Toledo, I always assumed that was where she had been raised. Hard to believe that with all the years that we have known each other, and the thousands of conversations we have had, that I was just now finding this out about her.

Anyway, she was very happy that Bryan and Joey would be able to grow up in such a nice atmosphere.

There go the tears again. This certainly didn't sound like she planned on moving back to Toledo any time soon. I rushed to get more tissues.

She then told me how much better the weather is there than in Toledo. It's the middle of winter and nearly every day is sunny with temperatures between fifty and seventy. She, Bryan, and Joey spend almost all day outdoors. She said they have had a little snow that lasted a few days but then it gets nice again. People were telling her that this was the worst winter they had ever seen and she just loved it.

Decent weather. I wondered if they had any computer related job openings down there. Toledo weather depressed me more every year I lived there. When I was younger, Toledo had a lot sunnier days than they did now. I attributed that to the power plant they built in Port Clinton. The Davis-Bessie Nuclear Power Plant must throw thousands of gallons of water into the air every day because it started causing gloom, lots of rain in the summer and a lot of snow in the winter. Some years it didn't seem like I'd see the sun from September until March.

I quit my daydreaming and went back to reading the letter. Their neighbors are quite far away, as they are living on an acre of land, which leaves them pretty much on their own. The land is flat so they're looking forward to starting a large garden in spring.

Her house is rather small with only two bedrooms, so Bryan and Joey have to share a room. The kitchen and living room are respectable sizes, plus they have a basement. There is an attached two-car garage and a lot of storage space. All rooms have new carpeting except for the bathroom and kitchen, which have new tile.

At their house in Toledo, or actually in Sylvania, they made a mess knocking down walls and building new ones to create new rooms or make old ones larger. Now they wanted to put a game room, a utility room, and a bedroom in the basement. I wondered why they didn't just buy a house the way they wanted it. Of course, I was thinking about building a bathroom in my basement, so maybe I don't have room to criticize.

She was happy that Debbie and I had managed to pay off all of our bills, except of course for our house. I was glad too, but wondered how long that would last. Joe was making more money now than they both did when combined when in Toledo, so they're out of debt too. They unloaded their newer car to get rid of the car payments, and bought a used VW Bug. They now pay cash for everything.

The Bug works out great since they live so far out in the country, saving them a lot of money in gasoline. Joe wanted to buy a truck so they could haul things, but Leslie was happy with the Bug. She did say that it's a little crowded in the Bug when they have to haul hay for their pony.

Then she told me they're living in a pet shop, but it sounds more like a zoo. They have two dogs, nine puppies, a pony, two kittens, and a goldfish.

They had made some friends and went to a company dance where she met more of Joe's friends and their wives. She had two girlfriends that she hung out with and attended a ceramics class every Thursday.

She'd been doing a lot of sewing and refinishing of some furniture. She got to do whatever she wanted, didn't have to work, and she had a nice place to live. She thought she had it made.

Knowing that she had all of that free time, and I was unable to spend any of it with her, made me very sad.

They had a lot of family from Toledo running down to visit them, so they didn't get a chance to be lonely.

Bea was the only female friend Leslie had at O-I. Bea was older, more matronly, and not threatened by Leslie's good looks. Leslie said she used to write Bea all the time, but had slowed down quite a bit because her letters were never answered. I knew how she felt. I used to write Leslie weekly but now only write once a month because she never sent me a letter, at least until this one. It seemed strange to me that she would ignore my letters and write to Bea, but maybe she's worried that Joe would get upset if she were sending me letters all the time. She talked on the telephone with Bea but that seemed to be dwindling as well.

The last conversation they had was mostly about how they hated the boss in the keypunch department. The boss was female and always seemed to be picking on Leslie. Probably some jealousy going on since all of the guys went after Leslie when she started working there. Now with Leslie gone, it's her friends that are being picked on. I'm not sure why that is.

Leslie was glad that things were going well for me at work and asked me to say Hi to everyone and tell them that she misses them.

She closed the letter asking Debbie to please write, too. Like there was much chance of that happening.

She gave their address and ended the letter with Love Joe, Les, Joey and Bryan. She could have left Joe off, but it was nice that she said, "Love." That was pretty much the only indication in the entire letter that she cared for me at all, even as a friend and I thought we were a lot closer than that.

I thought back to some of the times we had spent together. The night she offered to "KISS" me. The night we had sex we both regretted. She seemed to have drifted so far away and it made me very sad.

It was great hearing from her. Maybe she will stay in touch better than she did last year. It sounded as though she was getting along well in her new environment, which somehow saddened me.

I desperately wanted to write Leslie. Debbie and I were having some problems, and I'd love to get her advice on what I should do. Unfortunately, I'm afraid this is something that I'm going to have to deal with on my own.

Chapter 17

EARLY MARITAL PROBLEMS

Debbie and I got along great, and I loved her very much. However, I only had her word for it that she cared for me. She certainly never showed it.

With her being a virgin, I knew she lacked experience. I thought it would be fun teaching her how to please a man. Only problem was – she didn't have any desire to learn. Our intimate encounters could only be described as "having sex" – certainly not "making love." Two people have to be there to "make love" and Debbie never seemed to be there. Her idea of "making love" was lying on her back so I could take her. I'd do everything I could think of to try and please her. She seemed to love it when I'd go down on her but she wouldn't dream of returning the favor.

While attempting to arouse Debbie, I'd be hard and dripping lubrication all over the place. Deb would treat my pre-cum as an infectious disease she had to avoid at all cost. If it didn't hurt my feelings so bad, it would almost be funny.

After I had an orgasm, she would quickly jump out of bed to go cleanse herself, as though I had defiled her in some way.

I didn't have a lot of experience in this area, but her reactions left me longing to be with Nancy once again. Making love with Nancy was incredible, while having sex with Debbie left me feeling empty and unloved. Some nights I'd sob myself to sleep, wondering what the hell was wrong.

I tried talking with Debbie about how I felt. It was hard to get the words out, but they needed to be said. She seemed to understand, but nothing changed.

Months went by, and sex was still "the pits," so I asked Deb to check with her doctor, to see if there was a physical reason why she couldn't have an orgasm. I figured I wouldn't enjoy sex very much either if I never had an orgasm. Unfortunately, the doctor gave her a clean bill of health.

Nancy was the only woman I had ever had sex with that had an orgasm. I had heard that some women fake it, but I don't think she did. It didn't seem to be that difficult for her to achieve. She took a little longer than I, but if I could hold back, she would cum just fine. So, what was Debbie's problem? I could think of only one. She didn't love me like that. Was it just me, or did all men turn her off? Was she a Lesbian? I had no answers, just questions. All I knew for sure was that sex wasn't very pleasurable, so we didn't do it very often. She was "on the pill," so doing it to have children wasn't even a good reason. Once every couple of months, I'd try again, then be reminded why it took two months before doing it.

Along with my feelings for them, Debbie and Leslie had another thing in common: they're both terrible in bed. To be fair though, Leslie and I never made it to a bed.

Debbie and I started seeing a counselor to see if her problem was mental. We went about ten to twelve times. I don't have a clue how it was supposed to help her in bed. The questions seemed stupid and pointless. The counselor tried to make big issues out of little things. For instance, Deb, me, my mother, her mother - we all fold bath towels in thirds vertically and then in half over the towel bar in the bathroom. When I wash towels, I folded them the same way, then an extra fold in half to put them away in the linen closet. When Deb washed towels, she would fold them in half, then in half, then in half again, then put them in the linen closet. When it was time to put them in the bathroom, she would unfold them, and then refold them in thirds vertically, then in half over the towel bar. I tried to convince her she was putting forth twice the amount of effort she needed to. If she did it my way, it wouldn't be so much work. The idea seemed to irritate Debbie.

"You just think your mom's way is better than my mother's."

"If my mom does it the right way, then it is better than your mom's," I thought, but then said, "I don't know how my mother folds her towels. I don't care if my mother spends twice the amount of time folding towels as she needs to. I'm trying to be helpful."

Well, the counselor jumped on this, and made Deb understand I was trying to be helpful. There were about a half dozen other instances like that, and the counselor took my side on all of them. Big surprise. If you can think logically, you'll arrive at the same logical conclusion I do. These encounters did nothing to improve our sex. In fact, they were putting a strain on our entire marriage. Deb didn't want to go any more, and I had to agree with her that it was pointless.

Chapter 18

GOOD TIMES

Outside of the bedroom, everything was great. I loved Debbie, and she had replaced Leslie as my best friend. There were some things I didn't feel comfortable discussing with her, especially since she didn't seem to care about my feelings in those areas anyway, but I figured that it was probably normal for married couples to keep some things to themselves.

Dave's uncle was selling his 1973 Corvette, and Dave asked if I was interested. I told him I was, but I'd have to check with Deb.

"You've always wanted one. If you think we can afford it, why don't you get it?"

I researched the financing and insurance, and we bought the car. It was a white T-top coupe with a tan leather interior. It was fully loaded with power windows, power brakes, power steering, air conditioning, tilt/telescoping steering wheel, chrome side-pipes, four-speed manual transmission, and a 350 cubic inch V8 engine. Until I got married, I couldn't afford the insurance on one. I loved it. I called Leslie to tell her I finally had my dream car.

Debbie didn't know how to drive a manual transmission, but she was determined to drive "The Vette," so I took her out and taught her how. She was very coordinated and picked it up quickly, until her first stop on a hill, that is. Fortunately, there was nobody behind us. She was at cross streets, and I told her just wait until you're ready to go, then give it lots of gas. Traffic cleared, and she punched it. With tires squealing, and smoke billowing from the wheel wells, we shot across the intersection like a rocket.

"Not quite so much gas," I said, laughing.

We spent a lot of Sunday afternoons just going out for drives in that car. On Memorial Day weekend, we got on the expressway, and started heading out to her parents' house, where we were going to have dinner. The speed limit was fifty-five, so I cranked it up to sixty-three, figuring no police would bother me for going just eight over the speed limit in a Corvette. Well, I figured wrong. I saw him in my rearview mirror, two cars back. I maintained my speed, figuring he already had me. The car between us was going slower, and slower, so the officer sped around him, and then flipped on his lights and siren, signaling me to pull over. I pulled off the road onto the shoulder and stopped the car. I waited for the officer to come up to the side of my car then I lowered the window.

"Do you know how fast you were going?" the officer asked.

"Yes sir, sixty-three," I stated.

"Do you know the speed limit?"

"Yes sir."

"Let's see your license."

"Certainly," I said, as I reached into my back pocket.

"Uh, no you can't," I said, as I found my back pocket empty.

"Excuse me?" the officer said.

"I don't have my license."

"You're driving without a license?"

"Not exactly. I have a license. I just don't seem to have it on me at the moment."

"Is this your car?" the officer wanted to know.

I felt the words "no it's stolen," start to slip out, and then decided I may be in enough trouble all ready, and answered, "Yes sir."

"What's your name?"

I gave it to him, and he went back to his patrol car to check out my story. He came back about five minutes later, asked me to drive a little slower, and let us go on our way. At the next exit, I turned around and went back to get my wallet.

We finally made it out to her parents'. They were fixing something called "hobo dinner." The "hobo dinner" consisted of cabbage, potatoes, carrots, onions, and smoked sausage boiled in a pot. It was pretty tasty. In addition, we had corn on the cob and watermelon for dessert. I really enjoyed myself.

## Chapter 19

LESLIE'S SECOND LETTER

In early June I received my second letter from Leslie, dated June 5, 1976. It was a five-page letter. Actually, it was only four pages because she just said goodbye on the last page.

This letter she addressed to me and the salutation read "Hi Buddy." Her "buddy" is what I used to be before our first kiss. I thought I was a lot more than that to her now. I wondered if I was mistaken, or she was just being careful because she thought Debbie might read the letter. I wish there were some way that people could let you know what they're thinking without having to worry about somebody else finding out.

I had sent Leslie pictures of the 1973 Corvette I bought from Dave's uncle, so she writes to tell me that I'm now good enough for her to write to. I'd have bought it sooner if I had known it would get her to write more often. She says I owe her a ride. At least that gives me some hope that I'll see her again someday.

She commented on the stationary I used in my last letter and wondered if I was going to use the same in my next letter since nothing is too good for her. I wracked my brain to try and remember what was so special about the paper I had used for the last letter I sent her that she would comment on it. I couldn't remember. While Leslie's last two letters have been on printed stationary, I never really concerned myself with the paper, because it's what you write on the paper that makes it special. I just grab whatever paper is around. It might be some of Debbie's stationary or it might be index cards or just about anything else.

She said that the family has taken up camping and they have gone camping the past several weekends. They have only a tent, and no other equipment, but they have been going with a cousin of Joe's who has a trailer.

I haven't been camping since I was a Boy Scout. Debbie would never go camping as her idea of roughing it is staying in a Holiday Inn. I bet Leslie and I could think of all sorts of things to do alone in the woods. Unfortunately, it's not me that she's with - it's her husband. On the bright side, they're not alone.

They plan on going camping again on the fourth of July to a place called North Baltimore, Ohio. I've lived in Ohio my whole life and never heard of the place so it must be a pretty small town. She said that North Baltimore, Ohio will be celebrating their centennial while the entire country celebrates the nation's Bi-centennial, so that should be a lot of fun.

By then they expect to have a carrier on top of their VW Bug so they can carry their own camping equipment and supplies.

She mentioned something about a Computer Room Supervisor being ahead of her but I couldn't figure out what she was talking about. I couldn't remember saying anything to her about him, and I didn't know what anybody else had said.

She went on to say that she had been in Toledo the past couple of weekends and had thought about calling, but obviously she didn't. It saddened me to find out that she had actually been in town and didn't want to see me, or even hear my voice. She said she didn't have the time because they were camping, but she somehow managed to talk with her friend Bea from work. It amazed me that two such good friends as we were could drift apart so fast.

Leslie told Bea that she wasn't going to be writing her any more since she never wrote back. She thought Bea seemed relieved that she wouldn't be pressured into doing something she didn't enjoy doing.

She commented on Bea having a rough time at work and thinking that it was because she was a friend of hers. That seemed strange to me because I automatically think more of people who are friends with Leslie. Excluding her husband, of course.

Leslie mentioned that her Uncle Don was now working at O-I and had been for over a month now. She used to work with him at Toledo Hospital but had left there because the hospital didn't pay very well. She was happy that he would now be making more money.

She wanted to know what I'd been up to besides working, how Debbie was doing, and if she was still working at Hudson's Department Store.

Then Leslie said that maybe we could get together on one of their trips up here. After just asking about Debbie, I got the impression that she was talking about her and Joe getting together with Debbie and me. Something tells me that Joe would be just about as thrilled with that as Debbie would be. While I'd certainly be willing to meet Leslie, I doubted if there was any way that Debbie would want to see her. Her next sentence confirmed my suspicions. She said the trouble was that Joe's family always monopolized his time when they came up to Toledo. That didn't seem like a problem to me, because she could always come without him. In fact, I'd prefer that.

She went on to mention that Joe had gone into the Air Force in 1965 and his family never really got used to his being away. I guess his mother is really close with all of her children but Leslie didn't mention how many brothers or sisters Joe had. I briefly thought about asking her, in my next letter, how many siblings Joe had, but then I decided I really didn't care.

Leslie said she loved her mother-in-law as much as her own mother so she didn't mind that they spent a lot of time with his family.

After that, she said that Bryan and Joey were waiting for her to complete her letter so she would walk them to the store to get Popsicles, so she would have to go. She told me to take care and signed the letter "friends always."

I was glad she considered me her friend, and always would, but we had grown so close over the years that being demoted to just a friend really hurt. I consoled myself with the fact that even though she didn't want to get together while she was in town, at least she hadn't forgotten me entirely. I did, after all, get this letter.

After receiving that letter, I started hearing a song on the radio all the time. It sounded as though it had been written for Leslie and me. It was a song by the Three Degrees and it was called "When Will I See You Again?" The words echoed in my head.

When will I see you again?
When will we share precious moments?
Will I have to wait forever?
Or will I have to suffer and cry the whole night through?

When will I see you again?
When will our hearts beat together?
Are we in love or just friends?
Is this my beginning or is this the end?
When will I see you again?

Sweet, sweet, love of mine, tell me
When will I see you again?

It said everything that was on my mind. When will I see Leslie again? When will we share those precious moments? Are we in love, or just friends? Yes, when will I see her again?

Chapter 20

HAVING FUN

Summer in Ohio meant a trip to Cedar Point Amusement Park, in Sandusky, Ohio. They have the best roller coaster rides in the United States. Debbie and I decided it was a nice day for a ride, so we would take the motorcycle. There are two ways to get to Sandusky from Toledo: Route 2 and the Turnpike. Route 2 is usually the fastest, but it's only a single lane in each direction, so you have to be willing to pass slower vehicles. A lot of times you will run into long caravans of people afraid to pass, then you have to be able to pass a lot of cars at one time. Passing cars on Route 2 with a slow car is scary, but passing cars with my 750cc Honda isn't a problem. It's faster than any car on the road and can pass a car between heartbeats. The trip is approximately sixty-seven miles and usually takes an hour and a half. We made the trip in a little under an hour.

We had a good time, hitting all the major coasters, and a lot of the smaller rides. By late afternoon, it started to cloud up and looked like it would rain soon, so we decided we should head home. Just in case we didn't beat the rain, I thought it best to go back the Turnpike, because they had rest areas we could stop at if we needed to get out of the rain.

Fifteen minutes on the Turnpike and the heavens opened up. At the speed we were traveling, the raindrops felt like people were throwing rocks at me, but Debbie was well protected with me blocking the wind and driving rain. The rain was coming down so hard I had a stream flowing over my facemask, making it hard to see where I was going. I could feel the tires breaking traction and had to slow down quite a bit. We were thoroughly soaked in a matter of minutes, making it very cold.

I hadn't seen any signs to indicate how far away the next rest area was, so when I came to an overpass, I pulled off the road stopping under it. We had to wait nearly an hour before the rain let up enough so we could continue. We stopped at the next rest area we came to, and went to the rest rooms to wring out our clothes and dry them as best we could. It was still raining, but at least we could warm up a little before continuing. It took almost three hours before we finally made it home, but at least we made it safely.

Debbie's birthday was soon upon us. The whole country celebrates on her birthday. It's on July 4th – Independence Day. This year she turned twenty-two. I bought her a nice ruby pendant and a few other miscellaneous items. We spent the day at her parents' house. It rains nearly every 4th of July in Toledo, but for the nation's bi-centennial, it was a beautiful sunny day.

During the summer, I'd come home in the morning after work, grab a few hours of sleep and then lie out in the sun working on my tan. Some mornings, Joe, a co-worker, and I, stopped at a bar before heading home. Joe was single and didn't like to drink alone, so he kept buying me drinks so I'd stay. Debbie was at work by the time I could get home, so I didn't mind making a stop. We would shoot pool, play pinball, and talk about things on our mind.

One day the subject of Leslie came up. Although she was usually on my mind, I don't think it was me that started the conversation. Of course, being pretty polluted, I could be mistaken. Anyway, I learned that she and Joe (not to be confused with the Joe she's married to) went to school together. I know he told me the name of the school, but it slipped my mind. I was tempted to ask him later, but didn't want to appear to be too interested in Leslie.

Towards the end of summer, Joe and I decided to go to my apartment on our lunch hour. There wasn't any traffic at 4:00 a.m. so it only took 10 minutes to get there. When we got there, Joe was a little surprised, and I was shocked.

Debbie had left keys in the outside door lock so anybody could walk in. We did, and what we saw surprised us even more. Debbie's clothes were strewn all over the floor leading to the bedroom.

My first thought was that she had somebody in bed with her, so I burst into the bedroom. She was alone, and my banging the door open woke her up. I threw the keys at her and told her she had left them in the door lock.

Since I knew I couldn't please her in bed, I couldn't help wondering if someone else had been there already, or she was expecting somebody to show up later. I tried pushing these thoughts out of my head but I wasn't having much success because they hurt too badly.

Joe and I had a bite to eat, then headed back to work. I vowed I'd never surprise Debbie, by coming home in the middle of the night, again. If she was seeing somebody else, I didn't want to know about it. Just like with Leslie, I loved Debbie, and wanted her to be happy - even if it wasn't with me.

As quickly as it got here, summer was gone, and we were into September and our anniversary. I sent Debbie a dozen red roses at work and we went out for a fancy dinner that night.

## Chapter 21

LESLIE'S THIRD LETTER

In early October I received my third and final letter from Leslie. The letter was dated September 27, 1976 and it was four pages long. Of course, I didn't know at the time this was to be the last letter I'd receive from Leslie, but I did notice the letters were getting shorter all the time. I reasoned that if they kept getting shorter, eventually there wouldn't be anything left to send.

Like the last letter she sent this was addressed to me, her buddy. She started the letter saying I had probably forgotten about her since she hadn't written for so long, as if that were possible. No Leslie, I haven't forgotten about you, and it's not because I haven't tried. I love Debbie and I want our marriage to work but I'll always love you. That's a fact of life just as much as gravity. I could no more forget Leslie than I could forget to breathe.

She asked me to not answer this letter since she's so far behind in sending me letters. I just don't understand why she waits so long to reply. I enjoy writing, but I want an answer right after I send it. I want an answer minutes or hours later, not months later. Having to wait for a reply is so maddening.

The most exciting thing in her life right now is that her oldest son Joey is starting school. Joey won't be five until October so he had to be tested before they would let him start school, and he passed. Leslie is sure that Joey gets his brains from her. Not yet five and he has an IQ of 112 and a vocabulary of a six-year-old. Leslie is very smart. Her thought processes are very logical like mine and she has a better memory than I do. I had no doubt that Joey got his smarts from her.

She said that Bryan just turned four and he thinks he should be going to school too. She thinks both boys are growing up too fast. Her mother and brothers were down to visit with her over the weekend. It was the first time her mother had been there since she had left Toledo. Her mother told her she wouldn't stay away so long next time.

Leslie went on to say that Joe was scheduled to attend a class in November so she would probably see about taking Joey out of school and head to Toledo and stay with her mother for a week. Her husband wants her to go with him so maybe he isn't a complete idiot after all. I know I wouldn't want to go anywhere without her. Joe will be in class all day, and studying all night, so she doesn't think that would be much fun for her. She's looking forward to spending time with her mother so she thinks she will probably go to Toledo even if Joe objects.

They had planned on visiting Toledo last weekend but she talked her husband out of it. She just wasn't ready to see everyone. She was wondering if I ever get that way. Sure, there are a lot of times I prefer to not go visit a bunch of people, but if it gave me a chance to see her, I'd certainly jump at the opportunity. Why is it that people can't love you as much as you love them?

She said her sister-in-law was going to have a baby in December so she was hoping to make it up then, plus they would be in town for an early Christmas because Joe has to work on Christmas Day.

Leslie thanked me for sending the pictures of my Corvette. She wanted me to take good care of it because she pretends it's hers. It could be hers if only she'd marry me. Well, that's certainly a silly thought since now we are both married.

She said she had talked with Bea a while back and found out there was no more third shift keypunch department. Keypunch operators were once considered indispensable but now more data was being entered into computers directly via a keyboard and monitor. Punch cards were rapidly becoming obsolete.

Leslie had heard that the old third shift keypunch supervisor was now working in the computer room, as were some of the keypunchers that the supervisor thought highly of. Needless to say, Leslie wasn't thrilled with this. She started to ask me some questions regarding this situation and then remembered she had told me not to answer this letter.

Her dog had nine puppies about three weeks ago and her mice had six cute babies. Seems to me that one of her dogs had nine puppies when she wrote before. Leslie must emit some kind of energy that makes every animal around her horny. I know she has had that effect on me many times. She went on to say that I probably had a good idea of how small the mice were. At first, I wondered why she said that but then remembered she had been in my apartment several times with Dave. I didn't have mice but I did have hamsters, so yes, I did have an idea of how small they were.

Every family around them was huge. She called them baseball teams. She and Joe would like to have more children but she doesn't think she can get pregnant again. I don't know if that's just because they haven't had any more children yet, or if there was some problem, she never told me about. Both she and Joe were disappointed.

With Joey now in school, she started to get involved in school activities and said she now belongs to the MTA. I have no idea what MTA stands for. In Toledo there is a PTA in schools. That stands for Parent Teacher Association so I guessed that MTA stood for Mother Teacher Association. Last Tuesday she had the opportunity to popcorn for the kids. They had popcorn every Tuesday and she popped five hundred and thirty-five bags in one morning. She thought that was a lot of fun.

The school was having a Fall Festival on October 2nd and she had a hand in getting that going. She would be utilizing her craft making skills until her fingers fell off, as she put it. She included a bookmark she had made for Debbie. I don't think Debbie knows what a bookmark is. I'm not even sure she knows what a book is. I'm always reading something, but other than an occasional magazine, Debbie never reads.

Leslie then said she had to get back to bed because it was after midnight and Joey had to get up at seven-thirty to get ready for school, which naturally meant she had to be awake too. I liked the way she said she would have to get back to bed. I assumed that meant she had been in bed thinking about me. If it's not listening to a song on the radio, then lying in bed was where I usually thought about her too.

She told me to take care and signed it your friend, Les.

It sounded like she would be back for Christmas. I sure hoped that I'd get a chance to see her.

Chapter 22

HOME SWEET HOME

I realized that Debbie and I had become a regular working couple. Every day was the same: work, eat, and sleep. Saturday nights we would sometimes go to a movie, but most times, we would get together with friends to play cards. Sundays in the fall and winter you could find me in front of the TV watching football. Some Sundays Debbie would stay and watch football with me and some she would drive out to her mom's and they would go shopping together.

Thanksgiving Day was the same as last year. Two sets of parents, and two dinners. It worked out well that there were two football games on. I was able to watch one at my parents' and then one at Debbie's parents'.

I was able to talk with Leslie a few times while she was in town, but she couldn't get away to see me. Her mother managed to monopolize her time pretty thoroughly.

I was forced to do Debbie's Christmas shopping on my own, and it was so depressing compared to last year. Last year was fun and exciting. This year I was sad and downtrodden. Debbie liked the clothes I got her so much last year that I wanted to get her clothes again this year, but I felt out of place in the women's stores and only managed to find a few items I thought she would like. I bought her some jewelry. She had been talking about a diamond star necklace in the store window of Bailey Banks and

Biddle. She was so upset when it was gone. Of course, I had bought it, but she didn't know that. I couldn't think of anything else to get her, so I bought her items for the apartment.

On Christmas morning, the star necklace was her favorite gift. The clothes were next, and the items for the apartment were her least favorite. She said she liked everything, but I wasn't stupid. I knew I'd have to work on getting better at buying her clothes. We were gone the whole day, spending time with both sets of parents. They were lucky. They didn't have to get out in the freezing cold. One of these days, I'll be able to stay indoors where it's nice and warm, and people will come visit me.

New Year's Eve was spent with friends, and New Year's Day we were back with all the parents.

In early spring, Debbie and I started looking for a house. Our apartment was nice, but it was a long way from everybody, and we wanted our own house. My mother offered to lend us the down payment, so we had to consider what she felt was a worthwhile investment. That wasn't a big problem. My mom and I'd go out during the day looking at houses, and if we saw something we liked, then I'd bring Deb back to see what she thought about it. My mom and I probably checked out two-dozen houses, and I took Deb to see about six of them. She really liked a little story and a half in West Toledo that was about a half mile from my parents' house. It was my favorite, too.

The main floor had a living room, kitchen, bath, and two bedrooms. The upstairs was a finished dormer, done in knotty pine. The basement was also finished in knotty pine and had a bar. There was a door that led into the laundry room, which wasn't finished. The concrete block walls were painted a light yellow. The garage was large enough only for a single car, wasn't attached to the house, and didn't have an automatic opener. There was a ribbon driveway, where there were two concrete paths for the tires, and a grass strip between them. The house was finished with white aluminum siding, and next to it stood a fifty-foot TV tower with an antenna on top. There was a large backyard where I could plant a garden. Everything looked very well maintained. They were asking $43,500 and we offered them $35,000. We waited anxiously for them to accept or counteroffer. They finally came back with a $39,500 counteroffer, and we grabbed it. I couldn't believe it. We were going to have our own house - a "real" home.

The house was empty, so we were able to have closing quickly, and start moving in. The house was centrally located, putting us closer to work, family, and friends. I spent a lot of time working around the house. I planted a peach tree out back and started a small garden. I built a workbench in the basement, and I laid down new carpeting in the kitchen and bath. I installed a new kitchen sink with a garbage disposal. The kitchen cabinets were just cheap plywood that was finished in white paint. I repainted them using a two-tone process of light base coat and dark topcoat that simulated wood grain. They looked a lot better when I was done, although not as good as natural wood would have looked. Depending on how long we stay in the house, maybe that would come later.

The months flew by as we worked to turn our house into a home. Debbie and I worked on many homemade projects to decorate the house. We hooked rugs, we did string art, and Debbie did some counted cross-stitch.

In the summer, we did our annual trek to Cedar Point, but this time we took the Corvette. Taking the car was better anyway, because we could bring back boxes of Cedar Point's famous salt-water taffy.

Now that we had a house, I started talking about having kids. Kids weren't something Debbie wanted right away. I reminded her that we had been married for over a year, so it wasn't exactly "right away." She was insistent. She was young and wasn't ready for kids. OK, I thought, we can wait. I did however want children while I was still young enough to be able to get out and play with them. Teach them to ride a bicycle, throw a ball, and swing a bat. If we didn't have kids before I was thirty, I didn't see much point in having them.

Our birthdays came and went. Mine is fifteen days after hers.

Summer gave way to fall and we went out and picked apples. There had been a recipe in the paper for making Apple Butter jam in a crock-pot, so we decided we would try making some. It turned out wonderful and we did our first canning so it would last for months. I'm not sure why they call it canning, when we were actually putting the stuff in jars, but who am I to wonder why?

For our second anniversary, I sent Debbie two dozen roses at work. I wasn't sure how many years I could keep adding an extra dozen roses, but the thought was there.

Thanksgiving, Christmas, and New Year's just flew by. I think I blinked and they were gone.

Weather was starting to warm up a little, and I started working outside to get my garden planted with the cool weather crops. This year I was trying a new method of gardening called "Square Foot Gardening." There was a TV show on weekly that made it look really easy.

Chapter 23

THE PHONE CALL

The phone rang. I answered it. A voice on the other end asked, "Gary?"

I replied, "Yes."

"It's Leslie."

"No kidding," I said, instantly recognizing the voice of the woman I loved so much.

"I'm back!" Leslie said, her voice brimming with excitement.

"Back where?" I wondered, not knowing what she was talking about.

"Back in Toledo."

"Great! For how long?"

"Permanently. We moved back."

I was stunned. I had no idea they were even considering moving back.

"When can I see you?" I inquired.

"I don't know. Do you still go in to work at midnight?"

"Yes."

"Do you want to meet before work?"

"Sounds good, but I can't leave the house much before eleven. That's when Debbie goes to bed."

"OK. I'll meet you just after eleven, near your house. Pick a spot."

I gave her directions to a spot with easy freeway access. A spot that's somewhat secluded.

"See you tonight," I told her. "Can't wait."

"Bye," was all she said.

I thought, "Maybe I shouldn't do this. Debbie probably wouldn't approve."

However, I rationalized that Leslie and I were just very good friends. It's not as if we were lovers heading off to a secret rendezvous. If Debbie didn't know, it wouldn't hurt her. Besides, it's not like I could invite Leslie to the house; Debbie would definitely get upset if I did that. No, it was best to not let Debbie know that Leslie was back in town. There was no sense in getting her all worked up for nothing.

I knew I'd see Leslie. I had to see Leslie. The only thing that could prevent that from happening was Leslie. All I had ever thought about was seeing her again. Now that I had a chance to do that, there was no way I could pass it up. My heart raced in my chest. The thought of seeing Leslie again was all I could think about.

I anxiously waited for Debbie to go to bed and then left the house. It wasn't anything unusual. Some nights I stayed to watch the news; some nights I didn't. I arrived at the designated spot, and there was already a car parked there, with somebody inside. I couldn't tell who it was. I got out of my car, and their car door opened. A short woman exited the vehicle and walked toward me. It had to be Leslie, but she looked so different. Her hair was shorter, and she was wearing glasses. We said, "Hi," and started walking around the block, talking. We had been walking, and talking, for nearly half an hour. We were almost around the block when she stopped and asked, "Will you kiss me?"

I didn't say anything. For an answer, I pulled her into my arms, and our lips touched. "Oh, Yes," I thought. This is what I had longed for. I was so happy. I was burning with desire. I loved this woman so much. I drank in her sweetness and wanted more, so much more. Time passed far too quickly. I didn't want to leave her, but we both had to go to work. We made plans to meet again: next week, after work.

Chapter 24

WORTH THE WAIT

I didn't know a week could go by so slowly. At six years old, I thought it took forever for Christmas Day to arrive. The day I was to meet Leslie after work seemed to take twice as long to get here. All I could think about was holding Leslie in my arms. Kissing those beautiful, soft lips. Now that I knew how close she was, I ached to be with her. Debbie caught me daydreaming several times and asked what I was thinking about. I couldn't very well tell her that my arms and loins ached to be with another woman, so I told her I was thinking about some work-related problems.

The day finally arrived. I only had to make it through eight hours of work, and then I could be with Leslie. I couldn't concentrate on work. Leslie filled every thought. I don't know how I managed to do my job. The hours dragged slowly by. I wondered if Leslie was as excited about seeing me as I was about seeing her.

Finally, it was daybreak. The sun was slowly rising. It wouldn't be long now. Just one hour more. I watched the clock hands go slowly around. "Come On!!!" my brain screamed. I could feel my heart start to beat faster. I wanted to run out the door. My stomach was starting to churn. I was beginning to feel like I was going out on my first date. I was becoming a nervous wreck.

"This is silly," I told myself, "I've known Leslie way too long to get nervous about seeing her."

I started to think about the many times we had spent together, and I started to relax. Time started to move faster as I remembered all of the good times we had together. My watched beeped, bringing me back from my thoughts. Eight o'clock. I ran for the door. I ran across the parking lot, jumped in my Vette, and lit up the tires as I flew out of the parking lot.

We had decided to meet at Ottawa Park. I had spent a lot of time there as a kid, and I knew a lot of places where we could be alone. I was there in about five minutes. Leslie hadn't arrived yet.

"It's OK. Don't worry," I told myself. "She'll be here shortly."

I felt like I was going to explode. I got out of my car and started pacing. I heard a car pull into the lot behind me. I spun around and saw it was Leslie. My heart soared. "Thank you, God, for answering my prayers."

Leslie got out of her car, and I led her to a hidden trail that was barely noticeable. We walked down the path, our hands firmly clenched to one another.

"Why can't every day be like today?" I wondered to myself.

The day was warming up fast. We reached a small clearing next to a babbling brook. We found a place to sit, and we started talking. We talked, and talked, eager to hear what the other had been up to since we last talked. We were sitting close, and she smelled SO GOOD.

"What's that fragrance you're wearing?" I asked.

"Sweet Honesty."

"Who makes it?"

"Avon."

"I REALLY like it."

Nancy had worn "Andiamo." I had bought Debbie some, but it never smelled as good on her. A perfume smells different on every woman that wears it. I wondered if "Sweet Honesty" would smell this good on Debbie. Somehow, I doubted it.

We had talked for over an hour, when Leslie said, "You have more will power than I do."

"Me? Will power? If I had any will power, I wouldn't be here with you. No, I have no will power when it comes to you. I live to be with you. I'd do anything for you."

"Then make love to me."

I couldn't have heard that right.

"We tried that once. Remember?"

"I wasn't ready then. I am now."

"For what?"

"For you. I long to feel you inside me. Please kiss me."

I wasn't sure about the making love part. The bitter memory of the one time we tried that still haunted me. I felt sick every time I thought about it. But the kiss, yes, I could do that. I longed to hold her in my arms and kiss her.

We leaned over, and our lips touched. Instantly, I had no control. She pulled me into her arms. I had never known her to be so aggressive. She wanted me. She wanted me bad. I could feel myself getting hard. I was throbbing. I ached for her. She pulled me to her chest, cradling me in her arm like a baby. Her kisses made me dizzy. My head was spinning. I never felt so good. I jumped a little, as I realized she had her hand in my pants. She had already unbuckled my belt. Unsnapped my pants. And pulled down my zipper. I was so consumed by her kisses; I hadn't even felt what she was doing. Her hand was gently stroking me, and I could feel myself getting wet, as she prepared me to service her.

She let my head slip to the ground next to her, and she leaned over the top of me. She unbuttoned my shirt with one hand, while the other continued to hold me. She began kissing my chest, working her way down to my stomach. I wanted to explode as I felt myself being taken into her warm, wet mouth. I was sure she could feel me pounding, as I got harder than I ever thought I could. I felt huge. I ached for release. My body shuddered. Every fiber of my being ached for release. She pulled my pants down around my ankles, slipped off her panties, and mounted me. Oh GOD!!!!!

My body shook and twitched as she leaned over, now straddling me, and slipped her tongue into my mouth. I had died and gone to heaven. There was no other explanation for how I could possibly feel so good. As she started sliding up and down on me, I decided heaven couldn't possibly be this good. With her tongue in my mouth and her warm wet pussy wrapped around me, she continued to work me top and bottom until I exploded. I could feel a huge load squirt deep inside her. My body twitched spasmodically as she rode through my orgasm. I lay there spent, thinking we were through, and loving every second of it.

But I didn't get soft. What was she doing? It was an incredible sensation that I'd never felt before. Something inside her had a firm grip and was gently milking me. The intense throbbing was returning to my shaft and my jewels were starting to ache. Leslie then lay down on my chest, her legs now straight out between mine. She pressed her lips to mine, wrapping her arms around my neck. I couldn't breathe without inhaling her intoxicating scent. My head was starting to spin again. I'd never before felt like I so totally belonged to someone. I was Leslie's, to do with as she pleased.

She started to slide her entire body up and down mine. Just as I felt I was going to spring free of her, she would slide down and swallow me up again. Her tongue was once again in my mouth. I couldn't decide which felt more pleasurable. Top and bottom were being stimulated beyond anything I'd ever felt before. She started doing that thing inside of her again. It felt as though I was being held in a tight grip, and being squeezed until I pop. And pop I did. My body trembled again as the orgasm swept over me. So much for no multiple orgasms in males.

I couldn't see anything. My eyes had rolled back into my head. My other senses were being overloaded. My chest was heaving, screaming desperately for air. I could barely breathe. I don't know if it was the weight of Leslie on my chest, the exertion, or the fact that every breath was filled with Leslie. But I felt like I was going to die there and then.

"What a way to go," I thought.

Just then the crushing weight lifted from my chest. Leslie rolled off me, pulling me on top of her. She had her legs wrapped around me, holding me deep inside her. In this position, my eyes rolled to their normal position, and I opened them to look into her eyes. I don't think I've ever seen so much love before. She looked longingly into my eyes, then cupped my face in her hands, and pulled me down to her mouth.

I was starting to throb again. I still wanted this woman so desperately. I started to pump, thrusting myself deep inside her. She felt so incredible. In a matter of minutes, I came again. After the third orgasm, I shriveled up, and slid out of Leslie. I collapsed into her arms, exhausted. As we lay there entwined, holding each other tightly, my mind started to drift to the first time we had sex. As I started to regain my senses, I became panicky. What had we done? We shouldn't have done this. Was she crying again? I looked into her face, expecting to see tears. She smiled at me and said,

"I love you so very much," and pulled me to her lips. We laid there, half naked in the warm sun, not wanting to let go. I had never been happier and it was destined to get better.

I don't know how long we lay there in each other's arms, but eventually we had to pull ourselves apart and get dressed.

Leslie had a concerned look on her face as she asked, "How do you feel?"

"I feel incredible."

"I mean about cheating on Debbie. About committing adultery."

Oh... She really wanted me to see that. Right there in black and white, big as life, ADULTERY. I had broken one of the Ten Commandments. I was going to burn in hell for all eternity. Good news is, it wasn't the first one I broke. Is that good news?

"I don't see it that way," I started explaining. "I knew you before I did Deb. I loved you before I did Deb. I wanted to make love to you before I did Deb. I would have married you, if you had let me, and then I never would have met Deb. I love you. I want you. And, that's all that matters."

I thought to myself, "I prayed to God for this moment and he finally answered my prayer. Wouldn't it be wrong to not accept his gift?"

I also reasoned, "If Leslie was going to burn in hell, for committing adultery, I wanted to be there by her side." No matter how I looked at it, there was one simple truth. I'd never been happier than I was right then, and I was going to hold onto that feeling for as long as I could. I'd worry about Debbie if and when the time came. As for now, Leslie was back, she was with me, and the future looked bright.

Chapter 25

TOO LATE TO TURN BACK

I left Leslie and was on my way home when a song playing on the radio caught my attention. It was "Too Late To Turn Back Now" by Cornelius Brothers and Sister Rose. It wasn't so much the words of the song, but the title. The words went, "I think I'm falling in Love." I'd been in love with Leslie for a long time, but after that day, it was definitely too late to turn back now. I wanted her so badly that nothing else mattered.

I couldn't imagine letting a day go by without making love to her. It scared me a little that we may be risking our friendship. Up until now, we didn't care if we were seen together, because we weren't doing anything wrong. If we were caught making love, there would be a price to pay and it would probably be a higher one than either of us would care to pay. I loved Debbie, and I didn't want her to get hurt, but a life without Leslie was something I couldn't even contemplate.

I got home and was getting ready for bed when the telephone rang. I answered it. It was Leslie.

"I love you," she said.

That was the sweetest thing I had ever heard.

"I love you, too. Can I see you tonight?"

"I was hoping you'd want to."

"Of course, I want to. Eleven o'clock; usual place?"

"See you then."

"Good night."

It was almost noon, and I was saying "good night." I fell asleep hoping that someday we would be going to sleep in each other's arms, when I said "good night" to her. I slept and dreamt of Leslie. Dreamt of holding her in my arms and making love to her. I was usually up to have dinner with Debbie, but on this day, I slept through dinner, not waking up until after nine. I just couldn't tear myself away from the dreams of Leslie's loving embrace.

I woke up and saw how late it was. My first thought was, "Less than two hours and I'll be with Leslie." I showered, shaved, and got dressed. Deb saved me dinner, keeping it warm in the oven. Dinner probably tasted better three hours earlier, but at least it was nourishment, and I needed to keep up my strength for Leslie. I watched some television with Deb, but really wasn't paying any attention to what was on. To cover the fact that my mind was off thinking about Leslie, I kept yawning and acting tired and disoriented. At eleven, Deb went to bed, and I went off to see Leslie.

Leslie was standing beside her car when I got there. As I climbed out of my car, she ran up and threw her arms around my neck, pulling me down to her lips. Having just left Deb, my first thought was that I wished Deb was this happy to see me, then that thought gave way to passion and desire. With the memory of making love to Leslie still fresh in my mind, she had me instantly hard. She knew the effect she was having on me, and she loved it. She pushed closer to me, concentrating the pressure on the hardness between my legs, as her kisses made me dizzy.

Leslie pulled back a little and said, "I'm so happy to see you."

I glanced down at the rock-hard bulge in the front of my pants and said, "I'm so horny to see you."

She smiled and said, "I can take care of that." She grabbed my hand and led me down a darkened street. I could barely walk as every step caused my thighs to hit my throbbing jewels. After just a couple of houses, she pulled me off the sidewalk and leaned me against a tree. She had just undone my pants and released me, holding me in her small warm hand, when a porch light went on next door and someone came out of the house. They started walking toward the sidewalk, and we knew we would be seen if we stayed there. Keeping the tree between them, and us, we started walking down the street, with her still holding me in her hand. I glanced behind us and saw the person that had left the house was out walking their dog, and thankfully, they were walking in the other direction. I glanced at my watch, and saw it was time to head to work.

"We have to go," I said.

"OK," she said, releasing me.

Me and my big mouth. I gently placed my still swollen organ carefully into my pants, and put myself back together. We slowly walked back to our cars.

"I'm going to see you in the morning, aren't I?" I asked.

"We'll see," she said.

"Please, Leslie," I begged.

"All right."

I kissed her good bye, and slid carefully behind the wheel. Every push on the clutch to shift gears caused an uncomfortable smashing of the family jewels. I was still hard when I got to work, and now felt like throwing up. My first stop was the restroom. Thankfully, nobody else was in there. I ran some paper towels under cold water, rang them out, then stepped into a stall and locked the door. I pulled down my pants, waved the towels in the air to cool them down more, and then applied them to my private parts. The swelling slowly receded as the coolness put out the fire in my loins.

This was the second time Leslie had left me like this. Although, to be fair to her, she did offer to "KISS" me the last time she got me like this. This time was a lot more painful. I walked out of the restroom, glad that the swelling was gone. There was still a dull ache between my legs, but nothing I couldn't live with. I bought a cold Coke from a machine in the break room, and then reported for work.

I found out they were putting together a new department at work, and they wanted to know if I'd be interested in working there. It was going to be called the Quality Assurance Department. They would be responsible for ensuring jobs going into production were coded properly. That COBOL programs specified a BLOCK CONTAINS 0 RECORDS clause, and that proper block sizes were specified in the JCL, as well as proper SPACE parameters.

In addition to making sure jobs followed certain standards, the QA Department would be the first line in problem resolution should a job abend. It would mean more money, and the job sounded interesting, but the hours didn't sound very good. It was a swing shift working days 8:30-4:30 for eight weeks, then working midnight to 8:00 for eight weeks, and so on. I told them I was interested, but I'd have to check with my wife first. Actually, I had to check with Leslie first; Deb second.

Leslie called me at 4:00 a.m. to see how I was doing.

"After applying cold compresses to get the swelling down, I was OK," I told her.

She laughed.

I told Leslie about the job opportunity, and asked, "Will we still be able to see each other every day if I take the job?"

"I don't know about every day. We're going for a record two days in a row this morning. We should be able to see each other just as often as we do now. When you are on days, I can get a few hours' sleep, and then meet you for lunch. When you are on nights, we can continue to meet before and after work. What does Deb think?"

"I haven't told her yet. I wanted to know how you felt about it first."

"That's sweet."

"That's me, a real sweetheart."

"You are."

"I love you."

"I love you, too."

We talked a little while longer, firming up our plans for after work, and then said goodbye.

# # #

After work, I rushed over to our secret meeting place, to find Leslie waiting for me.

"Now I can finish what I started last night," said Leslie, as she threw her arms around me.

Our lips met, and once again, we were one. She then took my hand and led me down the path to our secret spot. My legs were weak, and shaking, in anticipation. Once we reached our spot, Leslie stopped and unfastened my pants, pulling them down around my ankles. I was hard, and already dripping, when she threw her arms around me and pressed her soft body against my manhood.

I tried to step backward to keep my balance, but with my pants around my ankles, I fell to the ground with her on top of me. She was smothering me in kisses, and my head was spinning. She worked her way down my chest, kissing me all the way and then started licking my lubrication. My body then trembled as she took me into her mouth. Her tongue started doing things to me I had never felt before. I was about to cum, and started shaking uncontrollably, when she stopped what she was doing, slipped out of her slacks, and slipped onto me.

She leaned over and slipped her tongue into my mouth, as she started sliding me in and out of her warm, wet pleasure zone. Her hair covered my face and every breath I took filled me with her sweetness. I couldn't stand it anymore, and I climaxed with moans of ecstasy. Leslie lay on my chest, with her head on my shoulder, as shivers ran up and down my spine.

I don't know how long we stayed that way, but I could feel myself deflating, and sliding out of her. I was glad she didn't make me cum again. I was still sore from last night, and thought it would have been more painful than pleasurable. I held her tightly in my arms, never wanting to let go.

As I lay there, I started wondering why I wasn't having trouble breathing. The last time we were like this, her weight was crushing me, and I couldn't breathe. Today she seemed as light as a feather - really strange. I listened to her soft breathing. With every breath she took, I could feel her breasts pushing against my chest. She's so relaxed. I think she fell asleep. I strained to see her beautiful face, but couldn't, so I rolled to my side and carefully placed her on the ground next to me.

The movement disturbed her and she opened her eyes, saying, "You feel so good."

"You feel pretty great yourself," I replied.

"You know, you aren't the smallest man I've been with."

What did she say? As far as I knew, her husband and Dave were the only other two she had been with, and they were both taller than me. Duh, she means length not height dummy. Not the smallest? I wondered if she thought she was giving my ego a boost. Not the smallest? Not exactly great praise about my pride and joy. I'm just average, but that's not something to be ashamed of, is it? I briefly wondered which one was smaller than me,

Dave or Joe, and then I imagined her having sex at age ten. Her nine-year-old partner was smaller than me. I smiled.

"Do guys actually worry about how big they are compared to other guys?" I wondered.

Then I said, "I'm getting hungry. Want to go get a bite to eat?"

"Sure."

"Any place special?"

"No. Anywhere is fine with me."

We went to a Denny's restaurant. I had a big breakfast. She ate light. After breakfast, we kissed and said our good-byes. As she was getting ready to drive away, I remembered Deb and the job opportunity I had to tell her about.

"Leslie!" I shouted to get her attention.

She braked her car and looked at me questioningly.

"I have to be up to have dinner with Deb, so I can tell her about the job opportunity. Can you call me late in the afternoon?"

"If I can have a kiss," she said, leaning out the window with her eyes closed and lips parted.

I reached down and kissed her lovingly. Some people would have called it a passionate kiss, but compared to most of our kisses, it wasn't much. Heck, it didn't even last a minute. Our lips parted, and I said, "I love you."

"Love you, too," she said, and then drove away.

I stood there watching her drive away. I had that empty feeling in my chest that I get every time I have to leave her. I drove home and climbed into bed. I could still smell Deb on the sheets. I pulled her pillow next to me, and wrapped my arm around it, imagining it was Deb. Then imagining it was Leslie. Then wondering as I drifted off to sleep if this made any sense at all. I loved two women. Two women loved me. And I have to sleep alone.

# # #

The phone rang at four in the afternoon, waking me from a dream about Leslie. How appropriate it was, that she was on the phone saying, "Time to get up."

"I wish I could hear your sweet voice without the annoying ring first," I mumbled.

"You sound tired."

"Not so tired. I was just having a dream that I was making love to you, and I'd like to get back to it."

"If you hurry, you won't have to settle for a dream."

That woke me up. "Really?"

"And truly," she said.

"I'll be right..." and the thought trailed off. "Damn," I said, "I can't. I wanted to fix dinner for Deb and tell her about the job opportunity."

"You'd rather fix Deb dinner than make love to me?"

When she put it that way. Cook or have sex? Cook or have sex? Why am I even thinking about this?

"That's silly. Of course, I'd rather hold you in my arms and make love to you than cook dinner. That's not the point. It's too late to meet you now. By the time I shower and shave and get there, it would be time to come home."

"But I want you so bad," she whined.

I could feel something start to grow between my legs.

"Don't do this to me. You know I want you, too."

"Debbie sure is lucky to have you."

"Wish she thought so."

It slipped out before I thought I shouldn't say those things to Leslie any more. Now that we were "together" I shouldn't be bothering her with troubles that Deb and I have. I quickly changed the subject.

"Will I see you tonight?" I asked.

"If you want to."

"I want to. More than anything. I love you so much."

"Love you, too. Bye."

"Goodbye."

I jumped in the shower and got cleaned up, then started fixing dinner. I was fixing fried chicken, mashed potatoes with gravy, and green beans. Fixing fried chicken for Debbie always reminded me of when we were dating. We would have our apartment doors open so we could talk with each other across the hallway. Deb and Karyn would be opening a can of tuna fish for dinner, while I'd be fixing a meal of fried chicken. Something just didn't seem right about that.

I heard Debbie pull in, and got everything on the table. I met her at the door with a kiss.

"Hi Hon," I said, "Did you have a good day?"

"No, not really."

"Well, come in and sit down; dinner is already."

"This is a surprise."

"I have another," I told her.

"What's that?"

"I have a chance to get on days - sort of."

"Sort of on days?"

"It's a swing shift. I'd work days for eight weeks, then midnights for eight weeks, back to days, and so on."

"Would you like that?"

"Eight weeks of being able to sleep at night with you, rather than by myself during the day? Yeah, I'd like that. Wouldn't you?"

"I guess so."

She sounded really enthusiastic.

"I told them I'd discuss it with you, and let them know tonight. They want someone to start on days next week."

Debbie didn't say anything else. I didn't know what to say. I thought she would be a little more excited about this. We had a quiet dinner, and my thoughts started drifting back to a time in our apartment when Joe and I had found Deb's keys in the door, and her clothes strung around the apartment. I had always wondered if there was more to that. And now she doesn't seem to be thrilled that she will have to sleep with me for eight weeks straight. I wondered...

Some guys drive themselves nuts worrying about stuff like this. I tried to picture Deb having an affair. I couldn't do it. In the first place, she doesn't like sex, so what would be the point? Of course, maybe it's just me she doesn't like having sex with? That was a possibility. No, that couldn't happen. Deb would never have the nerve to have an affair. I was pretty confident about that. My plate was empty; I looked to see how Deb was doing. She was finishing up as well.

"Was dinner, OK?" I asked.

"It was good."

"So, what should I tell them about the job?"

"Do what you want. You will anyway."

Nice attitude. She's right though. It's my decision. I have to live with it, and while I'd like her opinion, I'll do what I feel is best. Best for whom though? Would it be best for Deb? She won't tell me how she feels, so I can't answer that. Would it be best for me? Sleep would be a lot better. I could go for eight weeks of sleeping when it's dark outside, rather than trying to sleep when the sun is up and people are cutting their lawns, playing stereos, etc. Then there's Leslie, and I. What would be best for us? Right now, I'm seeing her before work and after work. That couldn't happen while I'm on days. We could meet for lunch. Might even be able to come to the house sometimes. Make love to Leslie here in my bed. Now that's a thought.

"OK. I'll take it then. It means more money, and we can use that."

We watched some television, and then I kissed her goodnight, and left to see Leslie.

# # #

The first thing Leslie asked me was "What did you decide about that job?"

I took her in my arms and said, "I'd miss this something terrible if I was on days. However, there might be something better."

"What's that?"

"I was thinking you would be able to meet me for lunch, and we could go to my house. I'd really like to make love to you in my bed."

"That's Debbie's bed, too."

"You don't think she'd mind, do you?" I said grinning.

"Not a bit," she laughed, as she through her arms around my neck, pulling me to her lips. As always, her kiss took my breath away, making me breathe faster and my heart race. I think that kiss lasted twenty minutes, as our hands explored each other's bodies. I wanted her so much. I ached to be inside her, but I knew that would have to wait until morning.

We eventually pulled ourselves apart, said goodbye, and left for work. Once at work, I told my boss I was interested in the job with QA. He asked for me to stick around in the morning and meet with the head of the new department.

"I'll die if I don't see Leslie in the morning," I thought to myself, "I need her so much."

Fortunately, the manager of the Quality Assurance Department arrived at seven-thirty and we were able to meet then. The meeting ran a little past eight, but I thought Leslie would wait ten to fifteen minutes to see me. When I got there, Leslie jumped out of her car.

"About time!" she nearly shouted.

"I'm sorry, love. I had to meet with the QA manager about that job. I'm glad you waited."

"I almost left."

"I'm really glad you didn't. I'd have missed you something terrible."

"You would?"

"You don't really have to ask, do you?"

"I suppose not."

"I need to hold you," I said.

She slipped into my arms, and I held her tight.

"It feels so good to hold you," I whispered in her ear.

She turned her head, kissed me quickly and said, "It feels so good to be held by you."

We eventually let each other go, and headed down to our secret spot. We didn't make love that day. Instead, we started making plans for next week. Plans for the day we would first make love to each other in a real bed.

Chapter 26

SWING SHIFT

My first day working 8:30-4:30 felt strange. I had worked either second or third shift ever since I started working full time nine years ago. Leslie called me early in the morning to see what time she should meet me for lunch. I told her I'd leave work at eleven-thirty, so I should be at the park by eleven-forty. I had to wear a dress shirt, slacks, and a tie while on days, so I wasn't sure how we were going to engage in our normal activities and still have me presentable to go back to work. I supposed, "where there's a will, there's a way."

When I got to the park, Leslie was still in her car, and told me to leave mine there and get into hers. I sat in the passenger seat and slid over to be close to her. Being able to get close to someone is one advantage that bench seats have over bucket seats like I have in my Corvette.

"Where we going?" I asked.

"You'll see."

She drove only a few blocks away, and then parked the car in a secluded spot where we couldn't be seen.

"Turn around and lay in my lap," she commanded.

I did as she instructed. She held me in her arms, my lips close to hers. I was expecting a kiss, but she reached down and expertly undid my pants with one hand. Then she instructed me to pull my pants down, which I did. As the blood caused me to rise, she wrapped her hand around me and began stroking. Now her lips sought out mine, and her tongue darted into my mouth. She had a wintergreen Life Saver candy in her mouth, and she passed it to me. I sucked on it a while, and then passed it back. I could tell I was getting slippery, as her strokes were now sliding smoothly over my shaft. I began moaning in pleasure.

"Cum for me baby," Leslie said, "cum for me."

A few seconds later, I did just that.

"Does that feel good?" she asked.

For an answer, I moaned and kissed her some more. I trembled as she milked every drop from me. From somewhere, she produced a bunch of tissues, and began wiping up the white puddle from my stomach.

I looked deep into her eyes and said, "I love you so much, so very much. Is there anything I can do to please you?"

"You just did," she said.

"If that pleases you, I hope I can make you the happiest woman in the world."

I never came in a car before. Before I met Leslie, I had never done it outside before, either. I'd only managed to have back-to-back orgasms once before Leslie, and she had given me three in a row. I loved being with her so much before we started having sex; now being with her was beyond words. I hadn't even noticed the radio playing in the car. Now the song playing seemed so appropriate. It was "Nice to Be with You" by Gallery, and it was definitely nice to be with Leslie.

I thought about Debbie, and how she was so different from Leslie when it came to wanting to please their man. Wanting to please me was something that Debbie had no interest in. Leslie, on the other hand, could write books about it. I remembered back when Debbie and I were engaged, just before we got married. I tried to slip a piece of hard candy from my mouth to hers. She almost threw up; it gagged her so much. You would think I had squirted dog shit in her mouth. How can you say you love somebody, and react like that, I wondered.

I pulled my thoughts away from Debbie, and back to this woman I loved so much. I twisted around so I could take her in my arms, and indulge in one of our most passionate kisses ever. Several minutes later, I pulled away and said the words we hated to hear.

"We better head back."

I pulled up my underwear and slacks, and put myself back together as well as I could.

Leslie started driving us back, and I just sat there staring at her, drinking in her beauty.

"What are you looking at?" Leslie wondered.

"The woman I love."

She smiled, but didn't say anything. We got back to my car, we said "goodbye," and I headed back to work. I finished up the day, and then headed home to fix dinner for Deb. Tonight, I was cooking spaghetti. I don't like ordering spaghetti when we go out for dinner. The sauce is always too thick, and the noodles are always over cooked. I start my sauce out with the Simon and Garfunkel song "Scarborough Fair" using parsley, sage, rosemary, and thyme. Then I add onion, garlic, oregano, salt, black pepper, red pepper, crushed tomatoes, mushrooms, and enough water so everything is covered. I like to cover it and let it simmer for a few hours, but it's not too bad once it's hot. When Deb came home, I had dinner all ready.

"Hi Hon," I said as she walked in.

Debbie saw dinner ready and said, "I could get used to this."

We sat down and ate, and I told her all about my day, well almost all of my day. We finished eating, and I cleared the table and did the dishes. I made some coffee, and we went downstairs to the family room to watch television and settle in for the evening. There wasn't anything special on, mostly reruns.

At eleven, Deb kissed me goodnight, and headed off to bed. I stayed up and watched the news, then headed to bed to join her. I slipped under the covers, and slid closer to her. I reached over to put my arm around her, and she turned over, pulling away.

"Great," I thought, as I retreated to my side of the bed.

I lay there thinking about Leslie, and wishing I were with her. I fell asleep as I imagined Leslie climbing into bed with me and smothering me in kisses.

# # #

I awoke wondering if I'd be able to see Leslie today. I shaved, showered, got dressed, and then went to make some coffee for Deb and me. I just had coffee; Deb fixed herself a piece of toast. We kissed and said goodbye, then headed off to the rat race.

I was at my desk only for five minutes when Leslie called.

"Can I see you today?" she asked.

"That's my line."

"Well?"

People were standing nearby, so I whispered into the phone, "I certainly hope so. I'm dying to see you."

"Same place?"

"I hate wasting time we could be spending together. Why don't you just pick me up at work?" I asked.

"People know me there."

"So?"

"So, they'll know I'm not your wife."

"So?"

"You're not worried that Deb will find out?"

"That I'm having lunch with you? No."

"You know how she feels about me."

"Not my problem. Are you going to pick me up out front at eleven-thirty, or not?"

"You sure?"

"Positive."

"See you at eleven-thirty."

We hung up, and I got busy working. Amazing how long three hours can seem. Eventually, eleven-thirty arrived, and I went out front to wait for Leslie. She was already there. I jumped in her car, and she sped away quickly.

"Slow down, or you're going to get a ticket," I cautioned.

"I didn't like being there. I was afraid somebody was going to see me."

"You have as much right in that visitor lot as anybody else."

"I know, I just don't want you to get into any trouble because of me."

"The way we're going, that's probably inevitable."

"You think?"

"Occasionally."

"I mean..."

"I know what you meant," I interrupted. "Thursday should be a good day to make love at the house," I said, changing the subject.

"You sure you really want to do that?"

She's so sweet, being worried about my getting into trouble. She worries about me like a mother hen. Must be her maternal instincts.

"I've never been surer of anything. I want to make love to you in my bed."

"Did you make love to Deb last night?"

"Getting kind of personal, aren't you?" I joked.

"Did you?" she asked more forcefully.

She sounded a bit jealous and I liked that.

"Would it upset you if I had?"

"Yes."

"Well, I didn't."

"Really?"

"Yes."

"Why not?"

"She didn't want me," I said truthfully.

"She doesn't know what she's missing," Leslie said, as she slid her hand between my legs. I could feel myself starting to grow at her touch.

"Pay attention to what you're doing," I cautioned.

"Doesn't it feel like I'm paying attention?"

"To your driving."

"Oh," she said, putting both hands on the wheel.

"Me and my big mouth," I thought.

"Are we heading any place in particular?" Leslie wondered.

"You're doing the driving," I reminded her.

"Is a repeat of yesterday, OK?"

"You kidding?"

"It's not?" she asked, sounding a little worried that she wouldn't be able to please me.

"Yesterday was incredible. A repeat would be heaven."

"Good."

A few minutes later and we were back in the same place as yesterday, doing the same thing. I won't bore you with the details. I love it when she says, "Cum for me baby." She wanted so much for me to be happy. Why the hell can't Debbie be like that? Why the hell am I thinking about Debbie?

There must be something wrong with me. I lay at home in bed with my wife, and I dream about Leslie. Leslie gives me an incredible orgasm, and I think about Debbie. No, it can't possibly be my problem; this has got to be the warped way that God answered my prayer for Leslie to be with me. It's the only thing that made any sense. At least that's what I told myself.

"Tomorrow, I want to drive by my house so we can see how long it will take us to get there during lunch hour traffic."

"You don't want to do this tomorrow?" Leslie asked.

"No," I lied, "I want to save myself for Thursday."

We got back to my work, and I instinctively leaned over to kiss Leslie goodbye. She banged her head on the side window as she jerked her head away, not wanting us to be seen kissing.

"This sucks," I said, as I squeezed her hand and left the car. I watched as she drove away.

I walked into work and was heading toward the restroom, to make sure everything was tucked into its proper place, when a co-worker asked, "Wasn't that Leslie, I saw you with?"

"Leslie who?" I countered, as I walked on by him, not even slowing down.

Leslie was concerned someone would recognize her. That certainly didn't take long. Oh well, it would give us something to talk about tomorrow.

I finished up the day at work, and went home to fix dinner. Today I decided to take it easy, fixing Salisbury steak, mashed potatoes and gravy, and frozen corn. The Salisbury steaks were already prepared in cooking bags that I just had to throw in boiling water.

The rest of the night was a "carbon copy" of the previous night, including the rejection in bed, and my falling asleep dreaming of Leslie in my arms.

# # #

Wednesday morning was the same as Tuesday, dragging on until I was finally able to see Leslie once more. I slid into the seat next to her and said, "Somebody saw you."

She spun around in her seat looking for the "somebody."

I laughed. "Yesterday," I said.

"What did they say?"

"They said, that it looked like Leslie I was with."

"Oh, no. What did you say?"

"Leslie who? Don't worry about it, it's nothing."

"Are you sure?"

"No," I said truthfully, "but don't worry about it anyway."

"Are we driving by your house?"

"Yes, but we can't take your car tomorrow. Someone may drive past, see a strange car in the driveway, and decide to stop."

"So, you want me to park along a side street, and you'll pick me up?"

Another one of the things I loved about Leslie. She thought the same way I did.

"That's what I was thinking."

"OK, pick a spot," she said.

We were a few blocks from work. I said, "There," pointing to a side street near an elementary school. "Park on that street, and I'll pick you up just after eleven-thirty."

"OK."

We drove on past my house. It's a busy street, so there was lots of traffic, but I didn't see a single neighbor.

"Looks clear," I said, "Hope it looks this good tomorrow. Only took ten minutes to get here, so we should have forty minutes to ourselves tomorrow."

"I can hardly wait," Leslie, said, "I want you so bad."

"You keep stealing my lines."

"What?"

"I'm supposed to say, 'I want you so bad,' nobody is going to believe it if you say it to me."

"You don't believe me?"

"Oh sure, I believe you. I'd believe anything you told me. I'm madly in love with you."

"Then what are you talking about?"

"I'm thinking that we have a romance going here that should be written down in history, just like Romeo and Juliet. I'm just hoping for a happier ending. After the book, I see a movie 'Leslie and Gary - The Untold Story' or something like that. We'll make millions, buy that mansion on the huge estate, and live happily ever after."

"You're a nut."

"I am nuts about you."

I directed Leslie to a secluded spot where we were able to do some intense kissing and heavy petting. Leslie held me in her arms, and released one of her breasts from its restraint. I caressed her nipple with my tongue, gently sucking on it. We wanted each other so much. But of course, we had to get me back to work. Tomorrow would be better - much better - I was sure of that.

Leslie dropped me off at work, and I daydreamed about her for the rest of the afternoon. I could still feel, and taste, her breast in my mouth. I wanted her so badly; a wet spot was starting to form in the front of my slacks. I had to go to the restroom three times to dry myself. I'm going to have to start wearing dark slacks all the time.

First thing I did when I got home was put on a dry pair of underwear.

For dinner, I fixed a tuna fish casserole. All night long, my thoughts drifted to Leslie. She was all I could think about. Tomorrow we will make love here.

"Who you thinking about?" Debbie asked.

"Nobody, why do you ask?"

"You seem pre-occupied tonight."

"They gave me a problem at work they want me to resolve. I can't figure out how," I lied.

I didn't like lying. I hate lying. But the truth would hurt her, and that was something I didn't want to do. Why do we always hurt the ones we love? Seems like I heard that somewhere before.

Eleven o'clock arrived and Debbie kissed me good night and headed off to bed. I stayed up and watched the news, then headed for bed. Tonight, I didn't even try to make it with Deb. I knew I wouldn't be able to. My thoughts were only of Leslie.

###

Dawn broke and I felt like a kid on Christmas morning. Today I'd unwrap the best gift ever. Debbie and I went through our morning rituals, and then left for work. I couldn't even think about work. Leslie consumed all of my thoughts. At eleven-thirty I flew out the door, ran through the parking lot to my car, fired up the Vette, and tore out of there. A short time later, I was by the school, and Leslie was waiting for me. She hopped into the car, and we were off. Six minutes later, I was pulling into my drive. I didn't see anyone around, so we got out of the car, and went into the house. I watched the street for a while, and then signaled an all clear. We then retreated to the bedroom.

Leslie sat on the side of the bed, leaning back. "You sure you want to do this?" she asked.

I looked longingly at this woman I desired so much, sitting on my bed, and replied, "I'm sure."

She sat up, unfastened my belt and pants and gave a quick tug. Pants and underwear fell to the floor. She grabbed my handle, and pulled me closer. She reached up and unbuttoned my shirt and yanked it from my shoulders.

I kicked my pants out of the way, and pulled off my socks. Standing there completely naked in front of the woman I loved, while she was still fully clothed, made me feel like I was totally hers. She owned me, and it felt great. Her hand was still holding me, and she pulled me to her mouth. Her warm, wet mouth engulfed the end of my throbbing organ. Her tongue was working its way up and down my shaft, and my groin was aching.

"I need you so bad," I moaned.

Without letting me go, she managed to undress herself. She released me, and lay down on the bed, spreading her legs slightly. "Take me baby."

I didn't have to be told twice. I climbed on the bed and headed between her legs, with the intention of drinking in her juices. She quickly pulled me away.

"That's strange," I thought, "even Debbie likes that."

I kissed her stomach instead, then worked my way up to her full breasts, which were still being restrained by her bra. I kissed her cleavage, and kissed along the top of her milky white breast. I tugged on the top of her bra until a nipple popped loose, then slipped it into my mouth. I played with the nipple, rolling it around in my mouth, licking it slowly. Leslie began to moan gently. I released her nipple and carefully covered it with her bra, making sure she wasn't pinched.

I leaned over and kissed her high on the neck, just below her left ear. She smells so good here. I took a deep breath savoring her fragrance. Even though I had planned on more foreplay, we were both extremely wet, and I slipped into her without even trying. I kissed down her neck, and over to her mouth, placing my lips on hers. Her tongue entered my mouth and began exploring. Leslie wrapped her legs around me, pulling me deep inside her, and I started to pump slowly. It felt as though a little hand was massaging the tip of my shaft. I squirmed in delight.

Leslie wrapped her arms around my neck, and whispered in my ear, "Cum for me baby."

I love how that sounded. I wanted to cum for her. I wanted to show her what she does to me. I wanted to show her how much I love her. I exploded deep inside her as the orgasm swept over my body. I shook uncontrollably as she held me tightly in her arms. Mmmmmmmm

"Her turn," I thought to myself.

I rolled onto my back, pulling her on top of me, while I was still hard inside her. She assumed a kneeing position on top of me and started sliding up and down my shaft. She started doing that thing again. Somehow massaging me deep inside her. I felt like I was going to cum, but I was determined not to let her make me cum again. Not until she did. I had to think of something else. Work. When I get back to work, I'm going to have t... God, she feels incredible. The roof. I need to find that leak on the roof and fix it.

I felt myself stepping back from the edge of an orgasm. I was safe for a while. I reached up and pulled Leslie down so she was flat on top of me and I held her tight. I let my hands caress her body, feeling the smoothness of her skin, the curve of her back, and her nice round buttocks. I firmly grabbed her hips and began sliding her up and down my rock-hard shaft. She squirmed in delight, and soon took over the work on her own.

I could feel myself being pulled back to the edge of an orgasm. Debbie, I wonder what Debbie is doing for lunch. For some reason, that thought pulled me even closer to the edge. Need to think of something else. My car. I should repaint my car. I can see the body seams and they should be smoothed out.

My thoughts came back to Leslie - how was she doing? She was pumping faster now. Her breathing was sporadic and she was moaning in pleasure. She let out a gasp and her grip on my shaft tightened. I only had to thrust a couple of times with that tight grip around me, and I climaxed right along with her. As I squirted deep inside her, her body shook; she let out a loud moan, and collapsed onto my chest. She was breathing deeply, trying to catch her breath. My body twitched as the last of the orgasm swept over me. I wrapped my arms around her tightly, never wanting to let go.

"You are incredible," I whispered in her ear.

"Me? You! I've never had an orgasm through intercourse before; how'd you do that?"

"With great difficulty," I said honestly. "I'm going to need a whole chapter for this," I said, referring to my plans of writing a book about our love story.

She looked up at me and smiled. We just lay there in each other's arms as time slipped away. I was going to be late getting back to work, but I didn't care. I couldn't dream of letting her go. She finally made the first move, having to get up to go to the bathroom. While she was out of the room, I wiped myself off, and got dressed.

Leslie came back in the bedroom, saw me dressed, and said, "I thought we'd go again."

The blood immediately started swelling my now soft organ. "Really?" I asked.

"No - just kidding."

"Don't do that."

"Sorry."

We left the house, and I drove Leslie to where her car was parked. When we got there, she undid her seatbelt and climbed over the center console, plopping down in my lap. She threw her arms around my neck, pulling my lips to hers. The kiss was incredible. After what we had experienced earlier, it was the perfect topping; like a delicious dessert after a wonderful meal.

Needless to say, I wasn't much good at work the rest of the afternoon. All of my thoughts revolved around Leslie. Thank you, God, for bringing her into my life. I love her so very much.

I couldn't concentrate on fixing dinner after work, so I threw some potpies in the oven. I don't think I said anything to Debbie that entire evening, as all of my thoughts were about Leslie, and I could no longer talk with Debbie about Leslie. Debbie went to bed at her normal time while I stayed up to watch the news. An hour, or so, later I realized I had been daydreaming right through the news, and the Tonight Show was now on. I turned the lights and TV off and headed to bed, wondering if my dreams could do justice to today's experience.

As I undressed for bed, I realized I could smell Leslie's womanly scent all over my privates. I thought of washing up before climbing into bed, but decided not to. I loved having Leslie all over me. I slid under the covers and lay on my back. I took a deep breath as I relaxed and realized I could smell Leslie's perfume on my pillow. How could Deb not smell that? Leslie had been lying on top of both pillows. If mine smelled of her, Deb's had too as well. I was wondering if there was anything I could do, when Debbie cuddled up next to me. She laid her head on my shoulder, and her hand on my chest.

As I started to grow, I thought, "I should have Leslie over more often."

I waited for her hand to slide lower, but it never did. Eventually I deflated and fell asleep with Debbie in my arms.

Chapter 27

STILL ON DAYS

Leslie and I continued to meet every day for lunch. I have no idea how I managed to keep my job, or my marriage, as thoughts of Leslie engulfed every waking moment. We continued to go to my house every Thursday, and each love making session was more incredible than the last.

Whenever she was just a little bit late in meeting me, I'd panic. What would I do if something ever happened to her? How would I survive? Losing her was my deepest, darkest fear. It scared me more than anything else in my life ever had.

On one Thursday, she was late. Thursdays were so special to us; I couldn't imagine that she would let anything make her late for it. Five minutes went by, then ten minutes. A cold dark fear gripped me. My stomach was churning, making me nauseous. Tears were starting to form in my eyes, and my hands shook, as fear gripped tighter.

Then I saw her car turn down the street. It was as if someone, somewhere, had thrown a switch. I went from total desperation, to soaring happiness, instantly. Leslie pulled up and got out of her car.

"You, OK?" she asked.

"I was just worried you weren't going to make it."

Should I tell her about the fear that had gripped me? Should I tell her I was scared to the pit of my stomach? Even thinking about it made me sick. I didn't want to think about it, and I certainly didn't want to talk about it. I said nothing.

We were heading over to my house when fear gripped me again.

"I can't go to the house today," I told Leslie, "I have this fear that something is wrong."

"That's OK, let's go someplace else."

I drove to a secluded spot we had used once before. When we got there, I said, "For some reason, I'm a total bundle of nerves today. Can I just hold you in my arms?"

"Certainly," she said, as she climbed over the center console to sit in my lap. I held her tightly, fearing that someday I may lose her, and dreading that day with all my heart.

We stayed that way a lot longer than we should have, and I was very late getting back to work. Fortunately, nobody noticed.

That evening I talked a lot with Debbie. I didn't want to think about Leslie. Thoughts of her kept turning to despair, and I couldn't stand it.

"Were you out this way for lunch today?" Debbie asked.

"No, why?"

"I came home for lunch, and I saw a car I thought might be yours."

Debbie was here at lunchtime. If Leslie had been on time, Debbie probably would have caught us in bed together. Thank you, God, for protecting us.

Knowing that the fear had saved us, I didn't mind it so much. In fact, I was happy to have it. Until then, I didn't think I'd be able to sleep that night, as fear consumed me. Now, I slept peacefully, knowing that God still had his watchful eye on me.

# # #

The next day, I told Leslie all about our close encounter. We decided we shouldn't be pressing our luck as much as we had been. For a while, we actually started to go out to eat on our lunch, but that was too costly and not nearly as much fun.

We often went for walks in the park. Just being with her, holding her hand, was as enjoyable as the incredible sex we had together. On one of our walks through the park, she was walking on my left, with her right arm around my waist. She then slipped her left hand into my pants pocket. I can barely get my big hand in my pocket, but her petite hand didn't have any trouble at all.

Through my pocket, she began stroking me to life. I was growing, and she pulled me free of my underwear, so I could grow to full size. As she manipulated me, my legs were becoming wobbly, and I leaned on her for support. Although nobody could see, she had used my magic wand to cast a spell on me, and was using it to lead me through the crowd. With the incredible pleasure she was providing, I'd follow her anywhere. I tried to keep my eyes focused, but they kept rolling to the back of my head.

Although I tried not to, since people surrounded us, low moans sometimes escaped me. I was trying to see where we were going, and saw two police officers walking toward us. Thinking we should try getting away, I tried to turn around, but Leslie held me firmly. Every step brought us closer, and I was worried, but there was nothing I could do. Leslie had total control over me. When they were right in front of us, they looked at us, then at each other, grinned, and kept walking. They knew she had me. Leslie led me to a secluded spot, where I could support myself, and then got serious about her work. A short time later cum squirted from me and dripped down my leg. "Oh, God," I moaned, as I slid to the ground totally drained.

Leslie showed up one day driving a new car. Actually, I guess it was an older car, but definitely classier. Now she was driving a 1969 Pontiac Firebird. It was black inside and out, a real classic. Leslie loved speed almost as much as I do, so I knew she loved the performance. It wasn't a "muscle car" but it still had plenty of get up and go. She took me for a spin, and let it fly on the highway. She was zipping along about ninety-five when she decided to back down to a more reasonable speed of seventy-five. Since the speed limit was fifty-five, I'm not sure the police would think it was reasonable, but at least they wouldn't cart her off to jail.

I had come close to that one time myself. I had driven my brother-in-law to a Detroit Tiger baseball game. Coming back, he asked if my Corvette could go. In response, I punched it. The speedometer jumped from sixty to one hundred almost instantly then climbed a little slower to one fifteen before I started backing off. As we approached a hill, I said, "There's probably radar on the other side of this hill." I didn't know for sure, but I started applying my brakes just in case. I was down to about seventy-two when the radar nailed me cresting the hill. The police chased after me and gave me a ticket for doing seventy-two in a fifty-five zone. I didn't think it was fair, since the speed limit used to be seventy-five along that stretch before the oil crisis several years earlier, but they wouldn't give me a break. I knew if I had come over that hill at one fifteen, I'd have been spending the night in jail.

# # #

Debbie came home from work one day with some good news.

"I saw Cheryl today," she said.

Cheryl was one of her best friends in high school.

"Oh yeah? How's she doing?"

"She's doing good. She's the office manager at Channel 100, and she says they need help."

"Are you thinking of applying there?" I asked.

"I was. She said they could pay me two dollars more an hour than I'm making at Hudson's, and I wouldn't have to be on my feet all day. Don't you think I should take it?"

"Go for it," I told her.

Channel 100 was a premium cable channel. Cable television was just starting to take off, and I thought it sounded like a great opportunity for her. Besides, it was clear across town, and I wouldn't have to worry about her coming home for lunch any more.

# # #

Debbie got the job at Channel 100, and Leslie and I returned to our Thursday lovemaking at the house.

Financially, Debbie and I were doing well. With my new job, and hers, we no longer had to worry about making ends meet every payday. Sex however, was another story. Thinking about Leslie kept me horny all the time. On days when we couldn't be together, I'd turn to Debbie for relief. I know how that sounded. I wish I could make myself sound like less of a heel, but the truth was that sex was never very good between Debbie and me and if anything, it had gotten worse. On the few occasions when she didn't reject me, she would just lie there performing her wifely duty. I felt like I was raping her, and I derived no pleasure from it.

I loved Debbie so much and wished we could have a more active sex life, but after nearly three years of marriage, I doubted if that would ever happen.

#

I met Leslie for lunch one day when she informed me, "I have a problem."

"What is it?" I asked, immediately concerned.

"My car is overheating."

Thank goodness, I thought it was something serious.

"Let me take a look at it," I said.

I didn't have to look hard. The ground was soaked with anti-freeze. I opened the hood to see which radiator hose broke. I couldn't find one; they all looked good. That probably meant a bad water pump. Not good. I could replace a broken hose in the parking lot, but not a water pump.

"I think it may be the water pump. We'll let it sit and cool down while we go to my house and get some jugs of water. With any luck, you should be able to get home, and then you can have Joe look at it," I said, referring to her husband.

"What's he going to do?"

"I don't know. Replace the water pump maybe."

"He couldn't do that."

"Well, maybe he could drive it to a dealer and have it fixed? Let's worry about that later. Right now, we need some water."

We hopped in the Vette and headed over to my house to get some containers of water.

"I sure hope none of my neighbors are home," I prayed.

But they were.

"Damn," I said, "the neighbors are home. Why don't you wait in the car while I get the water? That way if they say anything to Debbie, I can truthfully tell her what happened, and that we just came here for some water."

"That is why we came," Leslie observed.

"Yes, but I don't want them to be able to describe you to Debbie. So, keep your head turned away from the house next door. OK?"

"OK."

I got out and went to the garage. I had several old containers that anti-freeze had come in. I keep them around to put the used oil in, when I changed the oil in our cars. I grabbed six of them, and then filled them up with water from the garden hose. I loaded them in the car, grabbed a roll of electrical tape, and some hose clamps. I wanted to be equipped to plug a hose leak, just in case there was one I had missed. As I was getting in the car, I saw my neighbor in her kitchen window, looking out. I waved to her, and she waved back. I pulled out of the drive and headed back to the park and Leslie's car.

When we got back to her car, I carefully removed the radiator cap, and then started pouring water into the radiator. I had Leslie start her car, so the water could circulate, and I watched for leaks. After the radiator was full, I put the cap back on. There were still two completely full containers of water, which I placed on the floor of her backseat. I closed the hood.

"It doesn't appear to be leaking now, but I don't know how long that will last. Head straight home and call me when you get there. There are two gallons of water in your back seat if you need them. If you have any problems, call me and I'll come running. I love you."

I leaned in and gave her a kiss.

"I love you, too," she said.

I watched as she drove away, then asked God to look after her. I headed back to work to wait for her phone call.

Leslie called about fifteen minutes later.

"I made it," she said.

"Any problems?"

"None at all. It didn't overheat, and it doesn't appear to be leaking. I think you fixed it."

"No, I didn't fix it. You should have it checked out. Hopefully it will last for a little while."

"I'm sorry we didn't have a better time today."

"I'm happy any time I'm with you," I replied, "Will I see you tomorrow?"

"I hope so."

But Leslie wasn't able to make it that Friday. We talked on the phone over lunch, and I reminded her that on Monday, I was back working midnight until eight. Not seeing Leslie for one day hurt really badly, but with the weekend, this meant I couldn't see her for three days. THREE

DAYS!! I'd rather go without food or drink for three days, than three days of not being with Leslie. The ache in my heart was almost a physical pain.

Debbie had known me long enough to know when I was unhappy, and this bordered on depression, but she never said a word. I was glad. After all, what could I tell her? Not a thing, without lying.

## Chapter 28

MARRIAGE VOWS

Leslie and I were back to seeing each other twice a day, both before work and after work. Sometimes her husband, Joe, would be working afternoons. On these days, we were unable to meet after work, since he would be expecting her to come directly home. Therefore, we would meet in the afternoon, after he left for work. Friday, June 30, 1978 was one of these days.

We met at the park and headed to our secret spot. Suddenly, it was no longer secret. Other people were there.

"We should have them evicted," I joked, in a rather loud voice, hoping to chase them away.

"Shhh," Leslie said, as she pulled me away.

We walked around looking for another secluded spot, but it wasn't easy, people were everywhere. We were afraid that we weren't going to be able to make love that day, but with the weekend coming up, we weren't about to give up easily. We both needed the fresh memory of our making love to carry us through the weekend.

We finally found a spot that we thought we would try. It really wasn't all that secluded, but we didn't see anybody around, and we couldn't wait any longer. We were in each other's arms, stroking the flames with one of our burning kisses. I was running my hands up and down the smooth, tender skin of her back, pulling her tighter against my groin. I was growing rapidly, and when she could feel it, she started brushing her body back and forth over it driving me wild.

I stepped back and unfastened her shorts. I knelt before her and pulled her shorts and panties to the ground. I took her soft cheeks in my hands and pulled her closer, kissing her smooth flat stomach. I kissed her high on the thigh, and then tried licking her clit, but she pulled away. I reached up for her, and she joined me on the ground, falling into my arms. Our lips touched and the passion burned strong. Leslie pressed her body hard against mine, and I fell to my back, with her on top of me. She kissed me for several minutes, and then unfastened my pants. I raised my hips so she could reveal my manhood, and pull my pants and underwear down around my ankles.

She mounted me, and then lay flat on top of me, raising and lowering her hips as she rubbed herself against my love stick. She was working toward an orgasm, and I had to stay hard if she was going to get there. This wasn't going to be easy, as my body was already starting to tremble, on the verge of my own climax.

"Nice trees," I thought, "What kind are they?" Lots of clouds in the sky. "Are there any shapes up there?" I wondered. "Is that an airpppppp - Oh jeeze..." This hard not to think about.

She's getting close. Her arms are wrapped tighter around my head, my face buried in her chest. Ooo, I like it here. Shit, don't think about that. My body was twitching uncontrollably now. She best cum soon. I can't hold out much longer. Just then, her body started shaking through the spasms of a climax. Her little extra twitching made me cum right along with her, and we had the best mutual orgasm imaginable.

Whatever she does inside her, she began doing, pulling and stretching my love muscle, squeezing every drop of liquid from my shaft. It was exquisite.

We rolled onto our sides, panting. She still had a firm grip on me from deep inside her. The grip was making me throb once more, and I was soon ready to do her again. I wished that I could give her multiple orgasms, but considering the strain of giving her one, I thought I'd break something. That thought quickly faded as her tongue was in my mouth once more. She had me so hard all over again. I needed more relief. I rolled her onto her back with me on top of her. I began pumping slowly, and she wrapped herself around me, pulling me ever deeper into her body. My tongue started working its way in and out of her mouth, as my hard shaft slid in and out of her. She was moaning in delight, and I came once more. The spasms shook my body and I collapsed on top of her. She held me tightly as I tried to catch by breath.

I was completely satisfied, but didn't appear to be getting any softer. I propped myself up on my forearms, taking some of my weight off her. I looked deep into her beautiful eyes and asked, "Will you marry me?"

"Certainly," she replied without hesitation.

I did want her for my wife. I wanted her by my side for all eternity.

But there was one small problem - we were both married. Divorces take a long time, and I wanted her for my wife NOW. I looked around for something I could use as a ring, but found nothing. I took a few blades of grass, and wove them together, into a wedding ring.

"Here you go," I said, as I slipped the ring onto her finger. "I Gary, take thee Leslie, to be my wedded wife. To have and to hold from this day forward. For better, for worse, for richer, for poorer, in sickness and in health, to love and to cherish till death do us part. With this ring, I thee wed. Do you Leslie, take Gary, for your wedded husband?"

"I do," she said in the sweetest, softest, sexiest, most loving and tender tone I had ever heard.

"Do you Gary, take Leslie, to be your wedded wife?" I asked myself. "I do. Then by the powers vested in me, and under the eyes of God, I now pronounce you husband and wife. You may kiss the bride."

We kissed. Not a burning passionate kiss; but a loving, caring kiss. We held each other tightly for several minutes. We got dressed and started heading back to our cars, holding each other, not wanting to let go. We hadn't walked far when a stranger seemed to appear out of nowhere.

"Excuse me," he said. "I saw you two together, and wanted to tell you, I used to do that and now I have these," pointing to his two young children.

I smiled, thinking, "That would be awesome. Leslie, the mother of my children."

Out loud, I said, "Cool." I gave Leslie a quick kiss, and with my arm wrapped around her, we continued on toward our cars.

When we got to our cars, Leslie asked "So where are we going on our honeymoon?"

I quickly thought about all the places I'd like to take her. The Poconos, Niagara Falls, Hawaii, the Bahamas, and then I said, "I'm going home to fix dinner for Deb."

"How romantic," she said, throwing her arm to her forehead like a movie actress.

I laughed. I loved her so much.

We said goodbye, then got in our cars, and went our separate ways. It was the happiest, most romantic, day I had ever spent with Leslie. On the drive home, my eyes misted over, making it hard to see where I was driving. I was happy and sad, all at the same time.

I wondered to myself, "Will this dream ever become a reality?"

Chapter 29

PREGNANT?

A few weeks later, Leslie and I were out driving together, when she said, "I think I'm pregnant."

"Congratulations," I said. I knew she wanted more children, but didn't think she could have any more.

"I think it's yours."

"Really?" I asked, with a big grin appearing on my face, "That would be so neat."

"You'd like that?"

There was something about the way she said that. Like she wasn't expecting that to be my response. Did she really think she was pregnant? Or was she just testing me?

"Of course, I'd like that," I said honestly, straight from the heart. "I can't think of anything I'd like more."

A baby - WOW

She seemed distant.

"You're worried about it, aren't you?" I asked.

"Yes, I'm not sure what to do."

"Don't worry about it," I told her. "I'd love for us to get married and raise our child together. But if that's not what you want, I understand."

"You're so sweet."

"Never been accused of that before," I said.

Would you believe? Five minutes later the Paul Anka song "Having My Baby" played on the radio. I looked to the heavens and smiled.

I was elated. We were going to have a baby. I hoped it would be a daughter; a little girl just as beautiful as Leslie. She already had two sons. I'm sure she would love having a daughter. A baby! WOW.

I went and bought the Paul Anka record. I played that song a lot. Leslie was having my baby. It seemed too good to be true. The thought of the two of us together, with our baby, was just the most awesome thing I could imagine. How would it all work out? I didn't have a clue, but I was sure God would provide an answer.

As usual, I didn't much care for God's solution. Being "Almighty" - I expected more. A week after Leslie told me she thought she was pregnant, her period returned. If she had been pregnant, she wasn't any more.

It hurt me a lot. Leslie never really told me how she felt. I suspect she felt a little relieved, and that made her feel a little guilty. I didn't know what to do or say, so I just did what I always did. I held her tightly in my arms. And said what I always say; "I love you so very much."

Chapter 30

THE JOURNAL

Since we were now "married", we needed each other more than ever. We could no longer wait until the weekend was over to hear each other's voices, or hold each other in our arms. We became more daring with each passing day, risking everything for a few precious seconds together.

I started carrying a journal, writing in it whenever we were together, to record all of our most precious moments for the book I planned on writing. On those days when we couldn't be together, or even talk on the telephone, reading through the journal about our past escapades helped me cope.

It was now nearing the middle of July. We were unable to meet on Thursday because the water problem with her car returned. It had been holding water just fine since the day I filled it, so she hadn't bothered to have it looked at. We were also unable to meet that Friday morning because she was without a car. She had driven her husband's car to work Thursday night and had to go directly home Friday morning so he could go to work.

# # #

Friday was payday for me so I had to go to the bank after they opened at nine. When I got home, I couldn't stand the thought of not hearing Leslie's voice until Monday, so I called her. We talked most of the morning and then decided to get a few hours of sleep so we could talk in the afternoon. I set my alarm for two and fell fast asleep.

At two o'clock the alarm woke me and I got up and took a shower. I then went downstairs to the family room and turned on the stereo. When I couldn't be with Leslie, the radio was my constant companion. There were so many songs that brought back memories of her and things we have done together. While the songs usually made my heart soar and lifted my spirits, today was different. Very different. The song playing on the radio was "Don't Go Breaking My Heart" by Elton John and Kiki Dee. Listening to the song made me feel like someone had stepped on my grave.

The phone rang. I answered it. It was Leslie.

She could obviously hear the radio blaring in the background, because she asked, "What are you listening to?"

Is this just a coincidence, Leslie calling while this song is playing? I hoped so, but I somehow doubted it as chills ran up and down my spine.

"There is an Elton John song on the radio called 'Don't Go Breaking My Heart'," I told her. "It's giving me the chills and I'm breaking out in a cold sweat. Please don't break my heart, Leslie."

"You don't have to worry about that, I'll never leave you. I could never hurt you. I love you too much."

Tears were forming in my eyes as I said, "I love you so much, I couldn't stand it if you broke my heart."

"I won't. I promise."

I loved her and trusted her with my life. She had never lied to me and I didn't think she ever would. Although the song left me shaken, her words brought me comfort. As her words soothed me, we started making plans for the following week, and we told each other how much we wanted to be together.

# # #

Saturday, I was a nervous wreck. I wanted Leslie so badly. It had been two days since I last held her in my arms, and it felt like it had been two months. Debbie was going to lie out in the sun to work on her tan, and although I usually lie out with her, I stayed inside because I needed to hear Leslie's voice. I used cleaning the basement as an excuse to stay indoors, and called Leslie. We talked a couple of hours about nothing in particular. Then I had to say goodbye when Debbie came indoors.

# # #

Sunday morning, the intense longing I felt for Leslie was almost a physical pain. I felt like screaming – "LESLIE, I NEED YOU SO MUCH." I took a shower in the morning and then Debbie took hers. While Debbie was in the shower, I called Leslie. One of her sons answered the phone in a wee little voice. It had been a long time since I had been with her children, but I thought it sounded like Joey. I asked to speak with his mother. I could hear him run from the phone yelling, "mom telephone." A few minutes later, he came back and said, "She's busy – who is this?"

"Tell her it's her lover," I almost said, but then replied, "Tell her it's a friend."

I was running out of time. I heard Debbie turn off the shower. I waited and waited. I heard Debbie start the hair dryer. I only had about five more minutes before she'd be done and come looking for me. Finally, Leslie came on the line just as Debbie finished drying her hair and turned off the hair dryer.

"Hello," Leslie said.

"Hi love. I only have a few seconds. I just wanted to call and say I love you, and I'm thinking about you."

"That's sweet. I was hoping it was you."

I heard Debbie open our bedroom door. She was seconds from seeing me on the phone, and of course wanting to know whom I was talking with.

"Gotta go," I whispered, "Debbie's coming."

I hung up the phone quickly and opened the refrigerator door.

"Hungry?" Debbie asked.

"Not really, just feel like eating something, but nothing sounds good."

That wasn't exactly true. Leslie sounded delicious, but I couldn't tell Debbie that.

"Have anything special planned for today?" I asked, while thinking, "Please, go out and visit your parents, so I can call Leslie."

"I need to do some laundry; then I was thinking of lying out in the sun for a while. You have anything planned?"

"Not really, watch some TV, read a book. I might read my book while lying in the sun with you."

"That would be nice."

I went down to the family room, and plopped down in front of the tube. Flipping through channels, I found an old Abbott and Costello movie, and started watching that. I could hear clothes coming down the chute in the laundry room. Soon Debbie came down and started up the washer. She got a load of clothes going and then came in and sat beside me.

I kept trying to send mental telepathy suggestions to Debbie, "Go outside – Go outside" but it didn't work. She stayed inside with me. After the movie was over, I got up.

"Where you going?" Debbie asked.

"I thought I'd go lie in the sun and read my book."

"OK, I'm coming, too."

Great, now I'm getting her outside, but I need to be inside so I can call Leslie. I put on my swim trunks, grabbed a towel and my book, and headed to the backyard. I put the towel on the ground, and lay down on it. I started to read my book. I was into the "Executioner" series of books. I loved reading about all of the grief Mack Bolin was causing the Mafia. I wished they would make a TV series or a movie. I thought either would do really well.

Debbie came out and lay down beside me.

I read three chapters in my book. Debbie seemed to be content with lying there, so I decided I'd go in the house and call Leslie. I had just gotten into the house, and picked up the phone to call her, when I heard the door opening. Shit, Debbie's coming in, too. I quickly grabbed a coke from the fridge so Debbie would think I came in because I was thirsty. I waited and waited for her to go back outside, but she stayed. Giving up, I finally went back outside.

I read four more chapters in my book. Debbie seemed to be at peace in the sun, so I headed inside to call Leslie. I had just picked up the phone to call her when I heard Debbie coming in the house once more. I quickly hung up the phone, and ran to the bathroom, and sat on the toilet. "This is getting ridiculous," I thought, "why won't she stay outside?"

Debbie came to see what I was up to, then went back in the kitchen to get something to drink. I kept waiting for her to go back outside, but she never did. My legs were going numb sitting on the toilet, so I finally had to get up. I headed back outside to read my book. Debbie followed.

I read three more chapters, then headed inside once more. I was getting smarter. I looked outside before I picked up the phone. I saw Debbie on her way in. I started fixing myself something for lunch. Something that takes a LONG time. I decided to fix some spaghetti. It takes a long time for the water to boil, more time to cook, time to eat, etc. I had only gone half way through the entire process, when Debbie decided to go back outside. I immediately called Leslie. Thank God she was there. It was so good to hear her voice.

"I miss you so much," was the first thing I told her.

We talked for about an hour, before Debbie decided to come back in.

"Deb's coming, I have to go. Love you bunches," was the last thing I had a chance to say before I had to hang up on the woman I loved so much.

# # #

Monday, Leslie called me early in the morning.

"I have a lot of running around to do today," she said, "We won't have much time together. I have to be home by two because Joe and I have to go sign some loan documents."

"So, when can I see you?"

"Now would probably be best."

"Just tell me where; I'll be there."

"Why don't you pick me up at K-Mart, and we can go to the park? I don't want to drive too far. I'm afraid the car will overheat again."

"Be there in five," I said, as I hung up the phone. She was referring to the K-Mart discount store off Interstate 75. It's approximately halfway between my house, and Debbie's parents' house. It's a twenty-minute drive there, but I figured I could do it in ten if I drove over one hundred. She couldn't possibly be there in less time, so she would think I was there in five. I jumped in the 'Vette and burned rubber to the freeway; then I nailed it. I was doing one fifteen before I knew it; flying by all other vehicles. Weaving in and out of traffic at a hundred and fifteen miles per hour took all of my concentration. I had the radio on, but didn't hear a thing. When I pulled into the parking lot, there was no sign of Leslie. I could finally relax, and I started listening to the radio. I don't know who was singing the song, but it seemed so appropriate. The words went, "If loving you is wrong, I don't want to be right" and then there were other lyrics that went, "Your friends tell you there's no future in loving a married man. If I can't see you when I want, I'll see you whenever I can." The words were echoing in my head when I saw Leslie pull up next to me. I leaned over and opened the door for her. Leslie climbed in, and I was whole again. I don't feel complete when I'm away from her.

I headed for the exit wondering, "How can the presence of one person take you from feeling empty to full of life?"

I hopped back on the freeway, heading in the other direction. I wanted to shorten the commute as much as possible, since that meant more time with Leslie in my arms, but I was carrying precious cargo now, so I didn't exceed eighty-five."

I pulled into the park. I helped her out of the car, and held her tight. I don't have the words to describe how good that feels. The sex we share is incredible. But our love is so much more. I took her hand in mine, and we started walking through the park. I don't think either one of us had sex on our mind. Rather than head toward a secluded area, we stayed out in the main flow of traffic for both pedestrians and cars. We ended up on a hill, overlooking a three way stop. From where we were, we could see all of the traffic, and they could see us.

We started out talking. Leslie had this idea that since we were "married," we should have a place of our own. She was explaining her idea of obtaining a condemned house and restoring it, when somehow, we were in each other's arms. Our lips sought out each other's, and our tongues were searching familiar territory.

As usually happens, when I'm with the woman of my dreams, I became hard and the only thought I had was how much I loved her and how close I wanted to be to her. We began ripping at each other's clothes, and I mounted her. There was a family at a picnic table, no more than twenty-five feet away, but I didn't care. I had to have Leslie. Leslie was all I could think of. My one burning desire. We were both still "mostly" clothed, so I entered her through the pant leg of her shorts. I was barely inside her, but it was enough. I felt like the whole world was watching, but I didn't care. Leslie, Leslie, Leslie, was all I cared about. After five minutes of pumping, and grinding, I came. After the first squirt, I fell out of her, and I filled her shorts with my juices.

It wasn't the best sex I'd had with Leslie, but it was definitely the most dangerous, and that moved it to the top of the list. I collapsed into her arms. Having her hold me after sex almost felt better than the sex itself. Almost.

We lay in each other's arms for nearly half an hour, then decided we had best head back. I drove her back to K-Mart and her car, then said, "Goodbye."

I went home and got some much-needed sleep.

Leslie called and woke me up around three-thirty.

"I'm going to run some errands now; want to go with me?" she asked.

"Sure, but I won't be able to drive us. The only way I'll be able to get back home before Debbie will be if I'm on my bike," I said, knowing that to make it back through rush hour traffic, I'd have to weave in and out at high speed.

"That's fine. Meet you at K-Mart in ten minutes?"

"I'm going to need twenty; I have to shower first," I said.

"Better hurry," she said as she hung up.

"Count on it," I thought as I hung up the phone. It normally takes twenty minutes to get cleaned up, and twenty minutes to get there, and I only had twenty minutes total. I was out the door twelve minutes later, only eight minutes before I had to be there. At least traffic wouldn't be a problem on the bike. I was like a man possessed. The city streets I had to take to get to the freeway were either twenty-five or thirty-five mile per hour speeds. I was flying around, and between, cars at close to eighty. I hit the freeway, and opened it up.

I was pushing one-twenty as I came off the ramp and merged into traffic, zipping by cars like they were going backwards. The tight curve where I-475 merges onto I-75 is posted at forty-five miles per hour, and is a single lane. I backed down to ninety, and passed cars on the shoulder. Once around the curve, I opened it up again. I spotted a cop going the other way, and I know he saw me flying, too. I could tell he planned on giving chase.

"No problem," I thought, "at this speed, I'll be at K-Mart before he can reach an exit to turn around."

I pulled into the K-Mart parking lot, then went around to the back of the building, where Leslie was waiting for me. I parked my bike, and climbed in her car, checking my watch. Nineteen minutes – not bad.

"Been waiting long?" I asked.

"Nope, just got here."

Leslie was working on a macramé project, and needed some supplies. We checked K-Mart first, and she was able to get about half of what she needed there. We then went to a craft store, where she was able to get the rest of the things she needed. Then we went to a department store, so she could find some clothes for her boys. It was really nice, just spending the day with my "wife."

Leslie finished her errands, and we headed back to K-Mart. I took her in my arms and gave her a long kiss goodbye, then hopped on my bike, and flew back home. I didn't have to be quite as reckless going home, but I cut it close. I had just got in the house, and climbed into bed when I heard Debbie pull into the drive.

# # #

Tuesday, I didn't have much time with Leslie, because her husband was on afternoons. I picked her up at K-Mart around three-thirty, and we headed to the park. We walked back to a secluded spot and made love. When we were done, Leslie got dressed. I was working on getting dressed when Leslie started playing with me. She had me hard and excited all over again. I felt like I was going cum any second. I wanted to be inside her when I came, but she didn't want to take off her shorts again, so she slipped me in through the leg hole of her shorts, and then inside of her. I came seconds later. I was so peaceful and content. I love her so much. I felt like I had found my little slice of heaven, and I was floating on a cloud.

I happened to glance at my watch to see how much more time we had together. Oh, shit! It was four forty-five. Debbie gets off work at five. I figured it was at least a five-minute walk back to the car, possibly ten, followed by a ten-minute drive on the freeway, during rush hour, back to her car. Then a fifteen-minute drive home. Five minutes for a quick shower and then jump in bed before Debbie got home at five fifteen. I was in trouble. I needed thirty-five to forty minutes of time, and I had only thirty.

"Come on, we have to go," I told Leslie, "I don't think I'm going to be able to make it home before Debbie gets there."

Once again, God was watching over us. Debbie had to work overtime, and I was safely in bed when she got home.

# # #

Wednesday was my birthday. Leslie came over to the house early in the morning and handed me an envelope addressed to "*Baby*." I opened the envelope and there was a card inside. The outside of the card read, "*When we're together...*" and on the inside she had written "*Honey*" just above, "*... it's a great big, beautiful world!*" and beneath that she wrote "*I can't live without your love, your touch*" and she signed it "*Honey.*"

After I thanked her for the card, she proceeded to give me the best birthday present I ever had - her. We made love in my bed, for hours. I tried going down on her, but she wouldn't let me.

"I want to taste you; why won't you let me?"

"It's dirty. It smells bad down there. I can't stand the thought of someone doing that."

I didn't press the issue. For all I knew, her husband could have left something there. That's a disgusting thought.

When we were done, Leslie decided to take a shower.

"Come take a shower with me," she said.

"I'd love to," I said as I started heading to the bathroom with her. Then I had a fear sweep over me. "I better not. Debbie might decide to come home early since it's my birthday, and we'd never hear her."

As she was showering, I was thinking, "This is really dumb. I could be in the shower with the woman of my dreams, and instead I'm out here alone. So, what if Debbie comes home early. Is it going to be any easier explaining a naked Leslie in our shower?"

While I tried to convince myself to join Leslie in the shower, she finished and turned off the water. I went in to watch her dry off and get dressed.

"I have a present for you," she told me.

"You just gave me a great present."

"That wasn't much of a present. You can have me any time."

She went out to her car and brought in a macramé owl. It was really neat. She had been promising me one for two years and I was thrilled with it.

"This is going to be hard to explain to Debbie. I think I better hide it until I can think up a good story."

We left the house and headed to the park, where we fell asleep in each other's arms. I awoke with a start, sure that we had overslept. I looked at my watch and saw only fifteen minutes had past, and we still had an hour and a half left to spend together. I tried to go back to sleep, but the thought that we could have slept until dark scared me, so I just sat there and watched my lover sleep. She's so beautiful. I'm so lucky to have her. I couldn't take my eyes off her as she slept there peacefully. The hour and a half quickly passed by, and I had to wake her to leave.

"Time to get up sleepy head," I said as I gently shook her.

"How long was I asleep?" Leslie asked, somewhat groggy.

"Nearly two hours."

"How long have you been awake?"

"Nearly two hours."

"Why did you let me sleep so long?" she asked as she took a swing at me. "Our time together is too valuable to waste sleeping."

"I couldn't bring myself to wake you. You looked so beautiful lying there. Watching you sleep is something I've never done before, and may never get the chance to do again."

I could sit and watch her forever, and never get tired of her. I already loved her more than words could describe, and my love for her grew stronger every day. Although I wanted Leslie for my very own, I couldn't stand the thought of leaving Debbie, and breaking her heart – because I love her, too! Leslie felt the same way about leaving Joe.

Someday, Debbie and Joe will probably find out what we've been doing, and leave us. Then the problem will be solved, and I'll be free to take Leslie as my legal wife. I say legal, because in my heart, I already feel that she's, my wife. Although we are committing a sin, according to the bible, I somehow get the feeling that what we are doing has God's blessing. Ever since I came to realize that there truly was a God, I've felt close to Him. I know that He understands what we are doing, and forgives us, even though He may not agree with us.

We left the park, and I went home and back to bed. Debbie woke me up when she got home, and we went out to dinner to celebrate my birthday.

I had sex with Debbie before I left for work. It was mostly the same as always, but I had this strange feeling that I was cheating on Leslie.

## Chapter 31

LOVE IS BLIND

Thursday morning, Leslie called and woke me up at ten forty-five.

"Want to meet me at eleven-thirty?" she asked.

"Sure. At K-Mart?" I inquired.

"Yep."

"Could you bring some macramé books with you? Maybe if Debbie sees me making something, I'll be able to convince her that I made the owl. That way, I'll be able to hang it up without getting shot."

"Sure. I'll bring some Kool-Aid and rolls, too."

I showered and shaved, then headed over to K-Mart. I wasn't used to having so much time to get there, and arrived a bit ahead of Leslie. I sat and listened to the radio, waiting for my love. I expected to hear some song that made me think of Leslie, but the closest song was "Burning Love" by Elvis Presley. While my love definitely burned for Leslie, I wouldn't exactly describe it as "a hunk of burning love." I was trying to think of other songs that made me think of Leslie when she pulled up next to me.

I leaned over and opened my passenger door for her. She reached in handing me several macramé books, which I stowed behind me. Then she climbed in, holding a jug and a bag. She closed the door and we were off.

"I assume we're going to the park?" I questioned.

"Sounds good."

I drove to Ottawa Park, and once there, we headed back to our secluded area. We had a little picnic. I brought her a piece of my birthday cake, and I ate one of the pecan rolls she had brought for me. My birthday cake is the same every year. A white angel food cake sliced horizontally into three layers. A strawberry and Dream Whip frosting is then used between the layers and over the entire cake. I love it. We washed down the food with the orange Kool-Aid she brought, and then we made love.

Leslie managed to have an orgasm. It was only the third one she had ever obtained through intercourse, and all three had been with me. Naturally, I had one, but I held back too long, and missed the exquisite mutual orgasm experience we had shared previously.

For once, Leslie had to get back before me, so I wasn't rushed. After I dropped her off at her car, I took a nice leisurely drive home. I got back to the house around three, and climbed back into bed at three-thirty.

Just before five, the phone rang. It was my lover.

"Would you like to go see a movie with me tomorrow?" Leslie asked.

"I'd love to, but I didn't think you were going to be able to see me tomorrow."

"Change of plans."

"I like it when plans change for the better. See you tomorrow."

"Bye."

"Bye, love."

I fell back asleep thinking how great it would be tomorrow with Leslie. We were actually going on a date. All of the times we had spent together, and all of the things we had done together, and we have never had an actual date. Going to see a movie together – that was a date. I loved her so much. I couldn't wait for tomorrow.

#

On Friday, I picked Leslie up at K-Mart, and we headed for South Toledo and the Southwick Mall. We figured there was less chance of us running into anybody we knew if we stayed away from our familiar stomping grounds. The precaution probably wasn't necessary since normal people would either be working or sleeping, but we thought the extra discretion was worthwhile. Leslie wanted to see "Saturday Night Fever" and her husband wouldn't take her to see it, so we bought tickets for that show.

I don't know how we managed it with the armrest between us, but we managed to hold each other and cuddle throughout the entire movie. But then, Leslie and I managed to do a lot of things that I'm not sure how we accomplished. Being led through a crowd by Leslie pulling on my manhood and making love in plain sight of everybody were two things that quickly came to mind.

I was looking forward to us being on a date, but it was unlike any date I had ever been on. I'd never gotten so far with a woman on a first date before. It hadn't been dark in the theater for very long before Leslie had freed one of her breasts, and was pulling my face to it. I eagerly pulled her nipple into my mouth and began sucking on it hard, while my free hand caressed her still covered breast. I could smell her sweet perfume emanating from her cleavage and it was making me dizzy.

Leslie meanwhile was working on my pants. She had me completely undone, and freed me from the restraint. She was massaging me, and I was dripping in delight. Anybody walking by would have no trouble seeing me in all my glory. However, the theater was nearly empty, and we were near the front where most people wouldn't want to sit.

Repeatedly, she would bring me to the edge of an orgasm, and then somehow pull me back. I wanted to cum so badly, but it didn't appear as though she was going to let me. To tease me even more, she put her breast away, pushed me back in my seat, and wrapped her lips around my rock-hard shaft. I was trying hard not to moan, but I knew I was. My body was trembling as she took me ever higher to pleasure peaks I never dreamt existed, but she still wouldn't let me cum.

Every time I was about to explode, she would quit working me, and start smothering me in kisses. I was back to being a puddle of happiness and desire. I no longer had any free will. I was hers to do with as she pleased.

I knew there was a movie playing, but the sights and sounds couldn't break through the haze that surrounded me. All of my senses, except touch, seemed to have quit working. The sense of touch appeared to be five times more sensitive than normal. It felt as though the proper touch would rip a tremendous orgasm from my body, but she seemed careful not to give that touch. Was she intentionally torturing me or did it just seem that way?

The movie ended, and the lights came on, but we continued kissing. The theater cleared, but we continued kissing.

Finally, Leslie said, "We better go. Let's put you back together."

She zipped up my pants and fastened them. Leaving the theater, I could hardly walk with the massive erection between my legs causing pain at each step. I was weak and had to lean on her for support.

I couldn't believe how Leslie could turn me on. It was scary, the power she had over me.

"This was some date," I commented, as I held the car door open for her.

Is this what normal couples do at the movies? If so, Debbie and I have a lot of changes to make. Taking Leslie to a movie wasn't exactly what I had expected. Still, for a while, it made me forget that we were married to other people.

I drove Leslie back to her car, and then went home for some much-needed sleep. I fell asleep, still having the erection Leslie had given me in the theater. I had been tempted to give myself some relief, but figured Leslie had caused the problem and she could darn well fix it.

# # #

Saturday morning Debbie asked me, "What are your plans for today?"

"I was going through these macramé books, looking to see if there was anything I'd like to try making. I found this hanging tiffany lamp, and thought I'd try making it today. What do you think of it?" I asked, showing her the picture.

"That's really neat. Think you can make it?"

"Of course, I can do anything," I replied confidently.

"Where did you get the books?"

I knew she was going to ask.

"From somebody at work," I told her.

"Somebody male, or somebody female?"

"Female."

"Who?"

"Nobody you know. I barely know her."

"What's her name?"

"What's this? Twenty questions?"

"You avoiding the question?"

Debbie wasn't smiling. Did she somehow know I'd borrowed the books from Leslie? I hoped Leslie's name wasn't written on them somewhere and I'd overlooked it.

"No, I just don't see the point to the questions. You're acting like you used to when I'd talk about Leslie. Like you're jealous, or something."

I looked her in the eye, searching. She was still waiting for an answer.

"Bea," I said, hoping I wasn't digging myself into a hole.

It was the first non-Leslie name that popped into my head.

"Sounds like an old lady."

"To old for me," I agreed. "Want to go to the craft store with me?"

"No, you go ahead, I want to get the bathroom cleaned up."

I hoped Leslie hadn't left anything in there. I jotted down the supplies I'd need for making the lamp, then headed out. I swung by a pay phone and tried calling Leslie to see if she wanted to go with me, but there was no answer. I picked up the macramé supplies I needed at the craft store, and then stopped at a hardware store to get a light socket, extension cord, and a switch. I headed home to start working on the lamp.

I worked hard on the lamp all day long. I wanted to complete the lamp in two days. I reasoned that if Debbie saw me finish the huge hanging lamp in two days, then she would believe me when I told her I made the owl in one day.

# # #

Sunday, I worked on the hanging tiffany lamp all day. I was putting the finishing touches on it in the late afternoon. It looked fabulous. I was really pleased with how it turned out. In the evening, Debbie decided she wanted to try a macramé project and headed out to the craft store to buy some rings and things.

While Debbie was gone, I called my sweetheart, using our secret signal. When we hear it, we know the other person wants us to call them, if at all possible. I hung up and waited to see if she was going to call me. She called back a short time later.

"Hello," I answered the telephone.

"Why did you call? Joe's sitting right here."

"If Joe's there, you shouldn't have called me back," I told her.

"But I wanted to hear your voice."

"Debbie took off to buy some macramé supplies. I was thinking of you, so I decided I'd take a chance and call."

"That's sweet that you were thinking of me."

"Like I ever think of anything else."

Leslie didn't want to press her luck with Joe right there so she said, "Call me at work tonight."

"OK," I told her.

Leslie worked Sunday night through Thursday night while I worked Monday night through Friday night. I liked to stay up late on Sunday nights to start preparing my body for staying up all night Monday night. After Debbie went to bed, I sat down and started watching a late show. It ended at one-thirty, and I called Leslie at work.

"Hello," she answered in a sharp businesslike voice.

"Hi honey, it's me."

"I was hoping you'd call, but it's so late, I had given up hope," Leslie replied as her voice took on a warm loving tone.

"You should never give up hope. If there's any chance at all of seeing you, or talking with you, you should know I'll take it."

"I miss you so much."

"I miss you, too. Speaking of which, will I be able to see you later today?"

"I don't see how," she said; clearly disappointed.

"Bummer," I said, trying hard not to let tears fill my eyes.

We talked for nearly an hour, and then she had to go back to work.

"Good night, baby," she said, "dream about me."

"Night honey. I'm sure I will."

We hung up and I headed off to bed. Within minutes I was asleep dreaming about Leslie.

#

Monday was a drag. I knew I wasn't going to be able to see Leslie, but it still hurt. I couldn't stand being without her. I was so spoiled that I had to be with her all the time. When we were together, the time never seemed to be long enough, and when she had to leave, she'd barely be out of sight before I'd start missing her. I didn't know how long this situation could continue. I loved her so, and wanted to be with her all the time, but the only way I could see that happening was for us to break our spouses' hearts, and neither of us wanted to do that.

While I couldn't even think about hurting Debbie that way, days like this ripped at my heart and soul. When I couldn't be with Leslie, I'd be willing to do just about anything to change the situation. I think I'd gladly give up everything that I own. Give up everything that I've worked for my whole life. If only I could have Leslie by my side for all eternity.

The problem seemed to have no resolution. I prayed to God for an answer. Only He could possibly provide a solution for this seemingly irresolvable problem. The big question was whether or not I'd recognize His solution when it came. Or like it.

I managed to talk with Leslie for part of the day, so that helped to make Monday a little more bearable.

# # #

Early Tuesday morning, about twelve-thirty, Leslie called me at work.

"Can you take an early lunch?" she asked.

"Why? You don't get a lunch," I reminded her.

"I'm still at home. Joe was supposed to have been here by now, and he's late. He was in a golf tournament tonight, and he's obviously out celebrating. I called into work to tell them I wouldn't be in tonight."

"So instead of going to work, you want to spend the night with me?"

"Yes."

"Sounds terrific. One way, or another, I'll get out of here."

After that, we talked about a bunch of different things until her husband finally made it home two hours later.

"Joe's here; see you in a bit," she said as she hung up the phone.

I hunted up a co-worker and asked him to cover for me.

"I'm taking an early and very long, lunch. Will you cover for me? I'll pay you back when you need a favor."

"Will do," he said.

I left the building about three. Leslie arrived, and I hopped in her car. She drove us to the University Lanes parking lot where she found a dark, secluded spot. We climbed into the back seat, took our clothes off, and made love.

Have you ever made love in the back seat of a 1969 Firebird? If you haven't, don't start now. I certainly wouldn't recommend it to anyone that didn't have a doubled-jointed spinal column. Being less than four feet tall might make it easier as well. As it was, it was a somewhat painful experience. However, once Leslie had me excited, I had to do everything possible to obtain relief. I certainly didn't want to be left like I was at the theater. I pumped, twisted, pushed, pulled, and twisted some more. Somehow, we both managed to have an extreme orgasm. Not what you would call mutual, but still extremely pleasurable for both of us.

We both got dressed, then lay there in each other's arms recuperating. After a while, she had me lie down with my head on her breasts. She unzipped my pants and started playing with me. She kept it up, literally, for over an hour. However, I was too drained to cum again.

"I'm a failure," Leslie sighed.

"I wouldn't say that. You please me like no other woman ever could."

I got myself together and checked myself in the mirror.

"Holy shit, look at my hair!"

It was a mess. I tried combing it, but it didn't help. While I was trying to decide what to do, Leslie stepped out of the car, pulled down her pants, stooped, and started taking a leak.

"I didn't know you could do that," I said.

"Pee? Everybody does."

"Not like that, they don't. I thought you would pee on your pants trying that."

I had never watched a woman go in public like that, and found it both educational and exciting. I think I could probably cum a second time now, but it was after six and it had been daylight out for almost half an hour. I needed to get back to work.

Leslie dropped me off at six-thirty, and I hunted up my friend to let him know I was back.

"Looks like you've been sleeping," he said after taking one look at me.

"Definitely not sleeping," I assured him.

He grinned, "Was it good?"

I knew what he was talking about, so I admitted to him, "It was the best."

His grin widened.

When it was time to leave, I didn't waste any time getting out of there. I felt the fewer people who saw me, the better. I got home so fast; Debbie hadn't even left for work yet. I was trying to think up an excuse to explain the condition of my hair when Debbie said, "It looks like you drove home with your window down."

That sounded better than anything I was going to come up with, so I just said, "Yep," kissed her goodbye, and headed to bed.

Leslie called and woke me up at eleven.

"Rise and shine, baby."

"I need your help to get a rise that's all wet and shiny."

"Well, hurry then."

I hurried. I picked her up at K-Mart, and we went shopping. She had to buy a birthday present. For who just didn't sink in. She picked something up at JCPenney, and then we went to Burger King for lunch. After that, we headed to the park where she made me rise and shine. I got home just after four and climbed into bed, falling asleep almost immediately.

# # #

I had just got home from work Wednesday morning, when Leslie called, and we made plans for the day. She wanted a picture of me so I was going to stop and get some film for my Polaroid. We were also going to see about pursuing her idea for obtaining a house of our own.

I had "Call Waiting" and while we were talking, the phone beeped indicating that someone was calling me.

"Have to go, honey. I have another call coming in. Call me at two."

I hung up on Leslie and said, "Hello," after picking up the other call.

"Are you OK?" my mother asked.

"Sure, why?"

"You used to stop by every morning after work, while you're on nights, and you haven't been by for a while."

I could hardly tell her I was having an affair, and that was occupying all of my free time.

"I've just been awfully tired lately," I said honestly.

Leslie has definitely been running me down. I can see why so many older men die while having affairs. Two or three hours of sleep a day just doesn't cut it.

"I'll try to stop by soon," I promised.

I said goodbye to my mom and headed to bed, where I fell asleep as soon as my head hit the pillow.

My sweetheart called and woke me at two, and we arranged our meeting place. It occurred to me that if I was only getting two to three hours of sleep a day, Leslie had to be getting by on only one or two hours because it never seemed like she was sleeping.

I got to our meeting spot about ten minutes late, and she wasn't there. I was afraid that she had been there and left, so I drove around trying to spot her car. I didn't see her car anywhere, so I headed back to our meeting spot and there she was. She was there, but her car wasn't. She had her mother-in-law's car because hers had stopped on the I-75 interstate.

Once again, we were off and running to try and fix her car.

When we got there, I said, "Try starting it so I can hear how it sounds."

It fired right up. "Take it someplace public, close to your house; I'll follow you there," I instructed her.

She exited I-75 at the Lagrange St./Stickney Ave. exit and drove to the public swimming pool at Woodrow Wilson Park where she left her car. She jumped in my car, and we headed to Point Place. Point Place is an 862-acre area in north Toledo where the Maumee and Ottawa rivers meet Lake Erie. We found a nice romantic place along the water and sat there talking. We mostly talked about having a house of our own and what we were going to have to do to make that dream a reality.

Then we headed to McDonald's for some French fries and something to drink. While at McDonald's Leslie saw somebody she knew. Somebody she didn't want to be seen by. I think she said it was Joe's sister, but she was so panicky, I didn't question what she said. We just got out of there in a hurry because she was afraid that we'd been seen.

We headed back to Wilson Park and her car. I parked mine next to hers. We sat for a while, and then she undid my pants and started playing with me until I came all over the place. I lay there feeling totally drained.

"Do you feel better now baby?" she purred in my ear.

"Mmmmm," I moaned, "I love you."

And I did love her. I loved her beyond words.

I finally tore myself away from Leslie at five after five. Debbie would be home in five minutes, and it was going to take me at least a half hour to get home. I decided that I better go buy something, so she would think I had just run to the store. I bought some macramé hangers, and then went home and hung my owl on the kitchen wall.

Debbie liked my owl, but she would probably burn it if she knew that Leslie had given it to me.

# # #

Early Thursday, Leslie called me at work.

"Guess what?" she said.

"What?"

"One of the girls here asked when I was going to quit my affair and go on breaks with them, rather than spend all of my time on the phone with my lover. I don't think they really care that I don't join them; they just want the low-down on what's going on."

"Tell them they can buy the book in five years. By then our romance should have a happy ending."

We talked a little while longer, and then she had to get back to work.

After I got home from work, Leslie called me, and we made our plans for the day. I then went to bed, wishing she were with me.

Leslie called and woke me at two, and I rushed off to meet her. I brought along my Polaroid, so we went to Sears to buy film, but they didn't have the proper size.

Next, we headed to the Post Office to see about getting a Post Office Box. We figured we would need a mailing address before we would be able to buy a house of our own. Unfortunately, the Post Office had none available.

The woman there said that a P.O. Box would cost fifteen dollars for six months, and they needed to know our address. I was a bit nervous about giving out an address. That was the whole point of getting a mailbox at the Post Office, so nothing would come to either of our homes. Oh well. This may take more thought.

We then headed to Ottawa Park. There's a golf course there, but there was hardly anybody playing, since it had just finished raining. We went for a walk and found a semi-dry spot under a tree and started to make love. We were about halfway to the point of no return when Leslie punched me in the eye.

That was interesting. Never experienced that before. I didn't know what to think. I mean, I can understand a woman being dissatisfied with your lovemaking, but she doesn't usually punch you in the eye because of it.

"I'm sorry. Two golfers just walked by and I was trying to cover-up. I didn't mean to hit you."

I guessed I'd have to take her word for it, but I couldn't figure out what her hand was doing around my head when her pants were around her knees, and we were both standing up.

After a while, we decided to risk lying down on the wet ground since we were having trouble accomplishing anything standing up. We were just about at the point we were previously, when Leslie punched me in the eye, and this time a golf ball came whizzing over our heads, and landed about ten feet away.

Golf always seemed like a stupid game to me. Hit a ball with a stick and then chase after it. Besides that, the players often dressed strange.

Four guys were heading in our direction. I briefly thought about killing them so they wouldn't interrupt us again. However, I decided that would spoil the mood anyway, so we decided to leave. I drove Leslie back to her car and then headed home.

# # #

Debbie was scheduled for some minor cosmetic surgery at the hospital the following morning.

"Do you think you should spend the night at your mother's?" I asked her, "That way you won't have to do all that driving in the morning."

"That's a good idea," she said.

After Debbie left for her mother's, I called Leslie. We talked for nearly two hours, and then I went to sleep thinking about her.

# # #

On Friday I met Leslie at Ottawa Park. I had a little bit of time before I had to meet her, so I was able to buy some film for my Polaroid. We took several pictures of each other. I took one of her sitting down on the grass and one of her standing next to my Corvette.

One picture she took of me bordered on the obscene. Right there in public, she took my shirt off, and undid my pants. She reached into my pants, and pulled my underwear down, so they wouldn't show in the picture. I was having trouble keeping my pants up, so I had to lie down. She took the picture with my fly open down to my hair.

After taking pictures, we were both so horny that we couldn't stand it any longer. We hadn't come prepared to make love, so we didn't have a blanket with us. However, we were fortunate and found something that we could lie on. We went back to our secret spot and had an unbelievable lovemaking session. I held back until her orgasm started and then let myself go. We had a beautiful mutual climax. I can't begin to put down on paper how wonderful it would make me feel when I made love with her.

It's funny; I never really considered myself a sex oriented individual. I mean sex with Debbie seemed like more trouble than it was worth. I had been married for almost three years, and on average, had only made love to my wife once a month. Then there was the first time Leslie and I had sex that we both regretted. I just didn't think sex was an important part of a relationship and never dreamed that I'd cheat on Debbie. And now I was making love to Leslie every chance I got. She would often make me cum several times in one lovemaking session, and we frequently had multiple sessions a day. I couldn't believe the things she did to me. The way she made me feel.

Leslie was always complaining about how terrible her body looked. She had two children and had the accompanying stretch marks. She'd make such a fuss, and of course, I didn't even notice. I'd look at her and all I'd see was a goddess. To me she was unbelievably pretty. I knew Debbie would love to look like Leslie although I saw nothing wrong with the way that Debbie looked, other than that her hair was too short.

I used to watch old spy movies, where the gorgeous woman seduced the man to get what she wanted. I always wondered how a guy could be so dumb. I mean, you would think that a guy would know when a woman is too good for him. If such a woman all of a suddenly starts wanting to be with you every minute, she had to be after something.

I used to feel that way, wondering what it was that Leslie was after. She was definitely too good for me. Now it didn't even matter. I felt in my heart that she loved me the same way I loved her. But even if she were after something, she could have it. Hell, I felt like I belonged to her more than I did my own wife.

Lately, Leslie had been telling me that she thought I'd be the perfect husband. That sounded pretty strange to me, considering that she knew I cheated on my wife, and a perfect husband certainly wouldn't do that. But then again, I knew she cheated on her husband, and I thought she would make the perfect wife. I suspected we were in love, and love is blind.

Chapter 32

OUR ANNIVERSARY

It was early Saturday morning, and I was at work. Leslie didn't work Friday nights, and her husband was a sound sleeper, so she was able to give me a call. We had been talking for a couple of hours, when Operations called me to resolve a problem with a production job. Since that was what I was paid to do, I had to go.

"Call me when Joe leaves for work," I told her.

"I will," she promised.

We said goodbye, and hung up.

The production problems went from bad to worse. There was nobody scheduled to come in on day shift, so I had to stick around until all of the problems were resolved. I didn't get home and to sleep until almost one o'clock Saturday afternoon.

Since I got home so late, Debbie headed out to her parents' house, so I could sleep in peace.

Leslie called and woke me up at two-thirty.

We talked for a while, and then Leslie said, "Joe has to work a double shift tonight. He won't be home until Sunday morning. How about I come over after Debbie has gone to sleep?"

"That would be great, but I've only had one and a half hours of sleep. I'm not sure if I'll be able to stay up that late."

We kind of got off the subject, and Debbie got home before we got back to it. The more I thought about Leslie coming over after Debbie went to sleep, the more I liked the idea. By five o'clock, I was completely awake and dreaming about being with Leslie after Debbie went to bed.

I left the house, using going to the store as a pretense, and stopped at a phone booth to call Leslie. She wasn't home, but her baby sitter answered the phone. She said that Leslie should be home by seven-thirty. I was starting to get worried that I may not be able to see her later that night because I was taking Debbie to see "Saturday Night Fever," and the show started at seven forty-five. With twenty to thirty minutes of travel time, there was no way that I could call Leslie until after the movie, and that meant I'd have to wait until after Debbie went to bed.

With the memories of what Leslie and I had done still fresh in my mind, when we went to see "Saturday Night Fever," I thought Debbie and I should be more intimate. I tried cuddling with her, but she said, "That's uncomfortable. The arm of the chair keeps poking me."

After the lights were dimmed and the theater was dark, I reached over and started massaging her breast through the fabric of her clothes. She pushed my hand away.

"Not in public," she said.

This wasn't quite the memory I had of being with Leslie. I tried one more time. This time I slid my hand under her top, so it was hidden from view. Debbie acted as though ants had crawled up her blouse. She jumped away from my touch, swatting my hand away from her.

"Quit it!" she warned.

"Now that's inconspicuous," I thought.

"Watch the movie," Debbie told me.

I kept my hands to myself and watched the movie while my thoughts drifted to Leslie. I hoped that I'd be able to see her later.

When we got home from the movie, it was ten o'clock. I turned on the television and switched the channel to watch "Fantasy Island." Debbie usually went to bed by ten, but of course, on this night she decided to stay up and watch the show with me.

After "Fantasy Island," the news came on, so I watched that. Still Debbie stayed up.

The late show came on, and still, she wouldn't go to bed. I finally had to start ignoring her, pretending I was engrossed in the movie, so that she would go to bed.

I was finally able to call Leslie at ten minutes before midnight. The phone rang and rang; nobody seemed to be home. At midnight I tried calling again. Still there was no answer.

"Maybe she decided to spend the night at her mother's," I thought to myself.

I was letting the phone ring thirty to forty times. I was sure that if anybody were home, they would hear it ringing. I decided that since I was up anyway, I'd keep calling every ten minutes until the movie I was watching ended at one-thirty. Fortunately, I didn't have to wait that long. After just a couple of more attempts, Leslie answered the phone.

"Hello," she answered.

"Are you coming over?" I asked anxiously.

I knew it would be extremely risky having Leslie come over while Debbie was home, but I thought we could spend time together away from the house. Being with Leslie for even a short time was well worth the risk.

"I thought you were going to be sleeping."

"I thought so, too, but the thought of holding you in my arms has kept me going. Can you come over?"

"No. I had planned on taking my sons to my mothers to spend the night, but since you said we couldn't get together, I kept them with me. There's no way I can leave them here by themselves."

"Shoot," I muttered, clearly disappointed.

"Why don't you come over here?" Leslie asked.

I ran the odds of my accomplishing that successfully. I'd have to get in my bedroom, where Debbie was sleeping, to get my wallet and keys. If that were successful, then I'd have to get out the door, which makes its own noises. Then I'd have to fire up the 'Vette with its noisy side pipes, back out of the drive, and take off down the street. Travel time alone would be an hour. Debbie seldom sleeps through the night; if she got up and found me gone, I'd have a lot of explaining to do.

"I don't see how that would be possible. Deb would hear me leaving for sure."

"Oh, please, I need you so bad," Leslie, pleaded. "I want you to make love to me tonight."

Her words excited me. I was getting hard and I wanted her bad.

"Now you did it. I'm getting a hard on."

"Oh, come to me baby," she purred in my ear.

It sounded as though she wanted me as badly as I wanted her.

"I wish I could. I need to hold you."

"Are you standing, or lying down?" Leslie asked.

"I'm lying on the sofa in the family room, why?"

"Undo your pants."

"Excuse me?"

"Undo your pants so I can imagine I'm there with you."

I did as Leslie instructed.

"OK," I said.

"Now pull them down."

I did.

"OK."

"Now tell me what you see."

"I see a rock-hard shaft that wants you so bad it's drooling all over the place."

"Ooh, I want you inside me. Imagine me slipping you inside me."

"I'm getting a big puddle over here."

"That sounds delicious."

"My balls ache; I need you."

"Imagine my hand holding you tight, stroking you. Up and down."

"You're driving me crazy. We have to figure out how to get together. If not tonight, then some other Saturday night."

"Joe is going to be working next Saturday night. Would you like to spend the night with me?"

"That's a silly question. I'd love to spend the night with you."

Thoughts of spending an entire night with Leslie made me harder than ever. I ached to be with her.

Just then, I heard noises upstairs. Debbie had to be up. I looked at my watch and saw it was three-thirty.

"I have to go. I hear Debbie coming. I love you."

"Love you, too."

"Good night, love."

"Good night, baby."

I hung up the phone and grabbed some tissues to mop up the white puddle from my stomach, and my oozing organ. I just finished getting my pants pulled up and fastened when Debbie called down.

"Are you coming to bed tonight?"

"Right now," I said, as I turned off the television and lights. I headed upstairs and climbed into bed wishing that it were Leslie lying next to me, rather than Deb.

# # #

I tried all day Sunday to get free from Debbie. It wasn't until three-thirty in the afternoon, after she started to think about getting dinner ready, that I was able to head out on my own.

"We're short on money in our checking account. I'm going to the bank to transfer some money out of savings," was the excuse I used on Deb.

I went to the bank and used the ATM to transfer the money, and then on the way home, I stopped at a phone booth and called Leslie.

"It's about time you called," she said as soon as she found out who it was. "Where are you?"

"I'm at a phone booth."

"Can you meet me? I need to see you."

"I'm on my way to K-Mart. I'll see you there."

I hung up the phone, jumped in my car, and burned rubber. In ten minutes, I was at K-Mart waiting for Leslie. She pulled in a short time later.

"Here," she said as she handed me an envelope with what looked like a card was inside.

I opened the envelope, and took out the card. The outside of the card read, "*I thought about you this morning...*" When I opened the card, it continued, "*... And I smiled for the rest of the day.*" On the inside of the card, she wrote, "*My feelings for you are so deep and tender - nothing will ever take them away. I love you so very much! Happy Anniversary Sweetheart!*" and she signed it "*Honey.*"

That was so sweet. Typical guy; I'd forgotten it was one month ago that we exchanged wedding vows at Ottawa Park. That was June 30, 1978. Tears began forming in my eyes. I was so happy. It meant so much to me that she had remembered. I don't think I've ever been on the receiving end of something so romantic before.

She also had a present for me, wrapped in tissue paper, and tied with a bow. I unwrapped it to find a little statue of a boy and girl. There was a caption on the bottom that read, "*Me and you - You and me - That's the way – It'll always be*." Leslie added her own little artwork to the statue as well. On the girl's shorts she added the word "*HONEY*" because that's what it says on her panties. On the bottom of the statue, she had put the initials "*LVR*", which is what her initials would be if she were *legally* married to me. She had wrapped a little green ribbon around the statue and sprayed it with her perfume.

I cherished the moments we spent together so very much. We held each other tightly, telling each other how much we loved each other, and how much we cared. The words were nice to hear, but not necessary. The fact that we spent every available second with each other said it all. We were only able to spend about forty-five minutes together, and then I had to head home.

Driving home I was deliriously happy. I couldn't believe how happy I was. I knew I had never been that happy before, and doubted that I ever would be again. It was surprising how much a little gift like that can mean when it comes straight from the heart. I knew I'd cherish that gift always, and no amount of money in the world could ever make me part with it.

I stayed up late Sunday night so I could call Leslie at work, just to tell her how much I loved her.

Chapter 33

SLEEP OVER

Leslie called me Monday morning, and we made plans for the day. After we said goodbye, I headed over to my parents' house. I rummaged through a bunch of my old things, looking for my high school class ring. In high school, I never had someone special to give my class ring to. Now I had someone special, and I wanted her to have my ring. I found my ring and left the house, heading to Franklin Park Mall.

At the Hallmark store in the mall, I bought Leslie a card and a little kitten shaped candle that I thought was darling. Feeling a bit guilty, I also found a nice card for Debbie. Next, I went to the Max Davis Jewelry Store, to see what kind of necklaces they had. I wanted to buy Leslie a nice necklace, but everything I liked was more than I could afford.

I left the mall, drove home, and cleaned my class ring so it shined like new. Then I signed the two cards and put Debbie's card where she would find it. I then rushed out to meet my love.

I arrived at our pre-arranged spot-on time, but Leslie wasn't there. As time went by, I was starting to worry that she was having car trouble again. I was just getting back in my car to go looking for her when she finally arrived.

I handed her the card and candle, then took my class ring and slipped it onto her finger.

"With this ring, I thee wed," I said in the most sincere and romantic voice I could manage.

She gave me a loving smile and then said, "This candle is so cute."

"Now you can get rid of the other cat," I joked.

She opened the card and read it. I wasn't as imaginative as Leslie and couldn't enhance the card with my own words, but I thought it was a very romantic card.

"You are so sweet," she said, as she reached up to give me a thank you kiss.

We left her car there and went to see a movie. This time we stayed in my part of town. I really didn't think there was much of a chance that anybody we knew would see us. We saw "Foul Play," starring Chevy Chase and Goldie Hawn.

Just like our last movie, we did just about everything possible in the theater, except for having intercourse. She undid my pants, and had me out, getting me all excited. I had one of her breasts out and was caressing her nipple. We were running our hands all over each other's bodies. We kissed and cuddled and held each other tight. When we left the theater, I wasn't in quite such bad of shape as the last time, but I was definitely ready to take my lover.

We swung by my house to pick up a beach towel and then drove to the park, practically running back to our favorite spot. We made intensely beautiful passionate love. Leslie had a double orgasm, and during her second one, I let myself cum too. She was incredible.

#

On Tuesday, Leslie called me late in the afternoon. She had been working out at the spa at the Great Eastern Shopping Center, and asked, "Can you come meet me?"

"Certainly. Where are you?"

"Great Eastern."

"Great Eastern Shopping Center?"

"Yes."

"It's three-thirty. Are you sending a helicopter to pick me up?"

It's a long way away.

"You don't think you can make it?" She sounded disappointed.

"Would you be upset if I don't make it?"

"I'll cry."

"We can't have that. It's my job to put a smile on your face. Where at Great Eastern are you?"

"At the spa; near the middle."

"See you as soon as humanly possible."

We said goodbye, and I was gone in a flash. It was going to be hard enough getting there, but coming back I'd be fighting rush hour traffic. I decided that taking my motorcycle made the most sense.

I exceeded one hundred miles per hour a couple of times, but held my speed at ninety most of the way. There wasn't much traffic, so I was able to make good time. I think I set a record for the fastest trip to Great Eastern. I always thought it took an hour to get out here. Heck, it took me only fifteen minutes. Not nearly as far away as I thought.

I spotted Leslie right away. She hopped on the rear of my motorcycle, and we headed around back behind the stores, away from the people. I parked the bike and we got off. She was in my arms immediately, our lips pressed together. She pushed her body to mine, and I started to rise. I looked around for a spot where we could make love, but I couldn't find a suitable location. Leslie wasn't about to let a little thing like that prevent her from pleasing her man. She was willing to forego sex, as long as she could please me. It didn't seem fair to me when I was able to think, but once she started working her magic, I didn't care. As she stroked me, my legs got weak, and I had to lean on her for support. A short time later I squirted all over the blacktop.

"There baby," she said, as she squeezed the juice from me. She shook me off, and put me away. She pulled my pants back up, fastened, and zipped me.

"Feel better now?" she asked.

"Definitely removed all of the tension from the ride over. But you know I love just being with you. You don't have to please me every time we're together."

"I know, but I like to. I love it that you enjoy my touch so much."

"That I do."

We held each other tight and kissed some more. As usual, I couldn't tear myself away from this woman I loved so much, and I left myself very little time to get back home before Debbie arrived. I had to make it back home in the same amount of time I took getting there, but now I'd have a lot of traffic blocking my route. I rode on the lane divider most of the way so I could pass by cars blocking both lanes. A few times I had to pass on the shoulder. I was in the house only seconds before I heard Debbie pull into the drive.

# # #

On Wednesday a meeting that Joe was supposed to attend was cancelled. Since her husband was going to be home, Leslie wouldn't be able to meet me. She called me in the morning to break the news. Naturally, the thought of not seeing Leslie all day depressed me.

I went to bed and fell asleep wishing I could be with her.

I woke up in the afternoon and decided to head to a Radio Shack electronics store. To safely spend Saturday night with Leslie, I was going to have to be able to prevent all incoming phone calls from waking up Debbie. With my job there was always the possibility that work would call, wanting me to resolve a problem. I decided the best way to do this would be to rewire the phone line, so it was fastened with quick connect/disconnect alligator clips. Once I had the clips in place, I could disable the phone line in a matter of seconds. So, I was on my way out to buy some alligator clips.

I had just walked out the door when I heard the phone start ringing. I ran back into the house to answer it. It was Leslie.

"Hello," I said.

"Hi baby."

"Hi honey. I was hoping it was you."

"Joe went to the spa so I thought I'd give you a call."

"I'm glad you did. Another few seconds, and you'd have missed me."

"Where you going? Not off to see your girlfriend, are you?"

"Get serious; you're my girlfriend."

"I thought I was your wife."

"Well, you got me there. Wait. Pretend I didn't say that. You're my wife, my lover, my best friend, and my girlfriend."

"You're pretty good at fast talking."

"Obviously not good enough, or I wouldn't have to correct myself. I'm working on improving my skills though. This seems to be a requirement when you're having an affair."

She laughed. That sound pleased me so much.

"I was heading over to Radio Shack to pick up some alligator clips."

"What for?"

I explained to her my plans for rigging the phone line. We talked a little while longer, then I heard Debbie walking in the house and we had to quickly say goodbye.

# # #

On Thursday Leslie called me when I got home from work and we made plans for the day. I went to sleep excited about being able to spend most of the afternoon with her. I felt terrible that I hadn't been able to see her all day Wednesday.

Leslie was supposed to call and wake me up at one o'clock. When I awoke on my own at two-thirty, I was scared that something might have happened to her. I started getting scared if she was five or ten minutes late. She had never been an hour and a half late before, even when her car stalled on the freeway. I tried calling her house, but nobody answered. I called several times, worrying for over an hour about her, and then I decided to take a shower. As I was getting out of the shower, the telephone rang, and I rushed to answer it. I was so relieved to hear her voice that I didn't think to ask her why she was so late in calling.

"Can you meet me at the spa?" She asked.

I glanced at my watch and saw it was after four.

"I'd like to, but I'm afraid I'd kill myself trying to make it there and back in that short of time."

"OK," she said, sounding disappointed.

Of course, I was disappointed too. Two days in a row, I haven't been with my love. We talked about our plans for Saturday night and how we were looking forward to it. We talked until Debbie got home and I had to go.

It was payday for Debbie, so we went to Pizza Hut for dinner, and then she went grocery shopping. As soon as Debbie left for the store, I decided to call Leslie. I knew Joe was going to be home, so I used our secret ring. I waited for her to return my call, but after fifteen minutes, I figured she wasn't going to be able to call me. Five minutes later the telephone rang.

"Hello," I answered.

"Hi baby," said the woman I loved so much.

"Hi honey. What took you so long? I didn't think you were going to call."

"I was lying down, trying to get some sleep. Joe was bugging me to go to the store for him. I didn't want to go until I heard your call. Then it was a great excuse to get out of the house."

"Good for Joe."

"Debbie isn't home?"

"No, she went grocery shopping."

"When do you expect her back?"

"It usually takes her about an hour, so I guess we have about forty-five minutes."

"Want to come see me?"

"I'd love to, but I don't think there's enough time."

"OK, be that way."

We mostly talked about Saturday night, and had to say goodbye when Debbie got home.

I went and helped Debbie put away the groceries.

# # #

Friday morning, I was at work when Leslie called. After I found out it was, she, I said, "I have to see you today."

"I don't see how that's going to be possible."

"But I haven't seen you for two days."

"I know."

"I need to hold you in my arms. My arms ache for you."

"I'd like to hold you, too, but I can't."

"My lips long to kiss yours. I need you honey."

"I need you, too."

"Then you'll meet me?"

"I can't."

"Please, please, please, oh pretty please."

"Oh, all right."

She was obviously only agreeing to see me so I'd quit pestering her. She doesn't really want to see me.

"You really don't want to see me, so forget it," I said.

"Yes, I do."

"No, you don't. Let's just forget it."

"I really want to see you."

"Yeah, out of sympathy."

I was sorry I had put her on the spot. I didn't want her seeing me just because she felt sorry for me. That's not much of a relationship, so I refused to give in. I could just wait until our Saturday night sleep over.

"I really do want to see you," she said.

"I appreciate what you're trying to do, but I don't want to see you since you really don't want to see me. I love you too much for that."

"Well, I don't love you," she said, as she slammed the phone down.

The words cut, like a knife, to my very soul. I just sat there, holding the phone, while tears started running down my cheeks. I felt totally crushed. I was having trouble catching my breath. I felt my whole world coming apart.

Somehow, I had to fix this. I couldn't lose my love this way. I somehow managed to make it through the night, and then headed home after work. When I got there, I dug out an old B. J. Thomas album and started playing "Hooked on a Feeling." As I longed for Leslie, I listened to the words. The ones that kept haunting me were, "I don't believe them that you're in love with me." If Leslie had ever loved me, how could she hurt me so? I started crying again.

The phone rang. It was Leslie.

"I'm so sorry for what I said," Leslie told me, "I really want to see you."

I flew out of the house, and I met her behind K-Mart. She came into my arms, and our lips met. Everything was right with the world.

"Can we get out of here?" she asked, "I'm afraid somebody I know will see me."

"Certainly."

We climbed in my car and headed where she told me. It was close to where a girlfriend of hers lived. I parked the car in the street. It was a divided street, with a large median separating the two directions of traffic. We decided to cross the street to lie on the grass in the median. Leslie took her shoes off, and I was carrying her across the street when she saw her girlfriend driving down the road.

Leslie flagged down her girlfriend so she could introduce us. Her name was Diane. Diane was very pretty and my first impression was that she was a very nice person. Leslie thought Diane was prettier than she was. Some people may think so, but I wasn't one of them.

I'm a girl watcher. A song was written about me. On any crowded street, Diane would definitely rate a second, possibly even a third, glance. But when Leslie was around, I had eyes for no other.

Leslie gave Diane my phone number so she would call me if, God forbid, anything should happen to her.

I was glad she did that because I had given Leslie's number to a friend as well so he would call her in the event anything ever happened to me.

We spent the rest of the morning holding and kissing each other. It was starting to get late, so we headed back to K-Mart. Leslie had to buy some paint and supplies so I tagged along and then helped carry them to her car. Once she had everything loaded, we kissed and said goodbye.

On the way home, I stopped at a Radio Shack to buy some alligator clips.

Shortly after I got home, Leslie called, and we talked for a while. After we hung up, I went downstairs to the telephone junction box. I used the alligator clips to set up a quick disconnect. Now I could stop all calls coming in, or going out, in a matter of seconds.

# # #

Early Saturday morning, I was at work when Leslie called.

"Hi love," I said once I knew it was, she.

"Joe's working. Would you like to come over for lunch?"

"I'd love to."

"See you then."

"I can't wait. Bye love," I said as I hung up the phone.

I was supposed to take my lunch at four, but I couldn't wait that long. I left work before three. My mind was racing as I drove to her house. Leslie had told me several times that her house was in really bad shape. I think she said it had been condemned at one time. Anyway, I was preparing myself for the worst. Leslie and Joe bought their house for $2,500 and I paid twice that amount for my used car, so I could imagine what kind of shape it must be in.

When I arrived at her place, the condition of the house was the furthest thing from my mind. Holding Leslie in my arms, and tasting her sweet lips were what I longed for, and I filled myself with her love.

Once we were done saying hello, she asked, "Is a BLT OK for lunch?"

A bacon, lettuce, and tomato sandwich sounded great. I wasn't sure when the last time was that I had one.

"Wow, I get food, too?'

"If you're hungry."

"I am, but mostly for you."

"After you eat. You have to keep your strength up."

I grinned at her, "OK."

Leslie headed for the kitchen to fix my lunch, and I took a look around. The walls were dirty, the plaster was cracked, the ceiling had stains on it and loose plaster from where water had leaked, and there were broken windows. What you can see in a house usually isn't the worst part of it, so I imagined I was looking at the good points. They had been in the house now for several months. Although I didn't see it when they moved in, it was hard to imagine that they had accomplished much since they started renovating it.

I felt bad that Leslie had to live in a dump like that. I walked in the kitchen and tried to hide how bad I felt for her. "Nice little fixer upper," I told her.

"Do you still love me?"

Leslie had told me on several occasions that she didn't want me to see where she lived because I'd stop loving her.

"Yes, I still love you. I'll always love you."

She smiled, and went back to frying the bacon. I never liked Joe. What kind of a guy would treat Leslie this way? How can this guy stand to come home to a dump like this? It would be depressing enough if he was single, but to raise a family under these conditions was unforgivable. He must not have any pride at all.

I thought to myself, "One of these days Leslie will have the beautiful home she deserves even if I have to buy it."

My house was a small one and a half story, but compared to their house, it was a mansion.

Leslie finished making my BLT and I sat down to eat.

"This, tastes great," I told her after the first bite.

It really seemed to please her, that she had been able to cook for me, and I enjoyed it.

After I finished my sandwich, we went into her bedroom, where we made love on the bed. She was right; I definitely needed to keep my strength up. The lovemaking was beautiful, as always, but way too short. One of the things I really didn't enjoy was having to leave right away after making love. I was sure that Leslie knew better, but the way it would look to me, was that I just went over there for sex and left after I got it. Somehow, it just seemed dirty - not at all like our relationship should be.

We finished and got dressed.

"I have to go," I told her.

"I know."

"But I'll be back in less than twenty-four hours, and we can pick up where we left off."

"I'll be waiting."

I leaned down to kiss her goodbye, and she put her arms around my neck, pulling me toward her. I wrapped my arms around her, and pulled her close. I didn't want to leave. I never wanted to leave her. Holding her and kissing her should be wonderful, but I was sad because I had to leave. I pulled away and said, "Have to go," then gave her a quick kiss and I was gone.

I backed out of her driveway with my headlights off. As soon as I hit the street, a car several houses down the street turned on its headlights. The first thought that went through my mind was that someone was watching her house, and they were going to try following me. I couldn't allow that, so I took off quickly. Not fast enough to squeal the tires, but the side pipes made enough of a racket. I got to the freeway quickly and then nailed it. There was no way anyone was going to keep up.

After I got back to work, I started thinking that it might have been Joe in the car. Maybe he was just waiting until I left so he could go in and confront Leslie. I began to panic. I called her house, using our secret code, and then waited for her to call me. She never did. I tried to convince myself that she already fell sleep, and my short rings weren't enough to wake her, but it was no use. I was still afraid for her.

I swore to myself that if Joe ever did anything to hurt her, I'd take him apart with my bare hands. I knew that for the time being, there was nothing I could do but wait.

I finished work early and drove home. Debbie was still sleeping when I arrived, so I climbed into bed carefully so as to not disturb her. I was afraid I'd wake her up, and she would want a kiss, or want to hold me, or for the first time in our marriage want to make love. I wanted to be left alone - alone with my thoughts of Leslie. I loved Leslie so much. She was all I thought about any more. I'd gone way past the simple wanting her; now I needed her. I couldn't stand being without her for a single day.

Leslie called in the afternoon, waking me up. Debbie wasn't home so we were able to talk for quite a while. I was going to tell her about the car that may have tried following me as I left her house. I was going to ask her if Joe got home early. Both thoughts faded as Leslie talked about making love to me. We talked about spending the night together and finalized our plans. We talked until Debbie came home and then we hung up with the thought that in a few hours we would be in each other's arms.

Where I work, there were several people working over the weekend, and I told Debbie that I was scheduled to work as well. I don't get paid for overtime, so I didn't have to worry about coming up with an explanation as to why my check wouldn't be any larger.

Before I started getting cleaned up "for work," I went downstairs and quickly disconnected the phone line. I went and took a shower. All I could think about while I was in the shower was what if Debbie tried to make a phone call? She would certainly want to know what was wrong with the phone. However, as it had been since this romance began, God was with me, and Debbie didn't attempt to make a call. I finished getting ready, and when I was ready to leave, Debbie walked me to the door.

"I wish I didn't have to go to work tonight," I said as I kissed her goodbye. "I love you."

"I love you. Goodbye."

I left her and headed straight for my lover's arms. I felt like a heel, but knew I really didn't have any choice. I'd do whatever it took to be with that woman I loved so dearly. My mind had been telling me from the very beginning of this affair that what I was doing was wrong, but my heart just wouldn't listen.

I was the happiest I'd ever been and I intended to enjoy it for as long as I could, regardless of the consequences. I'd always been willing to pay the price for what I did and this was no different. If tomorrow Debbie and Leslie, both left me, because of what I was doing, I'd have no regrets. Joy has filled my life for now and that was all that was important.

I parked at our pre-arranged spot several blocks from Leslie's house. She was supposed to have been there when I arrived, but her car was nowhere in sight. The neighborhood was far from the best and I was more than a little nervous standing there alone in the dark. I wished that I had brought a gun for protection, but found a little comfort with the knife I always had in my jacket pocket. I prayed I wouldn't need it.

Leslie finally arrived and all of the tenseness left my body. I still found it hard to believe the effect she had on me. She drove us to her house, and I snuck out of the car and into her house.

"I have to finish washing some dishes. Then I'll be right with you," she said.

"OK," I replied, then went into the living room and lay down in front of the television to wait for her.

# # #

It was now just past midnight, so it was Sunday morning. I lay there, more or less, watching "Saturday Night Live." I say "more or less" because I'd quit watching television every time, I caught a glimpse of Leslie moving around in the kitchen. I couldn't keep my eyes off her, and the problem seemed to be spreading to my hands.

She finally finished in the kitchen and came into the living room to lie down next to me. We started out behaving ourselves really well. We watched some television and then we played some Yahtzee. Leslie kicked my ass at Yahtzee, so I wouldn't play anymore. I hate losing, especially to a woman. We watched some more television and then I don't know what happened.

Suddenly we were in each other's arms. We kissed and caressed each other to the point where we had to have one another. We started taking off each other's clothes and then headed into the bedroom. As we were getting ready to climb into bed, Leslie decided it was time to change the sheets. It was a really good idea since Joe sleeps with their cat, and I'm allergic to cats. However, I couldn't stop thinking that it made more sense to change the sheets when we were done, rather than before.

I don't think I ever mentioned it before, but my reaction to cats was so bad that if I didn't take allergy medicine before I was with Leslie, my eyes would start itching and burning and my sinuses would start running. She didn't even have to touch the cat before she came to see me. Even when she showered and put on clean clothes before we were together, I was still affected by the cat, just from her being in the same house with it. The way

I was affected, it was just as if I were allergic to Leslie, and it was terrible being allergic to someone you couldn't stand being away from.

We finally made it into bed. Tonight, Leslie had prepared herself so I could finally taste her sweetness. I longed to taste her so that was my first stop. She was right; that was nasty. It reminded me of my parents washing my mouth out with soap. I didn't stay long.

I worked my way up her stomach and to her lips. I tasted her sweet lips and we made wild passionate love. Making love to her was the most beautiful feeling imaginable. I couldn't begin to describe how good she felt. What made it even better was that she felt exactly the same way about me. A couple of times while we were making love, I had images flash through my mind of Debbie, lying at home in bed, all alone. I pushed those thoughts from my mind. There was no point in thinking about it because I was right where I wanted to be - in the arms of the woman that I wanted for the rest of my life.

After we finished our marathon lovemaking session, Leslie set the alarm, and we lay there holding each other. We fell asleep in each other's arms. When the alarm woke us, we got up and washed ourselves. When we were done getting cleaned up, I pulled her naked body next to mine.

"Careful, or we're going to have to wash up again," she chided.

"I'll take my chances."

She felt incredible. My arms just didn't feel right when they weren't wrapped around her. I sighed, and reluctantly let her go. We finished dressing in silence. We left the house and she drove me back to my car.

"Thank you, honey. I had a wonderful time tonight," I said, holding her one last time.

"Me too. I love you so much."

"Me too."

I kissed her one last time, then jumped in my car and drove away. On the way home I was crying, wondering why every night couldn't be as wonderful as this night.

I got back home about five-thirty. I went downstairs and reconnected the phone line, then stopped and had a scotch on the rocks. I climbed into bed next to Debbie and went to sleep hoping that I'd be able to see Leslie again, later in the day.

Chapter 34

THE WATER PUMP

I was going to be sleeping most of the day Sunday, so Debbie left the house at nine with her mother to take her grandmother back home. It's about a two-hour drive each way so I expected her home about one. Leslie called at one.

"I have to see you. Can you meet me?"

"I'm expecting Debbie home any minute. If I can get out of the house before she gets back, I can meet you. I need to shave and shower. Call me back at one-thirty, and I'll let you know for sure whether or not I can make it."

I got cleaned up as fast as I could and then waited for her phone call. When she called, I said "Looks like I'm going to make it. Where do you want to meet?"

"Over by Diane's house, where you first met her."

"I'm on my way."

I hung up the telephone, went out, and fired up my motorcycle. I flew over there, sometimes reaching speeds in excess of one hundred and ten miles per hour. I had almost twice as far to go as she did, and I arrived just after her.

"Will you take me for a ride?" she asked when I pulled up.

"Sure, hop on."

I took her for a short ride up to where there was a split in the median and came back down the other side of the street to the next split and then back to her car.

"That's fun. I miss riding with you."

"I miss having you back there with your arms around me."

I sat down on the grass median and she sat on my lap facing me. We talked and hugged and kissed the way lovers do until it was time for her to go.

"I finally had my car checked out. It needs a new water pump."

"Thought so," I said.

"They wanted $175 to replace it and said they would guarantee it for three months. I checked a parts store and they said that for $35 and my old pump they would give me a new pump guaranteed for life. Will you put the new one in for me?"

"Anything for you love."

"Is tomorrow, OK?"

"Sure."

"I love you."

"I love you, too."

We kissed goodbye, and she slid into her car and took off with tires spinning.

I watched Leslie until she was out of sight and then headed home. When I arrived, I was surprised to find that Debbie still wasn't home. I watched some television, and she arrived an hour later. We had dinner, and I thought about how I was going to break the news to her. I had to tell Debbie beforehand that I was going to have a woman over, just in case the neighbors said something to her.

I decided the direct approach worked best.

"I have a girl from work coming over tomorrow."

"WHAT?"

"I said, I have a girl from work coming over tomorrow."

"WHY?"

"I told her I'd replace her water pump for her."

"Why doesn't her husband do it?"

"She's not married."

Well, it sounded good **before** I said it.

"You're bringing a single woman into our home?"

I wondered if I was painting myself into a corner.

"No, I hadn't planned on bringing the car in here."

Being a smart ass sometimes helps.

"Why doesn't she take it to a service station?"

"She tried, but they wanted $175 to do the job. A new water pump only costs $35 so I told her she was getting ripped off and I'd do it for her."

"Well, I don't think it's right at all for you to be getting involved with someone at work like you were with Leslie."

"What involved? I'm just changing a water pump for her; I'm not taking her out to dinner. I had no idea you'd get this upset. I'm sorry. If I could call and stop her from coming over, I would, but I don't have her phone number and she'll be over tomorrow morning."

"Well, OK. But don't ever do this sort of thing again without first checking with me."

"Yes, mother," I said in the snottiest tone I could muster, while making a face at her.

Treat me like a little kid, will she? I probably had no right to be, but I was more than a little ticked. I thought she had some nerve telling me what I could do.

Debbie was so jealous of Leslie. I hate to think what her reaction would have been had she known it was actually Leslie coming to our house.

#

Leslie called me about eight-thirty Monday morning.

"Are you still going to replace my water pump?" she asked.

"Debbie was really upset when I told her I was going to replace your water pump."

"You told Debbie?"

"I had to tell her, just in case the neighbors mention you being here. Of course, I didn't tell her it was your car, just that I was replacing a water pump for some girl at work."

"Wise move."

"I thought so, but Debbie was so pissed, you'd think she knew it was you coming over. She even told me I had better not be getting involved with somebody from work, like I was with Leslie."

"She said that?"

"Yep."

"What do you want to do?"

"You mean after I replace the water pump?"

"You're still going to do it?"

"I told you I would. What time you bringing it over?"

"Is eleven, OK?"

"Great, see you then."

We said our mushy good-byes and hung up. I went over to my parents' house to visit with them for a while, and then came back just before eleven.

Leslie showed up a short time later, and I started removing the belts so I could get to the water pump. While I was working on her car, the telephone rang, and I rushed inside to answer it. It was Debbie.

"I've been trying to call you all morning. Where have you been?"

"Over at moms."

"Why did it take you so long to answer the phone?"

I ignored the question because I was tired of getting the third degree.

"Why did you call?" I asked in a somewhat irritated voice.

She gave me a snotty "Good bye," and slammed the phone down.

I went back outside to work on the car.

"Debbie's pissed," I said.

"That was Debbie?"

"Yep, and I'm not making any brownie points."

Leslie was a big help replacing the water pump. She worked on getting the parts cleaned, removing all of the old pieces of gasket. It was one of the most tedious and time-consuming tasks, and I hated doing it. I really had fun working on the car with her. I could never get Debbie to do anything like that. I couldn't believe how much alike Leslie and I were. Sometimes I swore we had identical brains. The only differences I'd seen were those caused by our upbringing and experiences. Logically our thought processes appeared to be the same.

After we finished replacing the water pump, we went inside and downstairs to the laundry room, where we had a wash basin, so we could clean the grease from our hands and arms.

We kissed and held each other.

"I have to take the old water pump back so I can get my deposit. Want to meet by Diane's after that?" Leslie inquired.

"Sounds good. I want to take a shower first. I feel all grimy from sweating out there."

She gave me a quick kiss, then said, "See you in a bit," as she walked out the door.

What's that saying about best-laid plans? As she was pulling out of the drive, she found out she had no power steering. I thought maybe a belt was loose, but they looked fine. Next, I checked for power steering fluid.

"You don't have any power steering fluid. That's not good. We'll have to take my motorcycle to go buy some."

I would have preferred to take my car but her car was blocking the drive. So, we rode my motorcycle to the store and bought some power steering fluid. When we got back, I poured the fluid into the reservoir, and just to be on the safe side, tightened the fan belt for the power steering. We went inside to wash up once again.

While inside, I showed Leslie the hanging Tiffany lamp I had made. Suddenly we were in each other's arms, our tongues searching the other's mouth. The kisses fell somewhere between a loving tender kiss and an all-out passionate kiss. I thought both of her arms were around me, but I felt the now familiar tug at my belt and my pants were no longer a barrier to her warm touch.

She knelt down and took me in her mouth. As her tongue stroked me my knees started to get weak and I sat down before I fell down. She kept running her tongue over me and taking me in and out of her mouth until I was ready to explode. Just before I came, she let me go, and pulled me down on top of her. While I was busy kissing her, she was busy undoing her own jeans. We both stripped off our jeans and in a short time I was inside her. Before the afternoon was over, she had made me cum twice.

I was a little sore after the second time and was ready to quit. She wanted to keep going. I suppose if she had insisted there would have been little, I could do about it. Whenever she wanted me, I was hers for the taking.

Chapter 35

DEBBIE SUSPECTS

It was early Tuesday morning. As usual, Leslie and I talked whenever we could at work and again after we got home so we could make our plans for the day.

"I'm going to the spa this afternoon," she told me.

"Call me when you get there and I'll come see you."

"OK. See you then."

"Night love."

"Night baby."

I hung up and then went to bed, where I fell asleep almost immediately, dreaming of course about Leslie. Leslie called and woke me at three-thirty.

"Can you come see me now?" she asked, sounding excited at the prospect.

I looked at my watch.

"It's already three-thirty. That's not enough time."

"You told me once that even five minutes with me was worth the trip."

"I did say that and seeing you definitely makes the trip worthwhile. I'll see you in about an hour, love."

I showered faster than I ever had before and then hopped on my motorcycle and took off. On the expressway, cars were nearly a blur as I zipped by them. I was quickly approaching a tow truck in the high-speed lane doing only seventy-five miles per hour. Of course, the speed limit was fifty-five but his seventy-five was a lot slower than my ninety-five so he should have been in the slow lane. As I got closer, I checked the right lane and found it clear, so I started passing the tow truck on the right. Just as I was beside him, he changed into my lane. Now I'm no physics expert, but I do know that two objects can't exist in the same place at the same time. I locked up both brakes, and the bike went into an uncontrolled skid at ninety-five miles per hour. I don't know about my life flashing before my eyes, but Leslie definitely did. I was damned sure not going to die without seeing Leslie one more time. Everything seemed to be moving in slow motion as I fought to gain control of the bike which was now weaving all over the road. My heart was racing. I'm not afraid of much, but I was scared I'd never see Leslie again. It seemed like an eternity, but I finally managed to gain control once my speed had decreased to fifty-five.

I wondered briefly if that was why the speed limit was fifty-five, and then I cranked up the speed. I tore around the tow truck, throttling up to one fifteen. I had lost some precious time that could have been spent with Leslie and I had to make it up.

When I was finally with Leslie, and still in one piece, I felt much better. We went around back, behind the spa, where we had been before but this time Leslie had brought a large towel with her. She laid the towel on the ground and we fell onto it in each other's' arms. As we embraced, our hungry lips pressed eagerly against each other's.

Leslie leaned over and whispered in my ear, "I want you to make love to me."

"Do I have to?" I asked.

I said what?

It wasn't because I didn't want her, because I did. It's just that after a near death experience it took a little bit of time for me to relax enough to the point where I could get excited. About when it was time for me to head back home, I was finally starting to get aroused.

"I'm ready for you," I said.

"I'll be the judge of that," she said, as she undid my pants and took hold of me. She caressed me until my juices were flowing freely and then said, "I want you."

I knew there wasn't nearly enough time for her to have an orgasm so I just let myself go and came quickly. I shuddered and collapsed into her arms. In her arms was the neatest place to be. I felt so loved there. I wanted to fall asleep in her arms, but I knew Debbie was going to be home before I was, and I best get back as quickly as possible.

"I hate leaving you," I told Leslie.

"Me too."

"But I do have to go."

"I know."

We kissed goodbye, and I headed home. I knew I was in trouble. Debbie was going to beat me home no matter how fast I went. "If only we hadn't made love," I started to think. Then common sense took over. Leslie wanted me and I wasn't capable of saying no. I wanted her as much as she wanted me. I'll just have to live with the consequences.

I had no idea what I was going to say when Debbie asked me where I had been. "I'll find out soon," I thought, as I pulled the bike into the garage.

I walked into the house and Debbie immediately demanded, "Where have you been?"

"I was joy riding on the freeway during rush hour - what a blast," were the words that popped out of my mouth.

#

It was Wednesday morning and I was on my lunch hour, driving over to National Family Opinion where Leslie works. We had only a half-hour to spend together, but it was enough time to hold and kiss one another. It was beautiful. It reminded me of many lunch hours that we had spent together in days long since passed.

I headed back to work happy after holding her in my arms and kissing her sweet lips.

Leslie called after I got home from work and we made our plans for the day.

"I'm reupholstering a chair and I have to go pick up some material and supplies this afternoon. Want to come along?" she asked.

"Anything to be with you," I told her.

"I'll call you early this afternoon and let you know when I'm heading out."

"OK, honey. I love you."

"I love you, too. Bye."

"Bye love," I said, hating to break the link between us.

I went to bed and fell asleep holding my pillow tightly, wishing it were Leslie in my arms.

I awoke with a start at one o'clock.

"Leslie should have called by now," I thought to myself.

I hopped in the shower to get cleaned up. When I was done, I puttered around the house nervously waiting for her call. Finally, about two-thirty she called, but she had bad news.

"I'm not going to be able to make it today," she said.

"That sucks. Why not?"

"Joe came home. He's packing. We're leaving town in the morning."

I think my heart stopped.

"What do you mean you're leaving town in the morning? When are you coming back?"

"Joe has to go out of town on business and he wants the family to go with him. A little vacation. He doesn't want me to go to work tonight but I told him I have to. After all, I can't miss that precious half-hour lunch with you."

"How do you expect me to survive that long without you?"

"I'll just have to give you some special loving to get you through."

We talked the rest of the afternoon until Debbie got home. I was so engrossed in the thought that I'd be without Leslie for so long that I hadn't even heard Debbie pull in the drive, and now she was in the house.

"Got to go," I whispered and quickly hung up the telephone. That was too close.

# # #

It was just after midnight on Thursday when Leslie called me at work.

"Guess what?" she asked.

"What?"

"I didn't go to work tonight."

My heart sank in my chest. I was devastated - crushed - I wouldn't be able to see her today. I wouldn't be able to see her and hold her in my arms until next week - agony.

"I want you to come over to my house for lunch."

I think my heart started going again. Pain and sorrow were quickly replaced by joy.

"I'd love that," I said with all my heart. "I'll get there as soon as I can."

I went searching for my friend to cover for me, gave him Leslie's telephone number, and asked him to call me if I was needed.

I left work at two-fifteen and raced over to her house as quickly as possible. I got to her house at two-forty. It was a warm summer night. She had the front door open and I could see through the screen door that she was sleeping peacefully on the floor. I opened the door quietly and let myself in. A thin sheet covered her and I could tell she wasn't wearing anything under the sheet. I did the Sleeping Beauty bit and woke her with a kiss. She came into my arms ready and willing. I took off my clothes and slid under the sheet with her.

The last two times we had made love she hadn't had an orgasm so I was determined that she would climax this time. I held back for a half-hour until she started pleading with me.

"Please cum for me, baby."

Who could resist a plea like that? I let myself go and the orgasm poured over me in a rush. My body rocked uncontrollably as waves of pleasure coursed through me. As usually happened when I was with Leslie, I remained hard after the orgasm, still wanting more of her.

I still wanted to please her so I began working her, forcing her against me and sliding her up and down my shaft. I worked her for forty-five minutes when she did it to me again.

"Please cum for me, baby."

I was about pooped out anyway, so I gave in to her wishes allowing the second orgasm to rip through my body at full force. As the climax shook me, I held Leslie tightly in my arms, never wanting to let go.

This double orgasm thing was getting to be a regular habit when I was with Leslie. Afterwards, we just lay there naked in each other's arms, enjoying every second. While we lay there peacefully, we heard a car pull into the drive and saw headlights pierce through the windows.

I felt a sickening feeling sweep over me.

I'm not sure which of us was faster but in what appeared to be one fluid motion we were both standing beside the front door looking out to see who was there. You can just imagine the relief we felt when we saw it was a milk delivery truck out front.

The sickening feeling, we had felt only moments earlier spoiled the moment.

"I better get dressed," I said.

We went into the bathroom and washed up. After I was clean, Leslie carefully dried my privates, and then powdered them.

I find Leslie very sexy. Debbie thinks sexy is the way you look. I've always thought it was the way you acted. Of course, that's not to say that you can't look sexy, it's just that you don't have to have a fantastic body to be sexy. I guess what I'm trying to say is that if I was completely objective, I'd have to say that Leslie doesn't have a gorgeous body. However, she certainly knows how to use what she has. Everything she does turns me on. To me she's the sexiest woman alive - or dead, for that matter.

It wasn't twenty minutes ago that I had cum for the second time within an hour and already she had me so excited that I wanted her again. However, I was only on my lunch hour and I had already been gone for over two hours. I got dressed and spent the next fifteen minutes saying goodbye. It was hard for me to leave her knowing that it would be a long time before I could see her again.

"There's no way that Debbie could possibly love you as much as I do. You have to believe that," Leslie told me.

"I do."

I did believe that. It wasn't hard. Sometimes I wondered if Debbie loved me at all because she certainly never showed it.

"If I wasn't with Joe, Debbie would have to fight me for you."

"She would, uh?"

"Yep, I'd show up at your door and tell her that it was you I wanted. I can't imagine a life without you."

"I can't imagine a life without you, either. I love you so much."

I kissed her goodbye again and then finally had to leave her and head back to work.

As I was finishing things up for the day at work, getting ready to go home, the telephone rang and it was Leslie.

"This is a surprise," I told her.

"I just had to call and tell you that I love you so much and that I'll be thinking of you the whole time."

"That's sweet. I'm going to miss you so much. I'm starting to cry just thinking about it," I said, as tears started running down my cheeks.

"I'm going to miss you, too. Good bye, baby. See you when I get back."

I sniffled, "Good bye honey. I love you so."

She was just leaving and the pain was already unbearable. I missed her so much.

"How was I going to get through the weekend?" I wondered.

I spent the rest of the day thinking about her.

# # #

Friday morning, I was at work trying to do my job and not having much success. My thoughts kept drifting to Leslie. When my telephone rang, I certainly didn't expect it to be Leslie, since she was out of town, but it was she.

"I'm so glad you called," I said after realizing it was Leslie.

"I can only talk a few seconds, but I had to hear your voice. I miss you so much already," she said.

"I miss you, too. I don't know how I'm going to survive without you."

"It won't be long. I'll be back Monday."

"That seems like a long time."

"I have to go. I love you."

"I love you, too. Thanks for calling. It made my day."

"Bye baby."

"Bye Leslie."

And she was gone. While at work, I usually removed my wedding ring and wore Leslie's high school class ring on a chain around my neck. Since I considered Leslie as much my wife as Debbie, I felt it was only fair that I honor her in that way. It was getting close to being time to go home, so after talking with Leslie, I removed her ring from around my neck, kissed it softly, and stored it safely away. I then put back on my wedding ring and headed home.

I tried sleeping but it was no use. I missed Leslie too much. My whole body ached knowing she was so far away. Leslie called me in the afternoon and was surprised that I sounded awake for a change.

"You sound wide awake," she said.

"I am. I can't sleep knowing you are so far away."

"Now I'm not. I'm right there with you, where I always want to be."

"I wish I could hold you. My whole-body aches for you."

"Just remember the last time we were together. It was so beautiful."

"Yes, it was."

"Now I don't want you getting sick on me. So, you get your rest. OK?"

"OK honey."

"Bye baby."

"Bye love."

The time on the telephone was much too short but after hearing her voice, I was finally able to fall asleep.

# # #

By Saturday evening, I was really starting to feel terrible. The ache in my heart from being away from Leslie was unbelievable. I couldn't even hide the pain I was feeling.

Debbie asked several times, "What's wrong?"

I finally told her, "I'm unhappy."

I guess that wasn't the right thing to say because then she asked, "Why?"

"I'm not sure," I started saying.

Yeah, right. I know why, I just couldn't tell her.

"Life just seems a waste," I continued.

A waste when I'm not with Leslie. I couldn't very well tell her that with everything I had going for myself, none of it meant anything without Leslie by my side.

Debbie kept questioning me, which only made things more difficult. I hated lying to her, and telling her everything was OK, when it really wasn't. Besides, rather than denying my feelings for Leslie, I'd rather be telling the whole world that I loved her.

I turned on the stereo to try cheering myself up. It only made me feel worse. The song playing on the radio was one by Lobo called "How Can I Tell Her?"

The words sounded as though I had written them about Leslie and Debbie.

> *She knows when I'm lonesome*
> *She cried when I'm sad*
> *She's up in the good times*
> *She's down in the bad*

Whenever I'm discouraged
She knows just what to do
But girl, she doesn't know about you

I can tell her my troubles
She makes them all seem right
I can make up excuses
Not to hold her at night

We can talk of tomorrow
I'll tell her things that I want to do
But girl, how can I tell her about you

How can I tell her about you?
Girl, please tell me what to do
Everything seems right
Whenever I'm with you
So, girl, won't you tell me?
How to tell her about you

How can I tell her I don't miss her
Whenever I'm away
How can I say it's you I think of
every single night and day

But when is it easy
telling someone we're through
Oh girl, help me tell her about you

How can I tell her about you?
Girl, please tell me what to do
Everything seems right
Whenever I'm with you
So, girl, won't you tell me
How to tell her about you

Every word in the song ripped at my heart. How could I tell Debbie about Leslie? How could I tell Debbie that it was Leslie I thought of every single night and day?

I turned off the stereo before any more songs came on reminding me of how much I missed Leslie.

I drank heavily that evening and went to bed early.

#

Sunday was even worse than Saturday for me.

Debbie asked me point blank, "Are you having an affair?"

I thought about how I should answer that. I couldn't deny it. I wouldn't dishonor Leslie that way because I loved her too much. I couldn't admit it because then Debbie would leave me and I'd be alone. Leslie loved me, but she was too afraid of losing her kids to rip apart her happy home. I didn't see I had any choice. I walked away without answering her.

Chapter 36

VACATION

On Monday Debbie and I started our vacation. We had decided to stay home rather than do any traveling and we were looking forward to a relaxing time away from work. Monday was pretty much a carbon copy of Saturday and Sunday with me missing Leslie, thinking about Leslie, wondering when I'd get to see Leslie, and generally feeling miserable.

Around five-fifteen in the evening, the telephone rang with our secret code. I rushed into the house to call Leslie back with our secret ring to let her know I had gotten the message that she was back in town.

She wasn't supposed to return my call but she did anyway. Just as the telephone started ringing, Debbie came in the house.

I picked up the telephone in the basement and said, "Hello."

Just after that, Debbie picked up the phone in the kitchen and said, "Hello."

Naturally, Leslie hung up. Good thing Debbie had said something before Leslie had. Debbie didn't say anything about the telephone call, but I kept wondering what she was thinking. With the strange way I'd been behaving, and since she had already asked me if I was having an affair, she had to wonder who that was. Or maybe my guilty conscience was working overtime and she just assumed it was a wrong number.

# # #

Tuesday morning, I managed to get out of the house early and went to a pay phone to call Leslie.

"Can I see you?" I asked anxiously.

"Not now. Joe is working afternoons so I have to wait until he leaves for work."

"Debbie asked me Sunday if I was having an affair."

"What?"

"You heard me."

"What made her think that?"

"I guess the fact that I was missing you for the past several days. You were all I've been able to think about. I missed you so much."

"You better get things patched up between you two. You need to love her up."

It sounded like she wanted me to have sex with Debbie. I really didn't want to, so I asked to be sure.

"You want me to make love to Debbie?"

"Yes. Definitely."

"I don't want to, but I will, if that's what you really want me to do."

"It is."

"OK."

"If you can get away this evening, I should be able to meet you."

"I don't see how I'll be able to, but I'll try," I told her.

We talked a little while longer and then said goodbye. I headed home with the intention of making love to Debbie as Leslie had requested.

I was so affectionate that I made myself sick. After lunch, I took Debbie in my arms and kissed her. I caressed her and started to undress her. I had her clothes off, and I still wasn't hard. I lay on top of her and tried to imagine that it was Leslie I was with. That wasn't easy considering the size difference. Debbie was 5'11" and Leslie was only 5'4" - but I did start to get hard.

I managed to slip myself inside her, and I started pumping, but it was no use. I could never understand how some guys could have sex just for the sake of having sex. That's all that this was. Sex just for sex. There was no burning desire like there was when I was with Leslie. Debbie would just lie there and expect me to do everything. I thought I'd find a hole in the wall just about as exciting. No matter what I did or thought about, it didn't help. I went soft inside of her long before I even thought about having an orgasm.

To Debbie this proved I was having an affair and she started crying. Leslie wanted me to make things right, so I tried.

"I love you," I told her, "I like holding you. I like kissing you. However, our lovemaking just doesn't please me. You have to DO SOMETHING besides just lay there. You have to let me know you care for me. You have to let me know you want me. You can't just lay there and expect me to rape you. I don't find that enjoyable. The only reason I have sex with a woman is because I love her and I want to be close to her. If all of our sex in the future is going to be just like all of our sex in the past, then I'd just as soon do without."

From that point on, things started going a little smoother between us.

In the evening, I needed to get away so I could see Leslie, so I told Debbie that I was going over to my parents' house to help my brother work on his car. Since I'd be busy, I assumed she wouldn't want to go, so I felt safe in asking her, "Do you want to go with me?"

"Sure."

That wasn't supposed to happen.

We drove over to my parents' house and arrived there at seven o'clock. I started helping my brother. We were having trouble getting some parts loose and discussed how much easier the work would be if we had an air compressor and some tools to go along with it, like an impact wrench. Debbie was standing right there, but I was pretty much ignoring her, wishing she hadn't come along. My brother and I started talking about going to Sears to look at air compressors.

"I'm going to walk home," Debbie informed me.

"Why?" I asked.

"I'm bored."

"You knew I was going to help Walt work on his car; why did you come along?"

"To get out of the house."

"OK, I should be home in a few hours."

"Hours?"

"Maybe it won't take that long. I'll try to hurry."

I kissed her goodbye and she started walking home. It was less than a mile and took less than thirty minutes to walk, so I didn't offer to give her a ride.

As soon as Debbie left, I was in the house and on the telephone calling Leslie. The phone rang and rang but there was no answer.

"Can you take me to Sears so I can check on a compressor?" my brother asked me.

I wasn't having much luck getting a hold of Leslie, so I said, "Sure, let's go."

I drove us over to Sears and while Walt checked out the air compressors, I looked for a pay phone so I could call Leslie. Her phone rang and rang and finally she picked up.

"Where have you been?" I asked, "I've been calling all evening."

Well, it seemed like all evening.

"I had some errands to run."

"Can I see you?" I asked. She didn't answer right away so I added, "PLEASE."

"How about nine at K-Mart?" she asked.

I checked my watch. It was close to eight-thirty.

"OK," I told her, "See you then."

I went and hunted up my brother. He couldn't decide whether or not he wanted to spend the money on the compressor, so we left.

I dropped Walt off at our parents' house.

"If Debbie calls, could you tell her that I just left?"

He gave me a "Why the hell should I do that?" look, but then said, "OK."

I rushed off to see the woman I loved and had been missing so much. I figured that I'd have a maximum of fifteen minutes to spend with Leslie. If I could drive fast enough and limit travel time to ten minutes each way, then I'd only need to account for thirty-five minutes. Five minutes of that I could explain as drive time home from my parents'. That left a potential thirty minutes of unaccountable time that I might have to explain to Debbie. Awkward, but not impossible.

Unfortunately, I blew all of my carefully laid plans when I stayed with Leslie for more than forty-five minutes. Every second past the first half-hour, warning bells were going off in my head, but I ignored them. I needed more time with this woman I loved so much.

It felt so good holding her in my arms that I really didn't want to leave when I did. As always, our time together was much too short.

"Please stay and make love to me," Leslie pleaded.

"We don't have time to go any place," I told her.

"We can do it in my back seat."

If she had a bed, I may not have been able to pull myself away, but her back seat gave me a way out.

"I don't think my back could take that right now. Besides, remember how my hair looked the last time? Imagine me trying to explain that to Debbie?"

She laughed. God, I loved that sound.

I smiled. "Kiss me goodbye," I said.

She did and I was off. I might have quite a bit of time to account for. I needed an excuse. I wracked my brain. A plan was slowly forming. I stopped at the grocery store and picked up a frozen pizza.

When I got home, I saw we had company.

"Where the hell have you been?" Debbie demanded to know.

Oops.

I started to explain, "Walt and I went to Sears..."

But she interrupted me to say, "I called your parents' house at nine o'clock and Walt said you had just left. I called back at nine-twenty and he had no idea where you were."

Oh, shit. Worst case scenario. I had to account for ALL of my time. Stopping to get a pizza sure wasn't going to account for that. "Hurry brain, think fast." I had painted myself into a corner and now had almost an hour to account for.

"Tell her the truth. Tell her you were with Leslie. Get the whole thing out in the open," the emotional half of my brain was saying.

This is the kind of help I get from my brain?

Hey, emotions - get out of my head - kick in the logic circuit.

"I was hungry, so I stopped at the store to get a pizza. I ran into a friend I hadn't seen for a long time, so we just talked for a while."

Sure, hope I was convincing.

"You talked for an hour?"

"It didn't seem like that long. I had no idea I was being timed, so I wasn't in any hurry. I'm sorry if I worried you."

That's a nice touch. Make her think that I think she was worried something had happened to me, not that she was worried I was with another woman.

She seemed to buy the story. Thank you, God. We then spent a pleasant evening with our friends.

# # #

Wednesday morning Debbie and I got up early and drove to Cedar Point Amusement Park. I had a good time with Debbie, but still spend a large part of the day wishing I were with Leslie. A couple of times I was free from Debbie when she went to the restroom, and I was tempted to try calling Leslie. I couldn't come up with a good reason to use on Debbie if she caught me on the telephone so I decided it was best not to press my luck.

It was a very hot muggy day and when we finally got home at midnight, all we could think about was taking a soothing shower. I dried my hair and while Debbie was drying her hair, I went downstairs to call Leslie at work.

"Hi Honey," I said as she answered the telephone.

"I was hoping you'd call, baby."

"I had to call and tell you that I was thinking about you all day and I love you so very much."

"I was thinking about you, too. I was thinking it wasn't fair that Debbie was with you instead of me."

"Does that mean you're ready to leave Joe?" I asked, although I knew the answer.

"You know I can't."

I didn't know she couldn't; only that she wouldn't. She was afraid she would lose her kids if she were the cause of the marriage ending. Back then, I didn't understand the bond that a parent could have with a child, because I didn't have children of my own, and I was never close with my parents. Therefore, logic told me that Leslie probably had only another fifteen years with her kids, so what was wrong with letting Joe have custody anyway?

"Leave them and come to me," I'd sometimes tell her, "Fifteen years with them versus a lifetime with me."

Of course, if she were able to bring her children with her that would have been OK with me. They were good kids, I liked them a lot, and whatever I had to do to make Leslie mine was fine with me. However, if she wasn't able to maintain custody then logic made the choice seem simple to me. I now realize how that choice must have been tearing her apart.

"I want to see you tomorrow," I told her, "I'll call you around noon."
"I'll be waiting for you," she told me.
I heard Debbie turn off the hair dryer and start heading downstairs.
"I have to go. Debbie's coming. I love you."
"Love you, too. Bye."
"Bye Honey."

# # #

Thursday morning, I quickly showered and went out to lie in the sun. I figured Debbie would come out and join me, and that way, when I made an excuse to leave, she wouldn't want to come with me. It worked perfectly.

I had planned on repainting my Corvette, so at noon I told Debbie, "I'm going to start working on the 'Vette. I need to go to the store to get some masking tape and other supplies."

"OK," she said.

I threw some clothes on, then took off on my motorcycle, and went directly to a phone booth to call Leslie. She answered on the first ring.

"Can you come see me?" I asked.

"Meet you at K-Mart in ten minutes."

I sped on over to K-Mart and met her in the nearly empty parking lot behind the building. I took her in my arms. We kissed, we hugged, and we talked a lot. We hadn't seen each other for ages, and we had a lot of catching up to do. After about an hour of talking, Leslie decided that was enough and started undoing my pants. She took me in her mouth and gave me so much pleasure I couldn't believe it. Every time she excites me it's better than the last. Every time I cum, I want it to be with her. I hadn't had an orgasm since the last time I was with her. She switched from using her mouth to using her hand and started kissing me passionately. It didn't take long before my body started trembling and I had an eruption unlike any other I had ever experienced. It was so beautiful and it felt so good just to lie there in her arms.

As always, I hated to leave her, but Debbie would be wondering where I was. I left Leslie and headed to the store to do the shopping I had told Debbie I was leaving to do. I finally got back home at two-thirty and Debbie was crying. I was concerned.

"What's wrong?" I asked her.

"Why were you gone so long?"

"I couldn't find what I went for and had to go to several different stores. Then on my way home I ran out of gas. I had to push the motorcycle to the gas station," I told her.

Then I decided playing on her sympathy might help.

"That would have been bad enough, but my knee is still sore because of you cracking it at Cedar Point, and now I'm in pain. Is that why you're crying? Because I was gone a long time?"

"We're on vacation so we can spend time together, and you just take off and leave me home alone."

I thought to myself, "You really didn't want to be with Leslie and me."

"I know. I'm sorry. I didn't expect to be gone that long. Please don't cry."

I took her in my arms and said, "I love you. It's still early, let's run out to your parents for a visit."

She quit sobbing and mustered an "OK."

We drove out to her parents' house, visited all afternoon, and then stayed for dinner. By the time we got home, everything was fine again. Debbie went to bed at eleven and I stayed up to watch the late show and call Leslie so we could make plans for Friday.

"Debbie gets paid tomorrow, so she'll be going grocery shopping. When she leaves, I'll give you a call," I told Leslie.

"I'll be waiting," she promised.

We said goodbye and I headed off to bed.

# # #

Friday morning as soon as Debbie left to pick up her check and go grocery shopping, I called Leslie. Her husband, Joe, answered the telephone. I just about shit. I didn't know what to do so I quickly hung up the phone.

After a while the telephone rang and it was Leslie.

"Guess what?" she said.

I took a wild guess, "Joe's home?"

"Yes, he quit his job."

"Are you going to be able to manage on your paycheck alone?"

"I doubt it."

"Smart man," I said, while thinking, "What does this guy use for brains?"

He already can't take care of his family the way he should and he up and quits his job.

"Why does she stay with him?" I wondered.

"Are you going to be able to meet me?" I asked.

"I don't think so. Not with Joe here."

"Please, I really need to see you. Can't you tell him you have some errands to run or something?"

"OK, I'll meet you. Can you meet me by Diane's?"

"I'll be there."

We met but could only spend a half-hour together. We mostly talked about Joe's dumb stunt, but did manage to sneak in a few long kisses and some tender cuddling. We had to part much too soon. I know because I was home before Debbie and didn't have to come up with any explanations of where I'd been.

The telephone rang with our secret code at eleven forty-five p.m. I wanted to call Leslie but Debbie was sitting right next to me so I couldn't. Debbie never stays up this late, but for some reason, tonight she planned on staying up as long as I did. I finally went to bed wondering why Leslie called. I hoped it wasn't anything serious.

# # #

Saturday I was only able to talk with Leslie once and it was very short. She had tried calling Friday night because she needed a sympathetic ear. Her husband's dumb stunt was weighing heavily on her mind. I wasn't sure what I could do but I told her I'd be there if she needed anything. I prayed that we would be able to spend more time together Sunday. If not in person, at least on the phone.

# # #

On Sunday Debbie left early with friends to spend the day at the German American Festival. I used working on my car as an excuse to stay home. As soon as they left, I used the secret code to call Leslie. I waited for her to return my call, which she did a short time later.

"Debbie's going to be gone most of the day, so I can spend the whole day with you if you can get away."

"I can't. The only time Joe will let me out of his sight is when I go to church. Will you go to church with me?"

Leslie was Catholic and I wasn't, so I was a little nervous about going with her but then I figured what the heck. I guess I'd do just about anything to be with her.

"I'd love to," I told her.

She gave me directions to her church. When I arrived, she was waiting in the parking lot for me. We walked in together with her hanging onto my arm. The service there wasn't a lot different from the services at my church. The biggest difference is that Catholics have communion every Sunday while we have it only once a month.

At this point, I had to fight back tears since Leslie refused to take communion because of her relationship with me. It hurt really bad, tearing at my soul.

I have strong religious beliefs, but they're quite different from other people. I don't just believe there is a God, I know there is a God. Because of the way he answers my prayers, I picture him in much the same way that George Burns portrayed him in "Oh God." Not a supreme dictator who lays down laws that must be rigidly enforced, or else. Nor a being who demands that we kneel in his presence, but a kind, all knowing, all forgiving, generous person. Yes, I said person. We were made in God's own image. We are exactly as he is, except that his capacity for good is greater than we can imagine.

At the Last Supper, Jesus Christ broke bread and poured wine. He said, "This do in remembrance of me." In my church, I'd have no reservations about taking communion because the spirit of Jesus Christ fills my soul. I can't, in my heart, feel that because I love Leslie, that it in any way affects my feeling toward the Lord. In fact, it has brought me closer to the Lord.

I'm sure that he understands the way Leslie and I feel toward each other and forgives us for what we do. I just wish Leslie could see it that way.

## Chapter 37

FOR ALL ETERNITY

Monday the vacation was over and Debbie and I were back to work. I was now back on days working eight-thirty to four-thirty. I spent part of the day bringing the notes for my book up to date and talking with Leslie. We planned on meeting after I got off work.

After work I rushed home to change clothes and headed out to meet Leslie. In order to maximize our time together, we decided to meet at a park near my house. It was a small park with a little kids' playground nearby. Leslie lay down a blanket and we sat down and began to kiss. The kisses led to a lot of hugging and touching as we pleased ourselves with the other's body.

Much too soon, it was time for me to go.

"Time for me to go," I said, as I stood up.

I was wearing shorts. When I stood up to leave, Leslie ran her hand up my leg and through the leg opening and began caressing my privates. As I grew, she freed me from my underwear, so I could grow to full size. She's an expert at arousing me and she had me throbbing in no time. Either my resistance is getting weaker around her or she's getting better all the time. Sometimes I wonder how she got to be so good at pleasing me. How does she know exactly where to touch me and how hard or soft to hold me? She magically seems to know when to stroke slow and when to go fast. It's almost as if she can feel everything, she does to me. She somehow knows exactly what I feel and what to do to bring me to the highest peak of pleasure before allowing me to cum.

I read a joke once that said God didn't make man with enough blood so he could use both his brain and his penis at the same time. When his penis swells, there isn't enough blood left for the brain to work. Sometimes I believe that's true. In addition to my brain, my legs don't work, once Leslie takes control of me. My legs buckled and I was back down on the blanket next to Leslie.

Needless to say, I didn't exactly leave right away. As a matter of fact, I stayed forty-five minutes longer than I should have. Obviously, the brain wasn't working as well as it should. I almost came a couple of times, but couldn't quite make it. I wasn't sure if I was having a problem or Leslie was somehow delaying my release. I was hanging on the edge of ecstasy as she had total control over me.

Then she whispered in my ear, "Please, cum for me baby."

I wanted to cum for her. I wanted to cum for her badly. I ached to please her. Why couldn't I cum? Leslie continued to build the pressure. I yearned for release, but it wouldn't come. Or more precisely, I wouldn't cum. I was really starting to hurt. What the hell is wrong with me?

"Please stop," I begged Leslie.

She must have thought I was joking. I'd have thought so if I were she. She continued to build the pressure higher.

"AHHHHGGG," I'm not sure what I said. "PLEASE," I told her as I pushed her hand away. I folded up in pain and to protect my privates from her touch.

"Oh, baby," she said, "Are you OK?"

"Not exactly," I said.

"I'm such a failure."

"It's not you that's a failure," I told her, "It's me. When I can't cum for the woman, I love more than life itself. When I can't cum for the woman I'll love for all eternity, then the problem is mine."

"Will you?"

I was still focusing on my problem.

"Will I what?" I asked.

"Will you love me for all eternity?"

In pain, I got up on my knees so I could look deep into her eyes. "Yes, Leslie. I will love you for all eternity - and then some."

We talked a little while longer and then when I couldn't put it off any longer, I had to leave. I was so horny on the way home I could have screamed. I kept thinking about Leslie and wondering why I was unable to have an orgasm. Then pictures of Debbie at home crying started going through my mind, and I knew what the problem was.

Last week I was late getting home a couple of times and when I got there, Debbie was crying. My subconscious was somehow associating my being late to causing Debbie pain, and the guilt was causing my problem.

Now that I was looking at the problem logically, it made sense. Logically, though, it seemed as though allowing me to cum within the first five seconds would have been much more preferable.

Chapter 38

LOST RING FOUND

On Tuesday I met Leslie for lunch. We had planned on going to my house to make love, so we headed in that direction.

I was nervous from the start. With Debbie being so upset and suspicious lately, it was hard telling what she was likely to do. And then Leslie showed up at work wearing blue denim short shorts and a red and white halter top, which left very little to the imagination. It would be a little hard to come up with a convincing explanation as to why I was bringing a woman dressed like that to my house. Did I say a little hard? More like impossible. As we started getting closer, I started getting more and more nervous about going there.

"I really want to make love to you in my bed, but this doesn't feel right today. The last time I felt this way Debbie came home for lunch."

"No problem. We can go to the park."

I headed over to Ottawa Park. Once we got to the park, I was lying on my back, more or less, with my arms propping me up. Leslie sat down on top of me, straddling me. She proceeded to unbutton my shirt and started rubbing my chest and stomach. Then she undid my belt and my pants. It didn't take long before she had my juices flowing freely. I was so excited that my body was shuddering uncontrollably.

Unfortunately, when you do this sort of thing in public, you have to stay aware of what's going on around you. While I was lying there and

Leslie was bringing me ever closer to a climax, I counted nine police cars driving by. I really didn't think they were after us, because they certainly wouldn't need nine police cars. Then again, they might have volunteered to come and watch. Anyway, once again, I was unable to have an orgasm. I was so damn horny that the pain was unbelievable. I had to have Leslie soon. I couldn't stand this much longer.

Tuesday night was really bad between Debbie and me. She was crying again.

When I asked her what was wrong, she said, "I keep getting this feeling that you wish I wasn't around anymore. You act as though you just don't want to be bothered with me. Would you be happier if I left?"

Would I? I didn't know. Would I be able to spend more time with Leslie? Maybe a little, but probably not enough to compensate for the loss I'd feel without Debbie around.

"I don't think so," I told her, being as honest as I could.

"But you're not sure?" she shot back at me.

"So much for honesty," I thought to myself.

"Maybe we should have a trial separation," she continued, "I just can't help feeling that you're having an affair."

I thought Leslie and I did a good job covering our time together, so I was curious.

"What makes you think that?" I asked her.

"I don't really know why. I just have that feeling."

I didn't know what to say. I suppose I could have said, "I'm not having an affair, so don't worry about it." But I really didn't want to deny my feelings for Leslie. So I just sat there and stared at her. She met my gaze for a while, then turned away. There wasn't anything she could do about her feelings, any more than there was something I could do about my feelings for Leslie. What can you do about a feeling?

I watched Debbie for a while, trying to fathom her thoughts. Tension was thick in the room, so I left her to her thoughts and went to watch some TV.

# # #

Wednesday, I spent a lot of the day wondering where the relationship that Leslie and I were having was taking me. I imagined what the past would have been like, and all the wonderful times that Leslie and I could have had together, had I only known her back in high school, and that made me sad. It made me want to make sure that we didn't miss the good times the future held for us. But then again, happiness was not guaranteed. There was a distinct possibility that if we hurt the ones we loved, just so we could be together, that we may never be able to forgive ourselves. That could cause us to turn on each other and make us more miserable than we were.

The questions were many and the answers few. No matter how I looked at the problem I could find no solution, only more problems. More and more I turned to God for an answer, but he seemed to be telling me that I knew all the possibilities and the choice was up to me. The questions remained. What should I do? What could I do?

Leslie met me for lunch and we drove to my house, but we didn't stop.

"I still don't feel like making love at my house. The thought of doing it there has been scaring me. I think it's best we don't go there until things are going a little smoother between Debbie and me."

"I'm happy anywhere as long as we're together," Leslie told me.

We drove around for a while and then pulled into an empty parking lot where we could park. We held and kissed each other until I had to get back to work. As always happened, after spending my lunch with Leslie, I went back to work with wet pants.

In the evening, I found a ring on the floor of our laundry room. I thought it was Debbie's so I asked her, "Hey Debbie, did you lose a ring?" MISTAKE!!!!!!!!!!!!

She came and took a look at it and said, "No, that's not my ring. What woman have you had in our house?"

"OK, smart guy, let's see you talk your way out of this," I thought to myself.

My mind raced as I tried to come up with an explanation. I first assumed that the ring had slipped off Leslie's finger when she had her hand in my pants. It was definitely better for it to show up down here in the laundry room rather than fall on the floor of our bedroom while I was undressing for bed. I didn't see how I could use that as an explanation. I searched my memory for some other possibility. Were there any other women over here? Sister, mother, mother-in-law? The only person I could remember being here recently was Leslie when I replaced her water pump. BINGO. That had to be when she left it here.

"The only female that I've had in the house was the girl from work when I replaced her water pump. She got grease on her hands and I had her come down here to wash up. She didn't say anything about losing a ring though. I'll take it to work and ask if it's hers."

Debbie seemed to think that made sense and didn't say any more about it.

I made the first move in attempting to break down the wall that was coming between Debbie and me. We had sex on the basement floor. I managed to stay hard the entire time, but I couldn't have an orgasm.

A couple of hours later, we went to bed and Debbie lay close beside me with her head on my shoulder. She began running her hand over my chest, down my stomach, and lower. Once again, we had sex and this time, I had an orgasm. Afterward all I could think about was that I hoped she didn't get pregnant. While I wanted kids, I couldn't be sure at this point that Debbie and I were going to stay together, so I told her, "I'd like you to go back on the pill."

Leslie called me Thursday morning.

"I found a ring you lost," I told her.

"I was wondering where I had lost it."

"You must have taken it off your finger while you were washing your hands the day, we replaced your water pump."

"No, I'm sure I had it after that. It must have slipped off when I had my hand in your underwear."

"I'm glad it showed up where it did. I don't think I could have explained how a woman's ring got into my underwear."

We made plans to meet for lunch and then said goodbye.

Leslie showed up at eleven-thirty and we went to the park. We just sat in the car holding each other. It felt so good to have her in my arms. Unfortunately, I had to go back to work.

After I got home from work, Leslie called and we talked. She was baking a cake and I was fixing dinner. It was just like a hundred other phone conversations we have had, except for one major difference. Her husband was sitting right there when she made the call. It made me feel really good that she wanted to hear my voice so badly that she would take such a risk.

Chapter 39

OUT DAMN SPOT

On Friday, Leslie met me for lunch and we went to the park. She brought me a piece of cake she had baked, and although I wasn't fond of sweets, I thought it was pretty good. It was nice knowing that Leslie could cook as well as Debbie.

More and more of our conversations were turning from "If we get married" to "When we get married." I would have loved for Leslie to be by my side in everything I did. She enjoyed doing the things I liked to do, such as working on my car. I couldn't get Debbie to do anything like that if I paid her.

Leslie was playing with me, through my clothes, when she asked me, "Have you ever had a blowjob?"

Both Nancy and Leslie had performed oral sex on me, but an actual blowjob that would give me an orgasm?

"No, I've never had a blowjob," I told her.

"We'll have to fix that."

She undressed me and knelt beside me as I lay on the grass. I didn't see how she could do it from that angle. I thought she would have to be between my legs, but she leaned over and took me in her mouth. God that feels good. She was doing some head bobbing like I had seen in movies, but she gave me the most incredible sensations when she quit doing that.

I wasn't exactly sure what she was doing because I had never felt anything like it before. After about ten minutes I came in her mouth. What an incredible feeling. She spit out my load and then apologized.

"I'm sorry, I can't swallow it."

"Oh Leslie, that was incredible. You don't have to apologize. You're the only woman who has ever loved me enough to give me such a wonderful gift."

I felt so incredibly loved. I sat up so I could take her in my arms and hold her tight, never wanting to let go.

But of course, I was only on my lunch, so we had to head back much too soon.

When I got back to work, there was an envelope on my desk. It was sent U.S. Mail and had no return address. The handwriting on the envelope looked like Leslie's. I opened the envelope and found a card inside.

On the outside of the card there were three mice. To the left of the first mouse was written, "*What's a day without laughter?*" and to the right of the mouse was, "*BORING!*" To the left of the second mouse was written, "*What's a day without love?*" and to the right of the mouse was, "*SAD!*" Above the third mouse was written, "*What's a day without you?*"

I opened the card and on the inside was written, "*IMPOSSIBLE!*" and below that was written, "*I miss you!*"

At the bottom of the card Leslie had written, "*Hi Honey! I love you! Can you feel me holding you? I am. Touch me - I need you!*"

She signed the card, "*LR*" - which of course would be her initials once we were legally married.

Friday night I started stripping the paint from my Corvette, with the intention of smoothing out the body seams and repainting the whole car.

# # #

Saturday, I continued working on my car. Several times throughout the day I was tempted to call Leslie and see if she would come help me, and to heck with what Debbie thought, but sanity prevailed and I didn't. Debbie had to run to the store, so I ran inside to call Leslie. We couldn't talk very long but I had a chance to thank her for the card she sent me. It was so good hearing her voice.

Saturday night was my ten-year high school class reunion and I spent a lot of time wishing it were Leslie I was going with. I didn't like being around large groups of people so the first half of the night was a real drag. I was extremely uncomfortable and at one time I almost gave Leslie a call to come and get me. I really didn't want to go to the reunion anyway and it was only because Debbie wanted to go that we were there.

It was a "Bring Your Own Bottle" affair, so I had brought along a bottle of scotch. After finishing about half the bottle, I was finally able to relax a little. We left the reunion early and stopped by our friends' place where we sat and talked some more.

Sometimes I felt Debbie was getting a little suspicious about Leslie and me, like when my friend's wife asked "How are things going?" and Debbie replied, "Not too well, I think Gary is having an affair."

I couldn't believe she actually said that. I let her comment slide right on by as if I hadn't heard a thing.

"Could I have another beer?" I asked my friend.

I didn't really need another beer. In fact, I think I was already over my limit, but it was all I could think of to change the subject.

Sunday, I worked on my car all day. My head was really pounding in the morning but the strenuous work helped to burn off the effects of the hangover. Debbie never left the house, so I couldn't go in and call Leslie. I thought about taking off on my motorcycle and going to a payphone, but after the comment Debbie had made the night before, I thought it made more sense not to. Although I was unable to see Leslie or even talk with her, I thought about her all day long.

Monday, I spent about four hours on the telephone talking with Leslie. She met me for lunch and we went to my house. I showed her my car, now with about half of the paint stripped down to the fiberglass.

"It looks like it's in pain," she told me.

We went in the house and made love. It had been much too long since I last had her and it felt unbelievably good. Making love to her was the most beautiful feeling I ever had. She was just finishing her period and when we were done, I saw we had left a small brownish red stain on the quilt. Before going back to work, I sprayed the spot with some pre-wash stain remover and threw it in the washer.

When I got home from work, I immediately threw the quilt in the dryer and left it in there until it was almost time for Debbie to come walking in the door. I pulled the quilt from the dryer and - PANIC! It was still very damp.

At this point, I didn't have much choice but to put it back on the bed. I figured that as soon as Debbie came home and sat on the bed to take off her shoes, she would notice that it was wet, so I decided to make the bed.

When Debbie got home and went in the bedroom, she said, "Hey, you made the bed."

"Yeah, I'm good for something," I replied.

After dinner, I tried talking Debbie into going out to her parents' house for a visit since I planned to work on my car. After she left, I figured I'd be able to finish drying the quilt. But she didn't want to drive out there all alone, so she stayed home all night. When it was time to go to bed, I was trying to think up an explanation for the wet blanket. I couldn't think up a single good story, so I figured if she asked why the blanket was wet, I'd have to tell the truth.

I'm not as foolhardy as this actually sounds. I figured she wouldn't believe the truth if I said it sarcastically, as though I was playing on her suspicion that I was having an affair.

We climbed into bed, and thank you God, the dampness in the blanket was barely noticeable. Whew!

Chapter 40

PLAYBOY

Leslie met me for lunch and we went for a walk in the park.

"Take your shirt off," she requested.

"I don't want to," I replied.

"Please, for me," she pleaded.

I felt uncomfortable walking around without a shirt on, but I said, "I will if you will."

Leslie was wearing a pull over top, and with one quick move, she had her top off. Well almost. I have quick reflexes so I was able to stop her but if I'd been a tenth of a second slower, she would have had it completely off. As it was, she had it up and over her head.

"Hey, I'm willing to take my top off, you should be willing to do the same," she said.

"OK, I said I would if you would."

So I took off my shirt for her. We went for a walk and stopped next to the road to have a nice long passionate kiss. People driving by were tooting their horns, yelling, and whistling at us. We eventually moved on so we wouldn't cause an accident as our kisses heated up.

We walked away from the road and across the grass where we ran across a neat looking tree, which we stopped to climb. Up in the tree we continued our kissing. Leslie unfastened my belt, undid my pants, and then slipped her hand inside my underwear. It felt so good when she touched me, but up in the tree, I felt like I was on stage and the whole world was watching.

"I feel like we're being watched," I told her, "Why don't you put me back together and we can go back to the car. I think we'll have more privacy there."

She put me back together and we went back to the car. Once inside, she undid my pants and pulled them down around my ankles. She took me in her mouth and made me hard and wet. After she had me sufficiently excited and I was dripping all over the place, she had me sit on her lap where she held me in her arms and continued to play with me until I had an unbelievable orgasm. After I came, it took me nearly ten minutes before I could catch my breath. I just lay there in her arms letting time slip by. I felt so incredibly at peace with the world. After Leslie made me cum like that, I hated for us to have to part, but of course, you guessed it, back to work.

I went back to work sure in the knowledge that Leslie controlled my destiny. I couldn't possibly live without her. If she forced me to choose between her and Debbie, the choice would be simple. I didn't want to hurt Debbie, and I'd do everything in my power to avoid that, but I couldn't live with the thought of never seeing Leslie again - never holding her in my arms - never tasting her sweet lips - never being able to make love to her. I'd never let that happen no matter what the price.

After I got back to work, I opened my lunch and found that Debbie had folded a piece of paper into a card. On the outside of the card, she had drawn four hearts and, in each heart, she had written a single word. The words were: *"Me - and - You - Forever."* On the inside of the card in large bubble print she had written: *"I Love You!"*

It was so sweet of her that it made me feel like a heel, but Leslie had always been and would always be, number one in my heart.

Just before I left work, Leslie called.

"Guess what?" she said all excited.

"You filed for divorce?" I asked hopefully.

"No, silly - LOF called. They want me to come in for an interview."

"That's great. I'm so happy for you."

LOF - Libbey Owens Ford Glass Company. My dad had worked there for as long as I could remember. Debbie's dad worked there in the factory. I thought she had applied for a factory job. It was hard work but I knew she could do it. Leslie had amazing strength for a woman of her size. We had arm wrestled once, and it took every ounce of my strength to beat her, and I was in pretty good shape. There aren't many people who could lift their own weight, but I could.

"Are we still getting together after work?" she asked.

Silly question.

"Of course," I said. "At the park by my house?"

"I'll be there."

"OK, see you in about twenty minutes. Bye Honey."

"Goodbye."

We hung up and I quickly finished what I needed to get done so I could leave. I raced home to change clothes and headed over to the little park by my house. On my way to meet Leslie, a song was playing on the radio. It was a song by Climax called "Precious and Few." The lyrics went:

Precious and few are the moments we two can share.
Quiet and blue like the sky, I'm hung over you.
And if I can't find my way back home,
It just wouldn't be fair.
Precious and few are the moments we two can share.

Baby, it's you on my mind, your love is so rare.
Being with you is a feeling I just can't compare.
And if I can't hold you in my arms,
It just wouldn't be fair.
'Cause precious and few are the moments we two can share.

And if I can't find my way back home,
Ah, it just wouldn't be fair.
'Cause precious and few are the moments we two can share.

Precious and few are the moments we two can share.
Quiet and blue like the sky, I'm hung over you.
And if I can't find my way back home,
It just wouldn't be fair.
Precious and few are the moments we two can share.

Leslie was there when I arrived and we quickly found each other's' arms and lips. We had only twenty minutes together but it was still beautiful because "precious and few are the moments we two can share."

As usual, I kept putting off having to leave her, and ended up staying ten minutes longer than I should have. When I got home, I had an explanation all ready for when Debbie asked me where I had been. Boy, was I pissed when I got home and she wasn't even there yet. As a matter of fact, she didn't get home for another half-hour. That's valuable time that I could have spent with Leslie. Debbie had been questioning me lately when I wasn't home when I should be so I thoroughly enjoyed jumping all over her case.

After dinner I was back to working on my car. Debbie left for the store, and I went in to call Leslie. We were able to talk for about ten minutes before Debbie got home. I spent all night working on my car, stripping the paint and sanding. I quit about twelve-thirty after I ran out of paint remover.

I really wanted to call Leslie. She had tried calling me late at night several times in the past week and she had told me to call her if Debbie went to sleep early. Debbie was in bed, but not sleeping. She kept getting up and asking me when I was coming to bed. I decided the risk of calling Leslie was far too great and headed for bed.

# # #

Wednesday, August 30, 1978 was Leslie's and my second anniversary. It was two months ago today that we exchanged wedding vows in the park while making love.

Leslie picked me up at lunchtime and we went to my house to make love. We both had cards for each other. On the envelope, she had for me, she had written, "*Sweetheart*." I opened the envelope.

On the outside of the card was written, "*It's hard for me to tell you just how much I love you...*" On the inside of the card was written, "*perhaps because the only true measure of loving, is to love without measure.*"

Leslie added to the inside of the card. At the top she wrote, "*Hi Baby!*" In addition, at the bottom of the card she wrote, "*Loving you is beautiful (and fun too!) Always Yours, Leslie.*"

Our lovemaking, like the day, was very tender and special. I wish I could have held her in my arms for the rest of the day, but back to work - DAMN!!!!

\# \# \#

On Thursday Leslie was unable to meet me for lunch because she had to go to LOF about the job she had applied for. I received a card at work from her. On the outside of the card was written, "*I love your hands...*" On the inside of the card was written, "*especially when they're touching me.*" At the top Leslie wrote, "*Baby!*" At the bottom she wrote, "*I'm yours and you're all that I want! Honey.*" We met after work for forty-five minutes. I thanked her for the wonderful card. It absolutely made my day. After our lovemaking session of the previous day, it was the shortest forty-five minutes I'd ever experienced.

\# \# \#

On Friday we met for lunch and went to my house to make love. When we got there, I brought the mail in and saw my new Playboy magazine had arrived. I started browsing through it and Leslie got really upset. She was so upset; she was walking out the door. If it had been Debbie, I'd have let her go, since neither she nor the magazine really did anything to excite me. But the choice of looking at pictures, or making love with Leslie, was no choice at all. I dropped the magazine like it was on fire, and raced after her.

"I'm sorry Honey, please don't go," I pleaded with her. "I love you. I certainly don't have any feelings for those pictures. Besides, you're as beautiful as they are."

And to me she was - maybe more so. We were in the doorway, with my neighbor's kitchen window maybe fifteen feet away. I didn't even think to see if there was anybody standing there. All I was thinking about was my love. I pulled her into my arms and kissed her passionately, my hands pulling at her clothes.

We retreated to the bedroom where I undressed her. As she stood naked before me, I told her, "I love you so much it hurts."

In response, she threw her arms around me and pressed her naked body against me. There was now a distinctive bulge in the front of my pants and she proceeded to undo me so it could spring free. She worked me with her hand for a little bit, then we fell onto the bed with me on top of her. I came within seconds of sliding deep inside her.

"I love you, baby," she said as she ran her hands down my back and over my rear. When she reached my thighs, she pulled up, pulling me deeper into her as she wrapped her legs around me. Apparently, I wasn't going anywhere just yet.

She started working her hips and doing whatever it is that she does inside of her. I stayed hard in her and she was working me toward another orgasm. I took my weight off her, shifting it to my knees and forearms, to allow her hips more freedom so she could slide up and down my shaft. I tried to hold back so she could climax, but I desired her too much, and the climax escaped me.

I collapsed into her arms, and still she held me tight, still massaging me from within. I knew if she kept this up, she would make me come again, but I had already been gone from work for an hour.

"I have to get back to work," I told her.

"Just one more time," she pleaded.

"I've already been gone too long."

"But it's a three-day weekend. It'll be forever before we can be together again."

I hadn't thought of that, maybe one more...

"I'm sorry, I really have to get back to work."

Did I just say that?

We got dressed and I went back to work. I briefly wished that I had been born a millionaire, so I didn't have to keep leaving Leslie to go to work, but then I realized that if I'd been born a millionaire, I probably never would have met her in the first place. Maybe working wasn't so bad after all.

Chapter 41

DARING RENDEZVOUS

I spent nearly all-day Saturday working on my car. I managed to talk with Leslie only once and it was shorter than short.

"I'll call you tomorrow during football," she told me.

Debbie would usually drive out to visit with her parents while I watched football, so I thought that would work out perfectly.

"Talk with you then, my love," I told her as I hung up the phone.

Early football games started Sunday afternoon at one. Leslie didn't call, but since Debbie decided not to go out to her parents' it worked out OK. About four o'clock, Debbie had to run to the store to pick up some things for dinner. I immediately called Leslie using our secret ring, but she didn't return my call. I was out in the garage working on my car around five, when the phone rang. Debbie answered it and whoever it was hung up without saying anything. I knew it had to be my lover, but there wasn't anything I could do about it.

Sunday night Debbie went to bed at eleven and I stayed up, supposedly to watch Sherlock Holmes on the late show. I immediately disconnected all of the phones in the house and hot-wired the phone in the basement so it was the only active phone in the house. I called Leslie using the secret ring. However, before she could return the call, I called her back and just let the phone ring. I was hoping the signal would let her know it was I, and she would make sure she answered the phone rather than her husband. As it turned out, I didn't need to worry, as she was home alone.

"I miss you, baby," she moaned in my ear, "I just have to have you."

"I want you, too, Honey. My arms ache to hold you."

"Can I come see you?" she pleaded.

I mentally pictured Debbie upstairs and Leslie coming over. Would Debbie get upset if we used the bed? I thought the possibility high.

"I don't think that would be a good idea," I told her.

"But baby, I need to feel you inside of me."

Damn, she's making me horny. I could feel the pressure building between my legs as my underwear started to cut into me. I reached into my underwear and rearranged things to allow me to grow to full size. I was already getting very damp down there.

"I want you so bad," I moaned.

"Then I can come over?" she pressed.

What was that about brain and penis not working at the same time?

"Yes, Honey, come to me," I told her. "Park on the side street at the corner and I'll come see you."

I just couldn't stand the thought of her willing to come be with me and me not grasping the opportunity. I needed her and the risk no longer mattered. I left the house quietly and headed to the corner to wait for my lover.

She arrived a half-hour later and we climbed into her back seat. I took her in my arms and our lips met. She smelled so good. She obviously had thrown on extra perfume before heading over and the fragrance had my head spinning, or was it that hand she had between my legs. As our tongues continued to play with each other, I removed her top and my mouth sought out her breast. As I licked her nipple, she shivered slightly and held my head tightly to her. I couldn't see what I was doing, so my hands fumbled at unfastening her shorts.

She appeared to be in a hurry to have me, as she let go of my head so she could remove her own shorts. Her stomach looked inviting so I bent over to kiss it and used my tongue to explore her navel. I started heading south from there, but she stopped me. She forced me onto my back, her naked body lying on top of me, her kisses delighting me. She stopped kissing me long enough to unfasten my pants and pull them off. She bent over taking me in her mouth making sure I was nice and wet. Then straddling me, she slipped me inside. I was so glad that I had agreed to let her come over.

I barely had enough room to lie on her back seat, but with her being petite, she had plenty of room to work me. She was really sliding up and down my pole. She would go up until just my tip was inside her and then she would come down and take all of me. It felt so good being with her. I enjoyed being on the bottom where I could see her beautiful face and body accented by the moonlight.

Sweat was beginning to form in her cleavage and I strained to lick it from her body. I could tell by the angle she was working me that she was more interested in making me cum, rather than in her having an orgasm, so I didn't try to hold back. I'm not sure I could have anyway. The risk of getting caught with Debbie so close, the smell of Leslie's perfume now mixed with her sweat, the moonlit night, and the woman I loved so much wanting to please me. The orgasm just ripped through me shaking every nerve fiber in my body. I gasped as the force took me by surprise.

"Oh, God, Honey," I started to say, but anything after that was lost as another wave of pleasure swept over me. My head was spinning. I was drunk on her love.

She bent over to kiss me and said, "I love you so much."

"I love you, too. You are so incredible," I said as I held her tightly to me. I wanted to go again, but common sense made me say, "I better go make sure Debbie is still sleeping."

Leslie lifted off me dripping sticky wet juices all over my thigh. Thankfully, she kept a box of tissues in her car. She dried me off enough that I was able to get my clothes back on.

"I'll be right back," I told her as I kissed her and took off toward home. There were only three houses between Debbie and me, so I was halfway home in about fifteen seconds. When I could see my house, I got a sick feeling in the pit of my stomach. Debbie was obviously awake because she had turned on the front porch light. I quickly turned around and ran back to my lover.

"Debbie's up. I have to go. Thanks for coming to see me. I love you so much."

I kissed her quickly and started slowly walking home trying to figure out what I was going to say to Debbie. I was sure I had Leslie's smell all over me, her perfume on my face and neck, and her womanly fragrance on my privates. I couldn't tell in the dark whether or not she'd been wearing lipstick. She had nice natural lip color so she didn't usually wear lipstick, but I'd seen her wearing bright red lipstick before. If I had bright red lipstick all over my face, I was fucked, and I wasn't going to enjoy the second time tonight nearly as much as the first.

My mind raced. What possible reason could I have for being out roaming the streets at night while Debbie was sleeping? The plan hadn't completely formed when my body started acting on it. I broke into a trot and forced myself to hyperventilate. As I turned into my yard, I could see Debbie looking out the front window. When she saw me, she left the window and headed for the side door to intercept me.

I couldn't let her have the upper hand, so I pretended that I hadn't seen her, and plopped down on the front porch. When Debbie realized that I wasn't coming in, she came back to the front of the house. She was more curious than angry after I made her wait at the side door. At times like that I was glad that I was proficient at both poker and chess. Both games have you trying to out maneuver your opponent by attempting to convince them that you are planning on doing one thing while in fact you have something entirely different in mind.

When Debbie opened the front door, I was sitting there puffing hard. You would have sworn that I had just finished running a mile.

"Where have you been?" she asked.

Duh - this is a great performance - figure it out for yourself.

"Take a guess," was my reply.

"Where did you go? I've been up a half-hour."

I sure appreciated her volunteering that information, now I knew how much time I had to account for. I figured I could account for a half-hour without too much trouble.

"I ran around the block," I started saying.

It's a large block, but it wouldn't even take Debbie a half-hour to run around it, and she knew it, so I provided a better explanation.

"I had to stop for a while because I thought I was going to die. After breathing all of the paint fumes and the dust from sanding my car, it was really difficult to breathe."

After a while I got up and went in the house and plopped down on the sofa.

I continued spinning my tale, "For some reason I just wasn't tired, so I decided to jog around the block to wear myself out so I could sleep."

"Are you ready for bed now?" Debbie asked.

With the smell of Leslie all over me? You have got to be kidding.

"No, not really," I said.

What a lie. It was after three in the morning and I could hardly keep my eyes open. Leslie had drained every drop of energy from me but I had to wash before I went to bed, or Debbie would know I'd been making love to another woman.

"I'm going to watch TV for a while," I said, hoping for a chance to wash up before going to bed.

Unfortunately, Debbie joined me. I was afraid she would be able to smell Leslie's perfume on me, so I leaned away from her, and acted as though I was doing that because my back hurt.

After a half-hour, I said, "I'm going to take a hot shower. Hopefully that will help me relax so I can sleep."

I climbed in the shower and let the warm water run over me. I ran my hand over my privates and held my hand to my nose. The sweet smell of Leslie was strong in my nostrils and it made me hard. I couldn't believe we actually got away with this. My thoughts drifted back to an hour earlier when Leslie and I were making love and it brought a smile to my face. I couldn't believe the things that I'd do, the risks that I'd take, just to be with her. How far would I be willing to go I wondered?

I finished my shower and climbed into bed. I leaned over and kissed Debbie, saying, "Good night." Then I turned away from her and fell asleep dreaming about Leslie.

## Chapter 42

KISS YOU ALL OVER

Monday, I tried all day to get a hold of Leslie. I expected her to call me to find out what happened with Debbie, but she never did. By the end of the day, I was getting scared that something may have happened to her. I wasn't sure what I could do, yet. All I could do was wait for either her to call, so I knew she was OK, or wait for Diane to call and say something had happened to her. Waiting wasn't my strong suit and the waiting was tearing me apart.

#

Early Tuesday morning at twelve forty-five the phone rang waking up both Debbie and me. I jumped out of bed to answer the phone. It was Leslie.

The first thing she asked was, "Can you talk?"

I wanted to say, "Yes." I wanted to know why she was calling in the middle of the night and why I hadn't heard from her all day. I looked at Debbie who was sitting up in bed staring at me.

"No, you must have the wrong number," I told her, and hung up the phone.

I went back to bed and lay there most of the night worrying about why she had called. Was something wrong? I wished that I had thought to tell Debbie that the call was from work, then I could have gone into the kitchen and talked with Leslie. I could even have told Debbie I had to go into work and then I could have met Leslie somewhere.

I was so afraid that she was in desperate need of my help and I had let her down. I tried to convince myself that if it were really something important, she would have told me she needed me right away or have at least told me why she called rather than just ask if I could talk. However, no matter what I told myself, I lay there worrying about her and wishing she were with me and safely in my arms.

In the morning after I got to work, Leslie called.

"I'm sorry I called and woke you up, but I thought you had been trying to reach me."

"You had me scared. I'm so happy to hear your voice and know that you're all right."

I was so relieved to hear that she was OK; I didn't even think to ask her where she had been all day Monday.

Leslie met me for lunch and we drove over to the park. We sat in her car the whole time with my arms wrapped around her. I had been so scared of losing her that I just wanted to hold her tight and feel her love flow through me. Leslie wasn't entirely satisfied with just being held though and attempted several times to ignite the passion with her burning kisses. While her kisses did arouse me, I really didn't want to do much more than hug and kiss. Soon it was time to go back to work.

#

I wasn't able to see Leslie all day Wednesday and I felt as though I was about to die. It seemed as though there was a song with the lyrics, "love is a hurting thing" and boy that was the truth. The pain was almost unbearable whenever I was away from her. I needed her so much. She meant more to me than anything else in the world.

I was able to talk with her a few times on the phone.

"Joe is going to be bowling tonight," she told me, "If you get a chance, call me."

Debbie left the house to run some errands at six-forty and I immediately called Leslie. Since she had told me that Joe wasn't going to be there, I let the phone ring a long time, but nobody answered. I decided to go out and work on my car, but I kept running inside every five to ten minutes to try reaching Leslie. She finally answered at eight-fifteen.

"Where have you been?" I asked. "You tell me to call and then you leave the house."

"I'm sorry. Today was the first day of school so I had to go out shopping for school supplies."

We didn't get a chance to talk very long because Debbie came home fifteen minutes later.

I worked on my car until after midnight and then I called Leslie at work.

"I just called to tell you I love you," I said.

"You're such a sweetheart," she told me.

I couldn't help the way I felt about her. In some ways I wished I could. As it was, someday I'd end up breaking Debbie's heart and I didn't want to do that because I loved her so much. I knew for certain that I couldn't be without Leslie in my life. She had been away for years and I didn't want to go through that ever again. We couldn't talk long so we said goodbye.

I went to bed and started drifting off to sleep. My mind was spinning with bits and pieces of memories. Memories of times that Leslie and I had spent together. There was the time before I really knew her that we had both gone to a party after work. I had got drunk and grabbed her ass. Then there was the time when we went out to lunch together and I kissed her for the very first time. The time when I went to a bar after work with a bunch of guys and she called me there just to say she loved me and missed me. Then there was a Christmas party that a co-worker threw and we both attended. She was trying to be inconspicuous about her feelings for me by spending time with all the other guys there, when I was the only one, she wanted to be with. She did such a good job of neglecting me that I got jealous and left. I don't get jealous, so that was a new experience for me. There was the first time we made love. There was the time when I was engaged to Debbie and I left her at midnight and went straight to Leslie's arms.

Millions of little pieces of memories all building up to the deep, tender love, which I now felt for Leslie.

# # #

On Thursday Leslie met me for lunch and we headed to the park. We were like young lovers holding hands and walking through the park. After a while we sat down by a tree and began necking. It was a sweet and tender moment like a new love starting to blossom. While our sex was out of this world, that wasn't all that our relationship was about. Sometimes it was nice to remember that we had been very good friends for years, before the sex started dominating our time together.

# # #

Leslie met me for lunch on Friday and we drove to my house. She was wearing shorts, so I wouldn't be able to use the excuse that she was someone I worked with. I was rapidly reaching the point where I wanted to scream at the top of my lungs, "I LOVE LESLIE." Sometimes I really wanted the whole world to know how much I loved her. This apparently was one of those times because I really didn't care whether anybody saw us or not. I was with the woman of my dreams and that was all I cared about.

I showed Leslie the progress I was making on my car. While we were in the garage my neighbor came home. I'm sure she saw Leslie with me but I really didn't care. We went into the house and made mad passionate love. Leslie had an orgasm during our lunchtime lovemaking session, which was a rare treat. It made me feel so good that I was able to please her that way.

# # #

On Saturday Debbie went shopping with one of her sisters to pick out an anniversary present for their parents. I called Leslie.

"Can you come meet me?" she asked.

"I need to work on my car."

"You'd rather work on your car than be with me?"

"OK, it was a temporary moment of insanity. Please forgive me."

"I forgive you."

"Where do you want to meet?"

"The park? Then you can make love to me."

Joy at the anticipation of being with her quickly turned to a burning desire. I could feel the blood pouring into my loins as I thought about making love to her.

"The park it is. Be there in ten minutes."

"OK, bye."

We hung up and I took off to the park on my motorcycle. I arrived just a few minutes before she did. After she arrived, we headed back to our secret place. We had our longest lovemaking session ever. It felt so good to be totally naked outdoors with our bodies entwined and the warm sun overhead. We were constantly switching positions first with me on top, then on our sides, then Leslie on top, then on our sides, and back again. Everything we did felt absolutely sensational. It seemed to take forever but she finally climaxed. The orgasm seemed to hit her as hard as the one I had the other day. She fell into my arms, her body twitching uncontrollably. I held her tightly. God, how I loved pleasing her.

Saturday night after Debbie and I went to bed, she decided she had something to say.

"We need to talk," she started out.

"About what?" I asked.

"I really think we should get a divorce, or at least be separated for a while."

I didn't say anything. It was her show, so I let her run it.

"Are the problems that we're having being caused because you're having an affair?" she wanted to know.

"How can I have an affair with my wife?" I wondered.

Leslie and I just had our second anniversary.

I said, "I really don't know what the problem is between us. Sometimes things seem to be going really well and other times they seem really bad."

"Things haven't been good between us for over a month," she informed me.

Debbie rattled on and on. I fell asleep while she was talking. After all, there really wasn't much I could say. We were constantly picking on each other, saying mean and hurtful things. I couldn't help feeling that I wasn't entirely responsible for the failing relationship. I felt that even if I wasn't seeing Leslie every chance I got, our relationship would probably be the same. Debbie was constantly picking on me and everything I said or did was wrong. If I asked Debbie to do something for me, she would say, "The only reason you want me around is to be your slave."

If I just did things for myself, she would still find fault. "What, you don't think I can do that?" she would say. Or if I just went to the store to pick up something, instead of asking her to go for me, she would say, "You don't trust me to bring back the right thing?"

It was like talking with an arguing wall. When I got tired of her picking on everything I said, I'd just start ignoring her. You guessed it - that upset her too. I just couldn't win. I seemed to be trapped in a revolving door with no way out.

# # #

Sunday I wasn't able to see Leslie. I worked on my car and watched football during the day. In the evening we went out to Debbie's sister's place for dinner.

Debbie's mother said, "I tried calling today and there was no answer."

"There was someone home all day," Debbie told her.

"Gary must have been at his girlfriend's," Valerie said.

"What has Debbie been telling her family?" I wondered.

"No, her husband was home today," I said honestly.

Everyone laughed thinking that was funny. I wondered what they would have done if they knew that was the truth.

# # #

It was Monday and Leslie was supposed to start her new job at LOF. She was going to be working afternoons, so lunch would be the only time that I could see her. She called around eleven in the morning.

"I'm not going to be able to make lunch today," she informed me.

"That's terrible," I told her, "Why not?"

"I have to stay and help Joe write checks to pay bills."

I paid all of our bills, so I assumed he must not be able to write.

"What time do you get off tonight?" I asked.

"Eleven. I should be home by eleven-thirty. Will you call me then?"

"I plan on it."

We said goodbye and I dug my lunch out of the brown paper bag. Eating lunch alone wasn't much fun. I missed Leslie so much. I ached to be with her - to hold her in my arms. The unhappiness of being separated from her made it hard to swallow and I choked on my sandwich a couple of times. I decided eating was too dangerous and threw my lunch away. The rest of the day just dragged by until eleven-thirty that night.

I called Leslie after work to see how her day went. Debbie was still up, so I called from the bedroom while she was in the basement. I was nervous with Debbie being up so we didn't talk for long.

# # #

On Tuesday, Leslie met me for lunch and we went to the park. Once there, she undressed me like she normally does and we sat in the car holding each other. Even if we weren't having sex, I think she enjoyed seeing the effect she had on me. One look told her how much I desired her. We started out kissing slow. Each kiss was more passionate than the last. The middle of summer and our smoldering kisses were starting to steam up the car windows. By the time I had to go back to work, she had my groin throbbing and me dripping with desire.

# # #

On Wednesday, Leslie couldn't meet me for lunch again. She and Joe were going to go pay off their house. That was one good thing about buying a dump – you can pay it off early.

She called me at work a couple of times and we talked for a few hours but I still missed her terribly.

I called her at eleven-thirty after she got home from work. We talked until nearly one-thirty.

"Debbie's going out of town with her parents this weekend. Is there any chance that you could come over and spend the night with me?" I wanted to know.

"I think I can probably arrange that. I'll let you know."

It seemed like a long time since we had made love and it had been even longer since we were able to spend a night together. We were both looking forward to it and hoped we could pull it off.

# # #

Leslie met me for lunch Thursday and we went looking for upholstery material so I could reupholster the door panels in my Corvette. I really wanted new ones but they were too expensive so I thought this would provide a classy custom look until I could afford new panels.

We couldn't find any suitable material, so we ended up at a record store where we both bought a bunch of forty-fives. Leslie also bought some blank eight-track tapes so I could record some songs for her.

We then went to McDonald's where we bought a milkshake and picked up two straws. We sat in the car and shared the milkshake. The setting was different, but it reminded me of the very first time I kissed her. My how far we had come.

# # #

Leslie met me for lunch on Friday. It was payday and I should have gone to the bank to cash my check but I had more pressing matters to take care of. Leslie and I went to my house and made wonderful love. I briefly wondered if satisfying our need for each other like this would spoil the plans we had for making love Saturday night. I really didn't see how that would be possible. I knew that I never got tired of loving and making love to Leslie, and I was reasonably certain that she felt the same way about me.

# # #

Saturday morning at eight o'clock Debbie left with her parents for Ashland, Kentucky. Ashland was where Debbie was born, her mother was raised, and her grandmother lived. I spent most of the day working on my car. My brother came over in the afternoon and we left for a little while to go to a Corvette Supply Store. Wouldn't you know it, the short time I was gone Leslie stopped by. She had left a note by the side door. I was upset that I had missed her. A short while later she called.

"Are the plans still on for tonight?" she wanted to know.

"I certainly hope so," I told her.

"I'll see you a little after eleven, baby."

"I can't wait."

Leslie showed up at eleven-fifteen. We took a long hot relaxing shower together. We washed each other, spending extra time cleaning and stimulating the private areas. I was erect and Leslie pressed her naked body to mine, squeezing my organ between us. I could feel it throbbing and wondered if she could feel it as well. We embraced and started the longest most passionate kiss I think we have ever had. If the shower wasn't already steamed up, I think our kiss would have done it. Being in the shower you couldn't tell it, but I was sure that both of us were so excited that we were dripping in anticipation.

We finished the shower and helped each other dry off. We wanted each other so much, but we wanted to let the passion build. We went downstairs and I turned on the stereo. It seemed as though every love song that reminded me of Leslie was playing on the radio.

We laid next to each other on the sofa, wrapped our arms and legs around each other, smothered each other in kisses, and caressed one another until we could stand it no longer. I turned off the stereo and we headed upstairs to the bedroom.

I turned on the radio next to the bed and we started exploring each other's body. Leslie was kissing my thigh, working her way ever closer to my throbbing erection, planting kisses all the way. I twisted around and strained so I could kiss her back and work my way down her spine and over one of her lovely creamy white cheeks. As our kisses were getting us extremely excited a song started playing on the radio. It was "Kiss You All Over" by Exile. The timing was so perfect that it immediately became "Our Song."

Leslie's kisses soon became licking and sucking and I was moaning in ecstasy.

"Leslie, I want you - I need you."

She quit preparing me and straddled me, slowly lowering herself onto my shaft. Heaven couldn't possibly be any better than this. To be so intimate with the woman I loved so much, what could possibly be better? I moaned louder as she pleased herself on my swollen love stick. I wanted her so much I didn't even think about holding back, which was just as well, because she came faster than she ever had before. Her orgasm started just before mine and we were swept along through fields of pleasure. We held each other tightly as waves of ecstasy poured over us. As the orgasm subsided, we continued our embrace and gently kissed one another. She put her head on my shoulder and we fell asleep in each other's arms.

#

We slept peacefully all night long and woke up Sunday morning still tightly embraced as though we were afraid of being separated. I'm not sure which one of us actually woke up first, but when we awoke to find our lover naked in our arms, we were both immediately aroused. We made love again and it was every bit as good as the previous night's had been. I silently prayed that someday we would spend every night and every morning with each other, just like this.

Leslie got up to take a shower.

"Come join me," she pleaded.

For some reason, I was starting to get nervous. Maybe Debbie was just wondering what I was doing or maybe she was on her way home. Something didn't feel right, and I'd learned to trust my instincts.

"I want to make sure nobody pops in unexpectedly. You go ahead."

She climbed into the shower and I went to open the doors to let some fresh air in and watch for any approaching cars. Once I was sure that there was no immediate danger, I went into the bathroom and watched Leslie bathe. When she was done, I sat outside the bathroom to watch her dry herself and put on her makeup. I just loved watching her. She was so beautiful, and to think that she loved me. I felt I was just about the luckiest man in the world.

After she finished getting cleaned up, she came and sat down next to me. We sat there holding and kissing one another letting time slip away. We were in each other's' arms when we heard someone open the front screen-door. My heart almost leaped out of my chest. It had to be Debbie. Seconds later I heard a thud on the floor and I realized the paperboy had just thrown the Sunday paper in the house. After that scare it took nearly fifteen minutes before my heart started beating normally again.

Leslie had told her husband that she was going to be working last night, so she had to be leaving, as it was almost time for that shift to be let out.

She left to head home and I went back to bed. I could still smell her on the sheets and wished that she were still with me.

I was only able to talk with her once in the afternoon.

"Last night was so beautiful," I told her, "My arms are already aching to hold you again."

"I love you so much," she said to me.

"I love you, too. I can't wait until we can spend another night together."

"Me, too. I hope it's soon."

We talked for a while longer and then she had to go. I went out to work on my car and fantasized about this woman that meant so much to me and I loved so dearly.

Chapter 43

SHIT HITS THE FAN

On Monday Debbie and I started our second week of vacation. I wasn't able to talk with Leslie until after she got off work, and then we talked for over three hours.

#

Tuesday was the day before Debbie's and my three-year anniversary so I told Debbie that I was going shopping and rushed off to meet Leslie. We went to the shopping mall. We had a super time just hanging out with each other. It felt so incredibly wonderful just to be out in public holding her hand in mine. I was able to pull her into my arms and kiss her a few times, but it was much too few.

We had lunch at McDonald's (I'm a big spender) and then we went shopping for Debbie's anniversary present.

Our time together ran out much too soon and we had to leave each other's company. I called her after she got off work, but she was exhausted so we talked for only about an hour.

#

Wednesday and it's Debbie's and my three-year anniversary. I was out working on my car when Debbie decided to go do our grocery shopping. As soon as she left, I called Leslie. We met and sat in her car each of us exciting the other beyond anything imaginable.

"Make love to me," she said.

I looked around. The only place to do it was in her back seat. We were in a parking lot. There were other people around. Not a lot, but I figured somebody would see what we were doing. After all it was in broad daylight.

"I want you, but I don't think that's a good idea with all of these people around here."

She undid my pants and pulled me into her arms holding me tight. She began playing with me until I came all over the place. We finally had to leave each other.

"Someday we won't have to leave each other," I told myself.

In the evening, my parents took Debbie and me out to dinner and then back to their house for cake and ice cream. We got home about nine and a short time later our best friends dropped by.

While they were visiting, Leslie called, or rather her husband called. Debbie answered the phone and Joe asked for me. Leslie then came on the line.

"Joe knows about us," she informed me.

"I was kind of able to figure that out."

"He gave me a choice. I can either stay with him, or I can leave. If I stay, I can never see you again."

I was waiting for her to ask if she could come to me. I was thinking, "Poor Debbie, she has to find out, on our anniversary, that I want another woman."

"I've decided to stay," Leslie told me.

I felt like someone had buried an axe between my shoulder blades. I could hardly breathe and the room started to spin. One knee buckled and I had to steady myself with the wall to keep from falling down. The whole time I had to act as though I was talking with someone at work about a problem.

"OK," I said as I hung up the phone and tears filled my eyes.

I rushed to the bathroom so nobody could see me crying. Sobs shook my body.

"This can't be happening," I told myself, "This has to be a nightmare."

I pinched myself hard - OUCH - that hurt. I didn't know if that really worked anyway. I yelled at myself to wake up. "God, please let this be a dream," I prayed.

Nothing changed – I didn't wake up.

"OK, this is real. I can't let Leslie just walk out of my life like this. What can I do?" I wondered.

"Nothing right now," I told myself, "Right now you have to pull yourself together and go visit with your company."

I thought to myself, "If I can pull this off, I should switch professions and become an actor."

I put cold water on my eyes hoping to get the redness to go away, dried my eyes, and then took several deep breaths. "Please, God, give me the strength," I prayed, and then went back to spend the evening with my friends.

"Did you get the problem fixed?" Debbie wanted to know.

"Not exactly," I told her.

"So, we can expect them to call back later?"

"I don't think there's much chance of that. But I may call them back later."

We visited with our friends and I tried to act natural while the fear of losing Leslie was ripping my heart from my chest. It felt as though a jagged knife was in my abdomen and somebody was twisting it. I wanted to throw up.

After our friends left, I chased Debbie off to bed, telling her I was going to call work back. I called Leslie at eleven-thirty. I could hardly talk I was so choked up. I was crying like a baby.

"Please don't leave me, Leslie," I sobbed.

"It's for the best."

"Then why do I hurt so bad?"

I really didn't know how I could survive without her. I'd just as soon end my life now as to spend the rest of my life without her.

"I need you, Honey," I continued to beg. "Please leave Joe. He'll never love you as much as I do."

"OK, I'll leave Joe," she finally agreed.

She agreed to leave Joe, but it felt a hollow victory. It didn't feel right that I had to talk her into it. Leslie had told me many times that she wouldn't leave me. Even if Joe found out, she wouldn't leave me. And still after all she said, she put me through all of this pain and anguish.

"Are you sure?" I wanted her to be sure.

"I promise. I'll leave him tomorrow."

I hoped she was telling me the truth but I didn't know what to believe any more.

"I love you. I'll call you tomorrow so we can work out the details," I told her.

"OK, I love you."

"Goodbye, Honey."

"Bye baby."

We hung up. Two late shows and a half bottle of scotch later, I was finally able to attempt going to sleep.

# # #

Thursday morning, I left the house early after telling Debbie I was going to the store. I stopped at a payphone and called Leslie.

"I want to see you," she told me.

We met to discuss what our choices were for the future.

"Joe was really happy until you called last night. After I told him I was leaving him, he said that if I insisted on doing that, he would call Debbie and tell her what's been going on."

"If that's a threat, it's the dumbest one I've ever heard. That would work out perfect for us. He calls Debbie and tells her about us. Debbie leaves me, and I'm free to marry you. I love you and I want you. If you feel the same way, let him call Debbie."

"Are you sure?"

"I'm sure. How did Joe manage to find out about us anyway?"

"I had everything from you in a shoebox and he found it. Your class ring, the picture I took of you, cards you had given me, letters you had written, everything."

"OK. Why didn't you just say it was stuff you had saved from years ago?"

"I don't know. I panicked and didn't think of it. All I could think of was we were caught. Are you mad at me?"

"I could never be mad at you."

I took her in my arms and gave her a tender, loving, not quite passionate kiss.

We said our good-byes and as we parted, I said, "Be strong, we'll make it through this. I love you."

I went on home and Debbie went out to her mother's. We were supposed to go out with a couple in the evening and my friend called to see if we could go out tomorrow night, too. I told him I wasn't very sure whether Debbie and I would even be together then, and gave him an overview of recent events.

Debbie came home and fixed dinner, but I didn't feel much like eating because my stomach was in knots. I wanted to tell Debbie about Leslie but I didn't know how to go about it.

I couldn't finish eating and Debbie was concerned that I might be coming down with the flu.

Fifteen minutes later the telephone rang. I answered it and some guy asked to speak with Debbie. I was certain it was Joe. I briefly thought about hanging up the phone, but Debbie had to find out about Leslie and me sometime, or Leslie and I could never be together. I handed Debbie the phone.

"It's for you," I told her.

I couldn't hear what Joe was telling Debbie, but I imagine the conversation went something like, "Hello, you don't know me, but your husband and my wife are having an affair."

Debbie kept asking, "Who is this?"

I didn't know how much Leslie had told Joe, but he seemed to be aware of some of the times we had spent together. He seemed to be providing Debbie with dates and times. Debbie had a look on her face as if she had seen a ghost. She argued about some of the information Joe was telling her, saying I couldn't possibly have been there.

Debbie looked at me terrified and asked the caller again, "Who is this?"

I told her, "It's Leslie's husband."

Debbie's expression was similar to that of a dam collapsing. She looked absolutely crushed. At first all she could say was one word, "ASSHOLE!"

Joe kept rattling on but Debbie told him, "I can't talk now," and she hung up the phone.

It seemed like kind of a childish thing for Joe to do, but I was glad he was that kind of person. Debbie had to find out sometime, and I couldn't tell her. Debbie and I spent the rest of the night crying.

"Do you love her?" Debbie wanted to know.

"Yes, I love her."

To Debbie that was the same as me saying I didn't love her. I kept trying to explain to her that I loved them both but she either couldn't or wouldn't understand. I guess that you'd have to experience it for yourself before you could truly understand what it's like to be in love with two people at the same time.

Debbie and I hardly slept at all. Over and over all Debbie kept saying was, "I don't know what to do. I just don't know what to do."

#

Friday morning the telephone rang and Debbie answered it. She handed me the phone and said, "It's Leslie's mother."

"Great, what does she want," I wondered.

"Hello," I said into the phone.

"This is Leslie's mother."

"Hi."

"I want to know what your intentions are toward my daughter. Do you plan on leaving your wife to be with her?"

Debbie had started packing a suitcase with the intention of going to stay at her mother's.

I said, "It doesn't look like I'll have to leave my wife. She's leaving me."

"Do you love Leslie?"

"Yes, I do."

"Do you want what's best for her?"

"Where is she going with this?" I wondered.

"Yes, I do."

"You don't want her doing something she'll regret do you?"

"No."

"Then don't you think she should be given the chance to see if she can save her marriage? If you love her, don't you owe her that?"

I didn't get any sleep during the night so my brain wasn't working real swift. I wondered, "Why is Leslie's mother asking me these things? If

Leslie is having doubts about leaving Joe, why doesn't she just tell me?" I had many more questions than answers.

"Is that what Leslie wants? A chance to save her marriage?" I asked.

"Yes, but she needs you to tell her it's OK. If you love her, tell her it's OK with you if she takes the time for her and Joe to try working out their problems. Will you do that for her?"

I saw where this was leading and I didn't like it one bit. Tears were now flowing down my cheeks. I loved Leslie so much I wasn't at all sure if I could survive without her. I thought, regardless of how I felt, Leslie's happiness was what was most important. If she decided that she had to try working things out with Joe, rather than be with me, then that was a sacrifice I'd have to make. I wished she had told me before my marriage was ruined, but either way, what she wanted was what I wanted her to have.

"Yes, I'll do that for her."

"Good, here she is."

Leslie came on the line. Since she was there, she had to have heard what her mother told me. I didn't hear her saying anything in the background like, "Don't listen to her. I want to be with you." Obviously, what her mother asked for was what Leslie truly wanted.

"Hi Honey," I said, as I glanced at Debbie glaring at me.

"Hi."

I noticed there was no "baby" along with the "Hi." She seemed to already be pushing me out of her life.

"I think you should take whatever time you need to resolve things between you and Joe," I said, almost choking on the words.

"Are you going to be, OK?" Leslie asked.

"I don't think so. Debbie's leaving."

"She'll be back. She just needs some time to get over the hurt."

Our marriage had been unraveling for a long time. I think this was just the "straw that broke the camel's back." I really didn't expect Debbie to ever come back. I didn't want Leslie feeling guilty about me though, so I agreed with her.

"Probably," I said.

We said goodbye and I hung up the phone.

"Is she coming over?" Debbie wanted to know.

"They're going to try saving their marriage. Do you think we should do the same?"

"We have nothing to save," Debbie said, as she grabbed her suitcase and walked out the door.

I was there by myself wondering what the hell had just happened. A couple of days earlier I had two women telling me how much they loved me and now they're both gone.

"What am I supposed to do now?" I wondered.

I went into the bathroom to get cleaned up. I tried shaving but wasn't doing a very good job. I was crying so much that I couldn't see what I was doing and my hand was shaking so badly that I cut myself five times.

The telephone rang. I prayed it was Leslie. It was my mother.

"What are you and Debbie doing this afternoon?" she wanted to know.

Between sobs I said, "Probably trying to save our marriage."

She could tell I was extremely upset and said, "I'll be right over."

I took a quick shower and my mom showed up a short time later. I didn't know where to start so I decided on the blunt approach.

"I was having an affair and Debbie found out," I told my mother.

My mom knew I loved Debbie, so to say she was shocked would be an understatement. I started telling her the whole story beginning with the first time I met Leslie five years ago. It took hours to give just a rough overview. Naturally, I didn't go into the intimate details.

"I knew she was trouble," my mother said, referring to the only time she met Leslie.

"Please mom, I love her. Don't say anything bad about her."

"What are you going to do now?" my mom wondered.

"I honestly don't know. I don't seem to have a lot of choices. Try to save my marriage, I suppose."

My mom held me in her arms trying to comfort me. It somehow didn't feel as comforting as when I was in Leslie's arms.

My mom left and I was alone again. I was in shock. I couldn't believe what was happening. I sat down and updated my journal with the events that had occurred over the last few days.

It hurt to think. I went back and lay down on my bed remembering all the times Leslie and I had made love there. I started sobbing uncontrollably.

I may have fallen asleep for a few hours. I got up in the early afternoon and tried calling Debbie.

Her mother answered and said, "She doesn't want to talk to you."

I had no idea whether it was really Debbie's feelings, or her mother's.

"It's probably best to give her more time," I thought.

I never drank in the afternoon, but I needed a drink. I went and fixed myself a scotch. I turned on the stereo hoping to find some happy music on the radio. The first song that played was "Three Times a Lady" by the Commodores - one of Leslie's favorite songs. I turned off the stereo and went back to bed. I just lay there crying. I'd never felt such pain before; such depths of despair. I kept trying to drown the pain with scotch but it seemed to have little effect.

A whole day went by and the worst pain I had ever felt was now tenfold. I ached for Leslie. I was going through withdrawal and didn't think I was going to make it. I needed relief from the pain and I saw none in sight. I went to the medicine cabinet to see if there were any sleep aids. I found none. I looked for something that would put me to sleep, permanently. There was nothing around. Every time I thought of Leslie stronger sobs would shake me. The pain was getting ever stronger. I couldn't take any more. I went to my dresser and pulled out my revolver. I always kept it ready for use, so there was no need in checking it. I sat down on the floor, my back against the bed. I turned the gun around so the barrel was pointed between my eyes. I put my thumb on the trigger and started to squeeze.

"Have to remember to squeeze the trigger, not pull it. I don't want to blow this and end up a vegetable," I told myself.

I slowly squeezed the trigger carefully making sure the barrel was pointed between my eyes at a slight upward angle so the bullet would penetrate my brain. I really didn't want to screw this up. I could see my thumb changing color as the pressure increased. The hammer was near its peak and just about ready to drop and put me out of my misery.

As images of Leslie and Debbie flashed through my mind, I thought about my book. "I guess our love story is going to have a tragic ending after all."

I tightened my grip on the trigger. Soon my pain would be gone.

"Who will write this love story once you are gone?" I heard a voice ask. Good question. Who?

I wanted the whole world to read about our love. It somehow seemed very important. Stop the pain, or tell the story? Which was easier? Which was better?

Ending the pain would be easier. I was about a half-second from that.

I wasn't sure I'd be able to tell the story. It just hurt too much.

I decided that someday I would tell the story. I carefully lowered the hammer and put the gun away. I felt as though I was going to explode and needed an adrenaline rush.

It was about nine-thirty at night and very dark outside. I went out and fired up my motorcycle. I took off like "a bat out of hell." The speed limit was thirty-five and I was doing three times that. I was just letting it rip. I really didn't care if I killed myself out here. I'd be happy with anything that stopped the pain. I flew through three red lights at over one hundred miles per hour. The second light was a narrow escape, but I managed to avoid being hit.

The speed was the antidote I needed. The pain had subsided at least for the time being.

I had quit smoking years ago to save money. Now seemed like the perfect time to start again. I stopped at a drug store and bought a pack of Marlboros. I headed home so I could light up. The first two cigarettes made me gag, but after that the deep inhales soothed my soul.

After the near-death experience, the nicotine, and the scotch, I was finally able to fall asleep. I slept for nearly twenty-four hours.

Chapter 44

NOW WHAT?

I didn't feel well when I woke up. I suspected I'd never feel well again. This just made no sense to me at all. I risked everything so Leslie and I could be together and we weren't.

"They've had enough time to try and fix their marriage," I told myself.

I called Leslie.

"I am sorry but the number you dialed is no longer in service," was the recorded message I received.

DAMN!!!

"Should I drive over to Leslie's?" I wondered.

No, she made her decision and I had to respect it. I just hoped that she'd come to her senses. For now, there were more urgent matters to take care of. It was late September and the days were going to start getting cold very soon. Debbie left with the only usable car and my motorcycle wouldn't be much use once winter set in. I had to finish painting my car and get it back on the road. I went out and worked on my car for the rest of the day.

In the evening, I tried calling Debbie. Her mom answered the phone.

"Is Debbie there?" I asked.

"She doesn't want to talk to you," her mother told me.

"That's too bad. I'm not hanging up until I talk to her."

Debbie came on the line.

"Leave me alone. I never want to talk to you again. I'm filing for divorce tomorrow."

She slammed down the phone. I didn't have a chance to say anything. I started crying again. I loved Leslie and she didn't want to see me. I loved Debbie and she hated me. Things weren't supposed to turn out like this.

I got my journal and sat down to read about all of the times Leslie and I had spent together. Tears and snot flowed freely. I went through almost a whole box of tissues. One entry I had made in my journal caught my attention.

I had written, "If tomorrow Debbie and Leslie, both left me, because of what I was doing, I'd have no regrets. Joy has filled my life for now and that was all that was important."

Did I still feel the same way, or did I have regrets? I regretted that things didn't turn out happier for me, but no, I had no regrets for what I did. I will love Leslie forever and I'm thankful for every precious second, I was able to spend with her. I put my journal away where it would sit untouched for several years.

#

Days just kind of ran into each other. I wasn't real sure where one ended and the next began. I'd go to work during the day and come home to work on my car until the early hours of the morning. Every night I'd wish that Leslie was still working nights so I could call her at work. Unfortunately, she was working afternoons at LOF and I didn't have a number where I could reach her.

One evening I came home from work and immediately noticed that all of Debbie's clothes were gone. I did a quick inventory to see what else she had taken. Our wedding pictures were gone. That pissed me off. She wanted to end our marriage and she had the nerve to take our wedding pictures. I called a locksmith and had the locks changed on the house. She wouldn't be taking anything else.

I finally got my car back on the road. I still had a lot of work to do: wet sanding the paint and buffing it out, but at least I no longer had to worry about the weather and riding my motorcycle to work in the rain or snow.

Debbie called - what a shock.

"How dare you lock me out of my own house?" she demanded to know.

"What do you mean your house?" I asked, "You moved out."

Her name was on the property deed. I suppose she could have had the authorities force me to let her in, but I damn sure wasn't going to make it easy for her.

"I need to get some of my shoes and things that I left there."

"Fine, bring back what you stole, and you can have them."

"I didn't steal anything. I only took what was mine."

"No, you stole my wedding pictures. You don't want the marriage; you have no right to the pictures."

"OK, I'll bring them back. Can I come over now?"

"Sure."

She hung up without saying goodbye. How rude.

Debbie showed up about twenty minutes later.

"Here are your pictures. I hope you enjoy them," she said as she practically threw them at me.

While she was collecting her stuff, I said, "Don't you think we should talk?"

"I have nothing to say to you. My lawyer will be doing all of my talking."

Bitch.

"Bills are starting to pile up. You're responsible for them, too. Are you going to leave some money to help pay them?" I wondered.

"No, that's your problem," she informed me.

Fucking Bitch.

She finished getting her things and walked out the door without another word.

# # #

The next day I went to the bank, explained my situation to them, and asked if it would be possible to get a bill consolidation loan using my Corvette as collateral. The loan was approved, and I was able to restructure my debt load so I could pay all of our bills with just my paychecks.

I received a letter from Debbie's attorney. She wasn't interested in the house, my car, or my clothes, but she wanted just about everything else. It looked as if I'd have to get a lawyer to protect myself. If Debbie wanted to be reasonable, I was sure we could reach an agreement on who got what, but if it was a fight that she wanted then I'd be happy to give her one.

# # #

Meanwhile, I was writing Debbie letters trying to convince her to come back to me. I was sending cards. I even sent roses. Four weeks after Debbie had walked out on me; I received this letter from her.

October 19, 1978

Gary,

I did receive your letters, and wish that you had not sent them, and also received the roses, but please do not waste your money due to the fact that you will be needing every cent you can save.
Why do you think I won't be happy if I don't come back, that is poor thinking on your part. Especially, when I have been happier the last month than I have been in a really long time. At least the past two years. I have not even missed you, and every time I think of you (which has not been often) and what you have done to me in the past three years I get ill. Right now, you say you will do this or that with me or for me, but that's out of desperation. I tried for three solid years, to accept your selfishness and childish ways, and believe me it was hard. I am sick and tired of trying to make things work out. There were many times I had thought about ending the whole thing, and I honestly feel it would have ended in time anyway, even if Leslie had not come into the picture. I just thank heaven that this all came to a head before there were any children involved.
Your mother told me that you have always been a selfish person, and after 28 years of being selfish, nothing or nobody is going to convince me that you will change. I catered to you right and left which was one big mistake I did make, besides getting married in the first place.
I have never been so sure of myself. I just wish I had been this sure three years ago, I hope that you are not expecting any sympathy from me, because I'm just sorry that you won't get it!!!!! Please Gary, if you want me to be happy, LEAVE ME ALONE!!!!!!!!!!!!!
I am doing things now that I have wanted to do for the past three years, getting things I need, and even cut my hair, and it is short. I don't even care to

be friends!!!!!!!!! I also can hardly wait to take back my maiden name, also, I did not move out on my own, to get away from my mom, my mom and I were getting along just fine, I just felt it would do me good as a person, to help me grow up to live on my own for a while.

From a person, who wishes to be left ALONE!!!!!!!!!!!!
Debbie (maiden name)

I couldn't believe that was how she felt. It's like we were in different marriages. Me selfish? This required an answer, then she could have her wish, and I'd leave her alone. I wrote her the following letter.

October 21, 1978

Deb,

I received your letter today and was glad to see that you have at least taken the time to read the letters which I have sent.

I'm also glad that you are finally able to say the things which you should have said years ago instead of telling everyone that you were happy. I wanted you to be happy and thought I was going about it the right way since you never said otherwise. My biggest mistake was trying to give you the world. I knew you were used to nice things so I got us an expensive apartment, I sold all of my O-I stock, (which I had been saving for a new TV, videorecorder, etc.), to buy nice furniture for you. You weren't happy with the apartment - so I bought you a house. When we got the apartment, I didn't want you having to go to a Laundromat all the time - so I got you a washer and dryer. I scrape and save all year long so that I can buy you nice things for Christmas. I always did my own washing and ironing, I was the one that defrosted the freezer in the apartment, I was the one that always cleaned the oven, I scrubbed the bathtub the majority of the time, I did the painting, I did the yard work, I maintained the cars, and I started dinner more than once. I'm not selfish, you just never appreciate anything. I kept twenty dollars out of each of my checks and the rest went for bills. Out of your $230 check I had you deposit $100 for bills and you bought groceries (maybe $80?). That left you with about $50 (maybe more). I carried my lunch to work and ate at my desk while everyone else went out. You would hardly ever take your lunch - you always bought it. I enjoy smoking but I gave *it up so I could put money away for your Christmas presents. Two teams asked me to bowl with them this year - but I said no because I wanted to have money to do things once in a while.*

You seem to think that I said I'd change and that this is out of desperation. I didn't mean to imply that I'd change, because there is no reason to change. I tried hard to make you happy and made many sacrifices trying to give you nice things and make things easier for you. You're just so selfish that you want everything and are willing to give nothing in return - not even affection.

What I said was that I realize that I should have spent more time with you - like going grocery shopping or helping with the dishes. And I said that after getting a bill consolidation loan that now we would have money to do things. I like to go out to eat and go to the movies. And I wanted to go to Lake Geneva last year - but I didn't get to because I bought the house for you. Where in the world did you ever get the idea that I didn't like to have fun. I gave up everything that I liked to do so I could give you nice things - and all you did was complain that we didn't have money. You're childish and immature - you're like a little kid that wants everything and cry when they can't have it.

And what am I supposed to be desperate about. Losing affection which I never got? Losing all of the nice things which I bought for you anyway? Losing the help with the yard work? Help cleaning the oven? The list is practically endless - as a wife you were all but worthless.

All you ever did was cook dinner (when I didn't) and wash dishes (and I was always pulling dirty glasses and dishes out of cupboards). The only thing you were really good for was running to the store when I needed something.

Logically, I should be glad to be rid of you. Unfortunately, I will always love you, and because of that I overlooked your faults - which were many.

There is nothing wrong with my thinking when I say that you won't be happy. O-I pays me because I do very well at thinking logically. Of course, you're happy now - you think like a child. You're with your mommy and daddy and don't have a care in the world. No responsibilities at all. The ideal life for a child. Unfortunately, sooner or later, children do grow up. You will have to face responsibilities. It would have been good for you to get out on your own - if it had been longer, and especially if you had been on your own and had to do without things to pay rent and utilities and buy food - like I did for two years before I met you. Life's not easy - and it never is. You have to make sacrifices.

I may not have gone about making you happy in the right way - but the intention was there and I did the best that I could without you letting me know what you really wanted.

You say that when you think about what I've done to you in the past three years you get ill - I don't even know what you're talking about.

I don't want your sympathy - I have no need for sympathy. You are losing much more than I. I won't have any trouble finding someone else - and it certainly won't be hard for her to be a better wife than you. On the other hand, you will never find anyone to love you as much as I do - it's just not possible.

I still love you and want you to be happy, and if it will make you happy for me to leave you alone - that's what you'll get.

There is no alternative but to dissolve the marriage now. You have a lot of growing up to do. Just keep one thing in mind. You asked me to leave you alone, so if you ever decide that we can be friends and do things together - you'll have to call me. Don't feel bad about calling me, I'll always be there when you need me. Regardless of what happens, I'll always be

Your friend,
Gary

Well, so much for my marriage. Debbie was definitely out of the picture. I was still hanging onto a slim thread of hope that Leslie would miss me and come to me.

A week later Leslie called.

"Did you and Debbie work things out?" she wanted to know.

"No. Our marriage is over. The lawyers are fighting over who gets what. I'm still waiting for you to come be with me."

"I can't."

"How are things going between you and Joe?"

"Better."

"Can I see you?"

"Joe's keeping really close tabs on me. The only time I'd be able to meet you is if you came to LOF and spent my lunch with me."

"Is tomorrow, OK?" I asked.

"Sure," she told me.

She gave me directions on how to get there and the time I should come, and then we said goodbye.

#

The next day I headed over to LOF to meet with Leslie during her lunch break. She was waiting for me when I arrived and slid into my passenger seat.

"Hi," she said.

"It's good to see you," I told her.

"I'm sorry," she said.

I didn't say anything. I wasn't sure what to say.

"Will you kiss me?" she asked.

I leaned over and kissed her. There was no passion in the kiss, no burning desire, no longing. I was afraid to let myself go. Afraid of the feelings I had for this woman who no longer wanted me. It was like a kiss that I'd give Debbie, short and sweet.

"Have you been smoking?" she wanted to know.

"Yes," I admitted. "I started smoking again. I've been smoking and drinking a lot trying to cope with losing you."

There was tapping on my car window. I looked up and saw a security guard standing there.

I lowered my window and he asked, "Do you work here?"

"No, I don't, she does," I said pointing to Leslie.

Leslie showed him her badge.

"I think you better leave the premises," the guard told me, "And Miss, if you expect to keep your job, you better get inside," he said to Leslie.

"I better go," Leslie told me as she opened the car door.

"I love you," I told her.

She was now outside the car, so she leaned in to look at me. "I love you, too," she said and then closed the door and walked away.

I drove away. On the way home a song started playing on the radio. It was a song by The Spinners called "I'll Be Around." The lyrics went:

> *This is our fork in the road*
> *Love's last episode*
> *There's nowhere to go, oh no*
> *You made your choice*

Now it's up to me
To bow out gracefully
Though you hold the key but baby

Whenever you call me, I'll be there
Whenever you want me, I'll be there
Whenever you need me, I'll be there
I'll be around

I knew just what to say
Now I found out today
All the words had slipped away but I know
There's always a chance
A tiny spark will remain
And sparks turn into flames
And love can burn once again

Whenever you call me, I'll be there
Whenever you want me, I'll be there
Whenever you need me, I'll be there
I'll be around

Damnedest thing, our whole relationship seemed to have revolved around songs on the radio. I got the message. I'd bow out gracefully. In case Leslie ever decided she wanted me; I'd make sure she could find me. I didn't know what else I could do.

#

I waited weeks to hear from Leslie but she never called. Thanksgiving was soon upon us and I spent the day at my parents'. I was in the living room watching football when I heard my mother and grandmother talking in the kitchen. They were talking about Debbie. My Grandma Rohr was commenting on what a terrible person Debbie was for filing for divorce rather than honoring her marriage vows. I really didn't need this. How could she think Debbie was in the wrong?

I walked into the kitchen and said, "Please don't say anything bad about Debbie. She is still my wife."

They apologized for talking about her and switched subjects. I went back in the other room to watch football. I was only half watching the game. I was feeling sorry for myself. I missed Debbie. She should be here with me.

The Christmas and New Year holidays were fast approaching and it wasn't a good time to be alone. I was worried that if I didn't find someone to share the holidays with, that I wouldn't survive them.

Chapter 45

PATTY

Debbie wasn't coming back to me. She had made that painfully clear. Now it was déjà vu all over again. Once more I had come to the realization that I wouldn't be able to marry Leslie. Wouldn't be able to make her my wife. Once again, I had to move on and find someone to fill the huge hole she had left in my heart and soul.

I wasn't looking forward to dating again. Actually, the dating wasn't the problem; it was finding someone that I wanted to date. I started hanging out at bars every night but didn't see anyone I wanted to be with.

I thought about women at work. I had dated several and been shot down by a few others. There was one woman there, Patty, whom I thought was very attractive. I had never asked her out because I was already with Debbie when she started working at O-I. I knew she had lived near my parents at one time, because we would frequently race each other home. Other than our street racing, I never had any interaction with her. I may have said, "Hi" on occasion, but never really talked with her.

There was a young lady who delivered mail to my desk every day. She frequently sat on my desk and talked with me. After Debbie had filed for divorce, I told her about my situation.

I knew her and Patty were good friends so I asked her, "Do you think Patty would be willing to go out with me?"

Mentally I was very fragile and didn't think I was up to another rejection.

"I don't know, but I'll try to find out."

# # #

The next day she came up to me and said, "Patty is very interested. She would love to go out with you."

My heart soared. I laughed at myself.

"You haven't even asked her out," I thought, "You better get her on a date before you start getting too excited."

I started watching for an opportunity when I could talk with Patty alone. When I saw the opportunity, I used the direct approach.

"Hi, Patty," I said.

"Hello," she replied.

"I was wondering if you'd like to go out with me Saturday night?"

"I'd love to."

"Great. I was thinking of dinner and a movie if that's OK with you."

"Sounds great."

"Is five-thirty OK to pick you up?"

"That's fine."

"Super. Then I just need to know where you live. I know you used to live over on Maxwell, but I haven't seen you head in that direction for quite a while, so I assume that you've moved."

"We're living in Sylvania now. I'll get you directions."

"OK, I'll talk to you later."

"OK, bye."

I headed back to my desk pretty happy that it went so smoothly. I hoped that Saturday night would go as well.

# # #

I was very nervous all-day Saturday. It had been about four years since I last went on a first date with anyone. I hated waiting around the house so I left home early and arrived at Patty's at five-fifteen. Her father answered the door and we exchanged introductions. Since I arrived a little early, she wasn't quite ready. She came into the living room still fussing with her outfit.

"I thought you said five-thirty," she remarked.

"I did. You don't have to rush; I was just looking forward to being with you."

She introduced me to the rest of her family and then left to finish getting ready. I talked with her parents for a while, and thank goodness they didn't ask me any embarrassing questions.

Patty came back a short time later and we left. From the first time we were alone together, I found her very easy to talk with. Debbie was the only other woman that I had ever felt so at ease with so quickly.

We arrived at the restaurant and ordered drinks. While we were sipping our drinks, I asked, "You know that I'm married, don't you?"

"Yes. But you're separated, right?"

"Yes, my wife filed for divorce. We're just waiting for the lawyers to come to terms on who gets what. I want her to get half of our belongings; she thinks I'm selfish. She wants everything."

"Are you serious?" she asked.

"Pretty serious. She has a car, so she said I could keep mine. We just bought the house, which means there's no equity in it, so I can keep that. And I can keep my clothes. Just about everything else she thinks is hers, even though I bought most of it with money I had before we got married."

"She doesn't sound very nice."

"She used to be nice. She's just mad at me right now."

"Why?"

How do I say this?

I took a deep breath. "I cheated on her and she can't forgive me."

"Oh."

Silence...

I finally broke the silence.

"I know how that sounds. It's really a lot more complicated than that. If you want to see me after tonight, I'll tell you the whole story. It's only fair that you know what kind of a person you're seeing."

"OK," she said.

We had a really pleasant dinner and then went to the movie. I was a perfect gentleman, opening doors for her, holding her chair, etc. After the movie, I took her home and walked her to her door. Now comes the moment of truth.

I told her, "I had a really good time tonight. I liked being with you and would like to see you again. I can't afford to wine and dine you like this every night with the divorce going on, but I was wondering if you'd like to come to my house for dinner tomorrow. I'll show off my cooking skills for you."

"I'd like that. I had a really good time tonight, too," she told me.

"I'll call you tomorrow and let you know what time and give you directions to my place."

"OK."

I wasn't sure whether or not I should kiss her goodnight, but I missed getting kissed, so I leaned over to kiss her. It had been so long since I had kissed a woman and it felt great. It wasn't a passionate kiss, but I felt she had passion in her. Her lips were slightly parted, warm and soft. The kiss only lasted a couple of seconds, but I thought about it all the way home and fell asleep dreaming about Patty.

I called Patty Sunday morning and gave her directions to my house and asked her to be there at four.

"I can cook just about anything, but I have two specialties: fried chicken and spaghetti. You can decide which one you want."

"Fried chicken," she said.

"Fried chicken it is. See you at four."

I fussed all day to make sure the house was ready for company. I set the table and placed some candles on it. I ran to the store and picked up an inexpensive bottle of wine and put it in the fridge to chill.

After Patty arrived, I asked her, "Would you like a glass of wine before dinner?"

"Sure, that sounds good."

I went in the kitchen and poured us each a glass of wine. Patty had followed me into the kitchen, so I handed her a glass.

"Dinner should be ready in about twenty minutes. Would you like a tour of the house?" I asked.

"Sure."

I showed her the house and when we got to my bedroom, I said, "and this is the play room."

She smiled - I saw it.

We finished the tour and I went back to the kitchen to finish preparing dinner. I placed everything on the table and announced, "Dinner is served."

"You're a really good cook," Patty told me, after she had tasted everything.

"Thank you."

After dinner, I rinsed off the dishes, filled our wine glasses, and went into the living room to relax.

"Last night I told you that if you wanted to see me again, I'd tell you all about why my wife filed for divorce. We've been married three years, but the story started several years before that."

I went on to tell her all about Leslie. How Debbie came into the picture. I filled in the gaps as best I could and then gave her my journal to read. It took her about an hour to read through it.

"You really loved her, didn't you?"

"Who?"

"Leslie."

"Yes, I did. I do. Always will."

"What if she decides she wants you?"

"It doesn't look like that's going to happen."

"But what if?"

"That's a mighty big if. But IF she wanted me, I'd still want her too."

"What if your wife wants to get back together?"

"That's even more farfetched than Leslie wanting me. Here, read this."

I handed her the last letter Debbie sent me. She read the letter.

"But what if she changed her mind? What if she decides she wants to save the marriage?" she pressed.

"There is no marriage. There's nothing left to save. I'd tell her to forget it."

We went downstairs to the family room to watch some television. I sat on the floor in front of the sofa and Patty sat down next to me. I put my arm around her shoulder and leaned over to see if I could get a kiss. She came willingly into my arms and her lips pressed to mine. Our tongues found each other and desire started to burn. Instinctively my hand reached up to caress her breast. It was the firmest breast I had ever felt. As I massaged her breast through her clothing, I could feel her nipple getting hard. I unbuttoned her blouse and slipped it from her shoulders. I reached behind her and popped her bra snap free and her bra slipped off. I took her nipple in my mouth while my hand massaged her breast.

I had missed having a woman in my arms and I desperately needed someone to love. Someone to love me. I hadn't expected to go so far so quickly. I suspected that reading my journal had an erotic effect on Patty and had got her somewhat excited.

I continued sucking on her hard nipple until she started to moan softly then my mouth sought out hers. As our kisses burned hotter, she started fumbling with my belt. I helped her out. She unzipped my pants and slid her hand inside. I was already hard. Patty started pulling my pants and underwear down toward my ankles. Soon I was free and erect. She took me in her mouth and started working me. It had been a long time since I had any sex and she had me ready to cum in her mouth in a very short time. Seconds before I was about to erupt, I stopped her.

I wanted her bad. I hadn't known her very long and I already felt like I was falling in love with her. I had to slow this relationship down so I was sure of how I felt. Everybody always talked about being on the rebound and if there was such a thing, I thought I'd probably qualify. After losing both Debbie and Leslie on the same day, I could very well be desperate for a woman - any woman. To be fair to Patty, I wanted to make sure of my feelings for her before we did something we would regret.

And what was Patty feeling? Was she just horny? Could she be falling in love already? Was she infatuated with the idea of sleeping with a married man? Was she hoping to land a husband and move into her own house right away? I had learned a lot about her in a very short time, but I didn't know her well enough to answer these questions.

I put myself back together. "I'm sorry," I told her, "I really want you but this just seems way to soon for me."

"I understand," she said as she slipped her bra back on.

"I wish I did," I said to myself. I watched her very attractive body as it was slowly covered up.

"You know about the women I've slept with, how many men have you been with?" I asked her.

"None; I'm saving myself for my husband."

I didn't ask her how she got to be so good at giving oral sex. I assumed it just came naturally. After all, Nancy couldn't believe she was my first woman because I pleased her so well. Then again, I guess Patty could give oral sex while still saving intercourse for her husband.

I wanted to get the discussion topic off sex. "Would you like to come over for dinner tomorrow? You can come over right after work. I'll fix my world-famous spaghetti."

"World famous, huh?"

"Definitely."

"Can't pass that up."

It was getting late and Patty decided she better head home, so I walked her to the door.

"I'll be worried about you," I told her, "So call me as soon as you get home. If I haven't heard from you within forty-five minutes, I'll be out looking for you."

"I will," she said, then she gave me a passionate kiss that left me wanting more, and she was out the door.

Thirty-five minutes later the phone rang. It was Patty.

"I'm home," she informed me.

"OK, thanks for calling."

"Good night," she said.

"Good night, Patty."

#

Monday, after work, Patty came over for dinner. She enjoyed the meal, and then we sat down in the living room to chat. There was one thing she wanted to know.

"After your divorce is final, what are your plans? I mean, do you plan on dating a bunch of different women, playing the field?"

"Although it's hard to believe since I cheated on my wife, I prefer to have only one woman. I'll want to get married again as soon as possible. What about you," I asked, "Do you want to get married?"

"Are you asking me?" she wondered.

"I wasn't, but OK, after my divorce is finalized, would you marry me?"

"Yes. Yes, I would."

My second proposal had snuck up on me just like the first one. I didn't mind proposing. I liked being married and having someone to share my life with. I did however, wish that my proposals had been a bit more romantic.

# # #

After that night we were inseparable. We spent as much time together as possible. The more I learned about her, the more I liked. I tried to tell myself that I was on the rebound, but I didn't believe it - I loved Patty, and I hoped we would marry as soon as my divorce was finalized.

This just kept getting better and better. Most people think you can love only one person and I was now in love with three women.

# # #

With Patty by my side, the holidays were a lot more enjoyable than I was expecting them to be. We exchanged gifts. Nothing real expensive but we were both happy that the other took the time to go shopping for them.

Patty switched jobs, giving up her programming job for a job as an auditor, and started working in a different location than I did. I was disappointed that I couldn't see her at work anymore, but at least I could see her in the evenings and on the weekends.

Patty was saving herself for her husband, so she didn't want to have intercourse, but we sure enjoyed pleasing each other orally. The first time I tasted her I was surprised at how delicious she was, and thoroughly enjoyed being between her legs and pleasing her, especially since she was pleasing me at the same time. I had never done it "69" style before, but with Patty it was great. We would please each other for hours.

Unfortunately, I was never able to have an orgasm this way, probably because I was trying so hard to please her. One night we got each other so excited that I said, "I need to make love to you," and she took me willingly. It felt so good to be inside her; so warm, wet, and tight. I had wanted her so much, for so long, that I came quickly. She held me tightly in her arms as my body trembled.

"I love you," I told her, as I kissed her lips.

"I love you, too."

I wanted to please her the way she pleased me, but she didn't do that thing that Leslie always did to keep me hard, and I went soft.

"Next time I'll hold back until she cums," I told myself. Assuming of course that there was a next time.

# # #

I needn't have worried. The next day she was all over me. She got me hard quick and slid onto me, pleasing herself by using me. I held back as long as I could. She seemed to be having mini-orgasms. She would catch her breath like an orgasm was starting to sweep over her, but then she would continue sliding up and down as if nothing had happened. I couldn't time my release to coincide with one of these mini-orgasms, or whatever they were, so I just relaxed, watching her beautiful body until the climax swept over me.

I loved her so much; I couldn't wait until my divorce was finalized so we could be married.

# # #

I was at work in early January when my phone rang. It was Debbie.

"Hi. It's me," she said.

"A voice from the past," I thought.

"What do you want?" I asked her.

"We need to talk out some things," she said, "I was wondering if you'd meet me for lunch."

It's true; we had a lot of things to iron out. Our lawyers weren't accomplishing anything very fast and I was anxious to have this marriage behind me so I could marry Patty.

"When and where?" I asked.

"Tomorrow, Pizza Hut, at eleven-thirty?"

"See you then."

She hung up without saying goodbye. Where did she get this bad habit?

I was away from my desk in the afternoon. When I got back, I had a message waiting for me. I listened to the message. It was from Debbie.

She said, "I've changed my mind, I don't think we should meet for lunch."

Short and sweet. OK, maybe not so sweet, but definitely to the point.

"She's as bad as the lawyers," I thought, "why can't anybody DO ANYTHING?"

I called Debbie at work. When she came on the line, I said, "Don't do this."

"I was thinking that maybe it's not such a good idea for us to get together," she informed me.

"Yes, it's a good idea," I told her. "We have hardly spoken to each other since September. We need to get issues out in the open so we can get by them."

"You still want to meet for lunch?"

"Yes."

"OK, see you tomorrow," she said, as she hung up the phone WITHOUT SAYING GOODBYE.

# # #

That night, when I was with Patty, I told her I was going to be having lunch with my wife.

"Why?" she wanted to know.

"The lawyers are dragging out this divorce so they can make more money. Hopefully, we'll be able to reach some agreements to get this over with."

# # #

The next day, I headed over to Pizza Hut, to meet Debbie for lunch. I hardly recognized her. Ninety-nine percent of the women in the world look better with long hair. I argued with Debbie every time she got her hair cut for our entire three-year marriage. Now it looked like she had it shaved and frosted.

I skipped the pleasantries. "Your hair looks like shit," I told her.

"I knew you'd like it, that's why I got it cut."

Do I really need this grief?

"So, what do you want to talk about first?" I asked.

"I want to move back home."

"Excuse me?"

I couldn't have heard that right.

"I think we should get back together."

I did hear her right.

"Why? You hated the entire three years we've been married. You said you couldn't wait to take back your maiden name."

I was confused.

"You hurt me and I wanted to hurt you back."

Very grown up and mature attitude.

"I'll have to give that some thought. I'm seeing someone right now," I told her.

"I know, I've seen you with her."

"Oh yeah? When?"

"A few weeks ago. You were driving down Douglas and I saw her in the car with you."

Douglas Road was a major thoroughfare near our house.

"Her name is Patty. We plan on getting married when I'm free."

"Oh."

That shut her up.

It was getting to be time for us to head back to work. I left a tip on the table and paid the bill. As we walked out to our cars, I said, "I'll give it some thought and call you."

"OK."

#

That night Patty was eager to hear what our lunch was about.

"Did you get things worked out?" she asked.

"Not exactly. She wants to get back together."

"Oh…" Patty said, obviously not too pleased with me. "What did you tell her?"

"I told her I'd think about it and give her a call."

"What's there to think about? You told me you wouldn't take her back."

"I know I did."

"I was saving myself for my husband, and I gave myself to you."

"I know you did."

"So, what's there to think about?" Patty demanded to know.

"I think I owe her a chance," I replied.

"I can't believe this," Patty said.

"Neither can I. I haven't made a decision yet. I need to give this a lot of thought. I know I don't want to lose you."

"You can't have us both."

"I know."

Patty left. She was upset. Who could blame her?

I needed a drink. I went and poured eight ounces of scotch into a glass and sat down in the living room alone with my thoughts.

I asked myself, "Forgetting all obstacles, if you could have anything at all, what would make you the happiest?"

Easy answer – "Leslie."

"Should I proceed with the divorce and then just wait for Leslie? Wait for someone that may never come? Just throw away the rest of my life?"

Emotionally, that made perfect sense. Logically, it made no sense at all.

OK, we're looking at this problem logically, so we'll throw that option out.

"Would I be happy married to Patty?"

Easy answer – "Yes." I loved her. I'd been very happy the last couple of months. I enjoyed being with her and our sex was really good. Not extraordinary like Leslie and I had, but it may grow to that point.

"Would I be happy if I stayed married to Debbie?"

Not an easy answer. I didn't stay married to her for three years because I was unhappy, so there was a possibility that I'd be happy, but that was the past. What would the future hold? Would she harbor resentment toward me because I had slept with Leslie? Because I had slept with Patty? Would she resent the fact that I loved both Leslie and Patty, and probably always would? Our sex life sucked. Could she change? Could she become more loving and show me the affection I needed? I doubted it.

Logic seemed to dictate that I proceed with the divorce and then marry Patty.

"Have I thought of everything?" I asked myself.

"You owe Debbie a chance," I heard myself say.

"Why?" I asked myself.

"Because you said, 'til death do us part'."

"But she can't change. She will never be able to show me love the way that Leslie and Patty both have."

"Maybe not, but you still owe her the chance to try."

I'm talking to myself. Either I'm losing my mind, or I've had too much to drink. I figured either was possible.

I had to see if there was a way that I could give Debbie her chance, without losing Patty. Maybe if we just dated, without actually getting back together. That should give her a chance to show her true colors, and then I could marry Patty. I wondered what Patty would say to that idea.

#

"I'm not going to wait for you while you date your wife. You can't have both of us. You have to make a decision," she told me.

"I don't want her back. I want to marry you. I just don't feel like I have a choice here. We've been married for three years. I hurt her deeply and if she wants to try and make things better between us I think I have to give her a chance. I know she'll be back to acting just like she always does within a month and then I can leave her feeling I gave it my best shot. Please give me that chance."

"Her or me, you have to decide."

"She's coming over tomorrow night so we can talk things out. I'll let you know after that what I decide. I love you."

"I love you, too."

#

When Debbie showed up, I was drinking a scotch and smoking a cigarette. She asked if she could have a scotch. She didn't like scotch, but I fixed her one anyway. She tried drinking it while making funny faces.

"Can I have a cigarette?" she asked.

"You don't smoke," I reminded her.

"I want to be the kind of wife you want."

"Who was this imposter?" I wondered.

I gave her a cigarette and held a flame for her to light it. She choked trying to get it lit.

She seemed to be willing to change, although I wasn't sure these changes were for the better.

"I've given this a lot of thought," I said. "Before I can allow you to come back, there are a few stipulations."

"What?" she wondered.

"First of all, you have to read my journal. It documents most of what Leslie and I did together. It'll give you some insight into why I was always running to her instead of you. Maybe that will help you change. Second, YOU HAVE TO QUIT FUCKING WITH YOUR HAIR. Third. You have to try a lot harder at pleasing me in bed. Our sex life is the pits. If you can accept those three things, you can come back."

I was fairly certain she wouldn't agree to those terms, but she surprised me.

"I agree. Where's your journal?"

I went and got it and handed it to her. As she read it, she would sometimes ask for clarification on some of my notes, and I'd explain in more detail what I meant. She read all of it. All of the intimate details of Leslie and me making love in our bed. Details of the many times I had deceived her to be with Leslie. How I even rushed to be with Leslie on our anniversary. Everything. I was expecting a violent reaction. There was none. She coolly and calmly accepted all the gory details. I wondered if the facts were easier to deal with than the scenarios her imagination was coming up with.

When she was done reading the journal, she said, "I'll let my hair grow and I'll try really hard to please you. Can I come home now?"

SHIT! Not what I expected. Not what I wanted.

"Yes, you can come home now."

I went into the kitchen and called Patty.

I had wondered how Leslie could leave me in favor of Joe when she was obviously not happy in her marriage. She was a lot happier with me and still she chose to remain with Joe. At the time it made no sense to me at all. The few months I'd spent with Patty were happier than any I ever had with Debbie. Still, I was choosing Debbie over Patty. I was doing exactly the same thing to Patty that Leslie had done to me. I still didn't think that Leslie made the right decision but at least now I felt I understood why she did what she had done.

"My wife is moving back home," I told Patty as tears ran down my cheeks. "I love you, and I'm so sorry if I hurt you."

She hung up the phone without saying a word. I never heard from Patty again.

#

The timing between Patty and me seemed to be off. It wasn't until several months later that I started hearing a song on the radio that reminded me of her, and then I heard it almost every day for a month. The song was "Sad Eyes" by Robert John. The words that kept replaying in my head were:

She's comin' home today

Try to remember the magic that we shared
In time your broken heart will mend
I never used you; you knew I really cared

Debbie moved back home and for the first three weeks I was sure I had made the right decision. She was a totally different person. She acted as though I was her entire reason for living and no matter how much time we spent together, it wasn't enough. She would sit close and wrap her arms around me showing me a warm tenderness I hadn't experienced during our entire marriage.

She seemed eager to please me in every way imaginable – even sexually. She would pull down my pants and take me in her mouth. The first time she pulled down my pants, it shocked me. I wasn't even hard, but as she took me in her mouth, I grew quickly. Once she had me ready, she would slip me inside her and slide up and down until I came.

In three years of being married to her, I had never been so happy, so content. Then she started throwing up all the time and the sex quickly faded. The thought of having sex made her ill. She went to the doctor. She was pregnant. I thought she was on the pill.

I felt trapped. Obviously, the only reason she was so interested in having sex with me was so that she could get pregnant and I'd be stuck with her.

The thought of having a child was kind of exciting though. I had always wanted children, but Debbie hadn't wanted any. Maybe this was just one more way she was trying to change for me? It seemed like she could have timed it a bit better.

Even though I was looking forward to having a son or daughter of my own, I still felt trapped. I wished that I had other options in case the marriage didn't work out. I wished that I still had Leslie in my life.

\# \# \#

A few weeks later, the phone rang one evening. It was Leslie.

"How are you doing?" she wanted to know.

"I'm doing OK," I told her.

Debbie kept asking me, "Who is it?"

"Leslie," I told her.

The expression on her face told me she wasn't pleased.

"Is someone there with you?" Leslie asked.

She obviously called to see if she could quit worrying about me and enjoy her own marriage. I didn't want her feeling guilty about what she had done to me, so I put on a happy face and told her cheerfully, "Debbie came back to me and she's expecting."

I couldn't tell her I felt trapped. Not with Debbie sitting there. I wasn't sure I'd have told her anyway since it might make her feel guilty about dumping me.

"That's great news," Leslie told me.

"We're pretty excited."

"I wish you the best always. Take care of yourself."

"You too," I said.

She hung up the phone. Doesn't anybody say goodbye anymore?

\# \# \#

The next day I started wondering why Leslie had called. She hadn't said. I assumed that she and Joe were getting along well, and she just needed to know that I was too. What if that wasn't the reason at all? What if she had left Joe and was finally ready to come to me? Would she have changed her mind after learning Debbie had come back and was pregnant? I'd have left Debbie in a heartbeat to be with Leslie. I had to know. How could I find out? Her mother. Her mother would know. I knew her mom wasn't listed in the phone book because I had tried calling there before. I had been to her house once. I wondered if I could find it.

During my lunch I drove to South Toledo in a desperate attempt to find where Leslie's mother lived. Damn! Why hadn't I been paying closer attention when Leslie drove me out there that one time? All the houses looked the same to me. I wasn't even sure I was in the right neighborhood.

Fear that Leslie was ready to be with me and I couldn't find her tore at my heart. Dear God, please don't let this be true.

I had to find her. If she and Joe were getting along, I didn't want to show up at her house and ruin things for her. What other options were there? I wracked my brain. A personal. I'd place a personal ad in the paper requesting that she call me. I placed the ad and had it run for a solid month. Leslie never called.

I never heard from Leslie again.

Chapter 46

WHEN WILL I SEE YOU AGAIN?

I struggled with the realization that Leslie was now out of my life - quite possibly for good. Debbie was pregnant with our first child and I was eagerly awaiting the blessed event. A few months earlier it appeared as though our marriage was over. Debbie had filed for divorce and the institution of marriage had been shaken to its very foundation. Now we had a child on the way. Who would have thought?

While I still ached over the events of the previous several years, that was the past and I was hoping for a brighter future. I sorted through all of the things I had collected over the years that reminded me of Leslie. Cards, letters, pictures, a Sweet Honesty perfume sample, and a few other odds and ends. I carefully tucked them away with my journal for a day when I could look at them without feeling so much agony.

There was one item that I knew would always cause me more pain than I could endure. The little statue of a boy and girl that Leslie had given me. ***"Me and you - You and me - That's the way - It'll always be."*** Reading the words. Viewing her added artwork. Smelling the perfume, she sprayed on it. Seeing "***LVR***" inscribed on the bottom. Being near it was pure anguish. What had brought me such joy when Leslie had given it to me, now threatened to drag me to the depths of despair. I had no choice. I had to get rid of it. I kissed it goodbye, said, "I'll always love you, Leslie," and threw it in the trash. I cried for hours.

Debbie and I started preparing the baby's room. We struggled to come up with baby names we could agree on. For a girl, I liked Jennifer, Rebecca, or my favorite - Corinna Yvette. When I jokingly told Debbie we could name our daughter Corinna Yvette and call her Cor-vette for short, she decided she didn't like the name. We never did agree on a girl's name, so it was with welcome relief that the ultrasound indicated we were having a boy.

We were taking Lamaze classes so I could be in the delivery room for the birth of our son. Debbie's due date was October 15th. The fifteenth came and went. As days turned into weeks, everyone we knew was suggesting ways to induce labor. We went for walks, for long bumpy rides, nothing worked. Three weeks after the due date Debbie started having contractions around 11:00 p.m. In Lamaze class we had learned about Braxton-Hick's contractions and how to identify this false labor. Following the instructions, we were given, we filled the bathtub with warm water and Debbie climbed in. The contractions never got any closer. They were still about five minutes apart. After nearly two hours they finally stopped. We hardly slept at all the rest of the night.

Roughly one week later, contractions started again. Why do these always start at bedtime? We tested for Braxton-Hicks's contractions but this time it appeared to be the real deal. Contractions kept getting stronger and closer together. When they were three minutes apart, I rushed her to the hospital. Debbie was doubled over and in obvious pain as we entered the emergency waiting room.

The receptionist asked why we were there. When I said, "She's having a baby," the lady looked at me like I was crazy. Granted, Debbie only gained twelve pounds so she didn't look pregnant, but you'd think they'd have believed me. When Debbie let out a near scream as a contraction hit, there was a sudden flurry of movement. They had her in a wheelchair and were whisking her away.

I started to follow but they wanted insurance information first. I provided them the information they requested, then they led me to the labor room where Debbie was hooked up to a monitor. A nurse was close by checking the readouts. I felt a sense of relief now that there were professionals taking care of her.

As a painful contraction hit, I tried talking Debbie through the breathing exercises we had learned, but she was in too much pain to listen. She was breathing way too fast and started to hyperventilate. She was getting dizzy and her teeth were tingling. The nurse rushed to get a paper bag and instructed Debbie to breathe into it. After a short time, her breathing was back to normal. We were there for hours and her doctor finally showed up to check her out. He said she still needed to dilate quite a bit more, so he was heading back to his office and would be back later for the delivery.

He was only gone 10-15 minutes when a nurse rushed in to check the monitor. She informed us the baby was in fetal distress. I didn't know what she was talking about, but it didn't sound good. As more staff rushed in to hover over her, I learned that fetal distress was a widely used term to indicate the baby's heartbeat was slow or erratic. This was probably due to the umbilical cord being pinched in some way. If allowed to continue the baby could suffer brain damage or even die.

They began prepping Debbie for an emergency cesarean and I was told I'd have to go to the waiting room. I headed to the waiting room in a daze. I was in shock. I wished that Leslie was there to comfort me. To hold me in her arms and tell me everything was going to be all right.

I reached the waiting room in need of a strong drink and was disappointed to find there were no scotch or beer dispensers in the waiting room. I was glad I had started smoking again. I lit up a Marlboro and took a deep drag. I felt the nicotine course through my bloodstream giving me quick relief from the crushing despair I was feeling.

I chain-lit two more cigarettes and decided I shouldn't be the only one worrying. I called our mothers to let them know I was at the hospital, the baby was in fetal distress, and Deb was being prepped for emergency surgery. I was talking with my mother when I started shaking uncontrollably as sobs wracked my body. I told my mother I couldn't talk anymore and hung up the phone. I wiped my eyes with the back of my hand and went searching for some tissues.

Just a few short months ago Leslie walked out of my life leaving me crushed and broken. Now I was at risk of losing my wife and son. I was scared to think of what I might do if I lost them too. I collapsed into a nearby chair and began a silent prayer.

"Dear Lord," I started, "Please don't let anything happen to my wife and son. I may deserve to be punished for what I did with Leslie, but please don't take it out on my wife and son. Debbie has suffered enough. She doesn't deserve this. Amen."

I briefly thought about promising never to love Leslie again but it was a promise I knew I wouldn't be able to keep. I was wondering if there was something else, I could say or do for forgiveness, when a nurse walked into the room and told me I had a healthy son.

"Thank you, Lord," I said softly enough that only He could hear.

The nurse led me to a dressing room where I slipped on a mask and gown. I was then taken into a room where I could hold my son. Tears ran down my cheeks as I held our beautiful baby boy in my arms. I hadn't felt such incredible love holding someone since I last held Leslie.

Debbie was in recovery and would be sleeping for a few hours so I headed home for some much-needed sleep. For the first time in months, I dreamt about someone other than Leslie. Visions of my son were the focus of my dreams.

As I mentioned at the beginning of this book, I think a person develops certain characteristics based on the name they're given. Two actors that I'd always admired were Robert Conrad and Robert Wagner. I wanted my first son to be named Robert. The fact that Debbie's dad was named Robert made it a natural selection. One small problem. If your son's first name is the same as one grandfather, his middle name better be the same as the other grandfather. So, my first son was named Robert William - after his grandfathers.

The eighties were a very tough time for me. I never received much attention from Debbie and now with a baby in the house there was even less.

"Can there be less than nothing?" I wondered.

I was starving for affection. I knew many husbands felt abandoned by their wives after a baby is born. I wanted to be better than that. I struggled to rise above what I felt were petty feelings but my thoughts turned to Leslie and the love we had shared. It seemed as though every song on the radio reminded me of her.

It would take an entire chapter to list all of the songs of the eighties that reminded me of Leslie. These were some that hit me the hardest: "Please Don't Go" by K.C. and the Sunshine Band; "We Don't Talk Anymore" by Cliff Richards; "Just The Two of Us" by Grover Washington and Bill Withers; "Your Kiss is on My List" by Daryl Hall and John Oates; "(There's) No Gettin' Over Me" by Ronnie Milsap; "Lady" by Kenny Rogers; "Nobody" by Sylvia; "Here I Am" by Air Supply; "Never Gonna Let You Go" by Sergio Mendes; "Always Something There To Remind Me" by Naked Eyes; "You and I" by Eddie Rabbitt and Crystal Gayle; "Truly" by Lionel Richie; "I Can Dream About You" by Dan Hartman; "Missing You" by John Waite; "If Ever You're In My Arms Again" by Peabo Bryson; "Against All Odds" by Phil Collins; "I Just Called To Say I Love You" by Stevie Wonder; "Easy Lover" by Phil Collins and Phillip Bailey; "Part-Time Lover" by Stevie Wonder; "One More Night" by Phil Collins; "Saving All My Love For You" by Whitney Houston; "Secret Lovers" by Atlantic Starr; "Invisible Touch" by Genesis; "No One Is To Blame" by Howard Jones; "Just To See Her" by Smokey Robinson; "Got My Mind Set On You" by George Harrison; "Didn't We Almost Have It All" by Whitney Houston; and "Hungry Eyes" by Eric Carmen.

And of course, all of the songs from the seventies that reminded me of the times Leslie and I were together were played often throughout the eighties.

I frequently found myself back at Ottawa Park hoping to find Leslie there. I also spent time by "our" K-Mart and by Diane's house searching for her. I even drove passed her house on occasion. Some days I didn't even remember driving to these places. It was as though I had gotten there in my sleep. As though my sub-conscience knew I was dependent on Leslie and was trying to fulfill the need. When I was awake, I couldn't stop thinking about her and when I slept, she would haunt my dreams.

#

Two years and eight months after Robert was born, my second son was born. This delivery went much smoother than the first. I dropped Debbie off at the hospital the night before, went home to get a peaceful night's sleep, and then went to the hospital in the morning for the delivery. I wanted to name my second son after some television characters. My two favorite characters were James West and James T. Kirk. I talked Debbie into naming our second son James. I noticed that kids in school named David seemed to have a lot of friends, so I wanted David as his middle name. James David was the name I wanted for my second son. Debbie had a relative named David James, so it was a natural.

When my sons were babies and changing frequently, I carried pictures of them in my wallet. Today I have pictures of my family by my desk at work, but I don't carry pictures of them in my wallet. The only pictures in my wallet are those of Leslie. Leslie gave me these pictures years before I first met Debbie and I've carried them in my wallet ever since. I figure that I see my family daily so I don't need pictures of them in my wallet. I may never see Leslie again, so pictures of her are the ones I choose to carry. Every so often I take out her pictures and pray that one day I'll see her again.

I can't bear the thought of never seeing Leslie again. The hope that I will one day see her again is what keeps me going day after day. When I still lived in Toledo, every year I waited for the new Toledo phone book to come out so I could see if Leslie had her number listed, and every year I was disappointed.

I had told Leslie several times that our love had to be written down in history and I'd been keeping daily notes in my journal so I could write a book one day. At the time I had thought it would take five years tops for the book to be written. I had expected the two of us to be together and the writing of the book to be a happy experience. A time for us to reflect on all the good times we had shared. As it turned out, it was almost five years before I could force myself to even look at my notes. Then reading them hurt so much that I only managed to get through a quarter of them before I had to call it quits. Five years after that, reviewing the notes still caused terrible pain and the steady flow of tears prevented me from accomplishing very much.

In 1988 I was losing my job, and couldn't find another in Toledo. I was forced to look out of state and managed to find work in Phoenix, Arizona. I was concerned that Leslie might want to reach me, so I started paying extra to have my Phoenix home phone number published in the Toledo phone book.

Shortly after moving to Phoenix, I started writing a computer adventure game called "Searching for Leslie." "Legend of Zelda" hadn't been produced yet, but it was that type of adventure game. If you reached the end of the game, and knew where the real Leslie was, you could win a one-thousand-dollar prize. Unfortunately, I was writing the game for an Apple *//e*, and by the time I had gone far enough into development, the Apple computer was fading from the scene. Much better graphics could be found on an IBM PC, but I didn't have a clue how to write a game for an IBM PC. I shelved the project until I could learn to program on an IBM PC. The project remains shelved.

When the Internet became popular, I started doing searches for Leslie. I found lots of hits, but none was the Leslie I was searching for. I started doing Internet searches about every other month, praying that one day I would find her.

When the Internet site www.classmates.com started, I was one of the first individuals to register. I wanted to make sure that Leslie would be able to find me that way if she tried. Nearly every month I'd go to that web site and search for her. I did manage to find someone with the same maiden name, that graduated the same year I did, but she was in a different city. I emailed her just to be certain and of course she wasn't the Leslie I'd been searching for since 1979.

Just in case Leslie was looking for me, I made my own web page and registered it with every Internet search engine I could find. I also left my name, phone number, and email address on every list I could find. I was fairly certain that Leslie wouldn't have too much trouble finding me if she were trying. I only wished that she were trying to make finding her easy for me.

#

Several years ago, I did an Internet search for everyone with her maiden name listed in Toledo. I then used www.MapQuest.com to check the location of every address. I found one located in South Toledo that was in the area where Leslie's mother lived. I tried calling the number and Leslie's mother answered the phone.

"Hi, I'm an old friend of Leslie's and I'm trying to reach her," I said.

"She doesn't live here," her mother told me.

"Do you have a number where she can be reached?" I asked.

"Yes."

"Could I have it, please?"

"No."

"If I leave my name and phone number, would you have her call me?"

"No."

"Why not?" I asked.

"She has remarried, she's happy, and she moved out of town."

"I'm happily married myself. What does that have to do with anything?"

"I don't think it's a good idea."

"Won't you let her decide for herself? Just take my name and number and give her the message that I called. Let her decide whether or not she wants to call. Will you do that?"

"Why should I?"

"Please," I begged.

"I'll take your name and number, but I'm not promising anything."

"That's all I ask. Thank you."

I left my name and phone number. Leslie never called. I like to think that if her mother had given her the message that I was trying to reach her, she would have called.

# # #

Internet growth continues to mushroom at an amazing rate. Every day new sites come online with more information. I believe it is just a matter of time before I find Leslie. I have to find Leslie. I have far too many questions that need answers. The most pressing is why she didn't call me after she left Joe. Or did she? I wonder what Leslie's reaction will be when I finally manage to locate her. Will she be happy to hear from me? Or will she be angry that I invaded her privacy? My spirit is restless and I can find no peace until I come to terms with my past.

# # #

September 2000, Debbie and I celebrated our twenty-fifth wedding anniversary. They have been good years. Hell, they have been great years. If I had never met Leslie, I would be perfectly content. But I did meet Leslie and I can't help thinking about her, and what might have been.

I once told Leslie, "I will love you for all eternity."

After more than twenty years, I see no reason to doubt that statement. I love her as much today as I ever have and as I grow older; I become more fearful that I may never see her again.

Friends tell me I'm crazy to still love Leslie this way.

They say, "If she loved you as much you loved her, she would have been in touch by now. She has obviously left you in the past and you should do the same with her."

It's hard to fault their logic as my logic reaches the same conclusion. However, my heart doesn't buy it. Regardless of her reasons for not calling me, I can't believe she lied to me when she said, "There's no way that Debbie could possibly love you as much as I do. You have to believe that." I believed her then and I believe her now. I may be delusional but I can't believe she will ever be able to forget me any more than I'll ever be able to forget her.

I have but one regret and I'm afraid it may haunt me for the rest of my life. I wish I could go back in time to when I last talked with Leslie. I wish I had told her one last time that I loved her - that I'd always love her. I wish I had asked her to stay in touch so I didn't spend the rest of my life wondering where she is and worrying about how she's doing.

# # #

After I started writing this book, I began to worry about how Leslie would react to it. Debbie hasn't been thrilled with me writing it and she is hardly mentioned. I was worried that Leslie would be upset and decided to contact the Data Research Private Investigation firm in Toledo to try to locate Leslie prior to publication. They seemed to think there are Federal laws preventing them from giving her the opportunity to review the manuscript and gave me this response:

> *Interesting story but we're not really comfortable with it being a permissible purpose (under federal law). As such, we feel it's best to error on the side of caution and, sadly, won't be able to help you with this search. Good luck with your book.*
>
> *Data Research, Inc*

Naturally, I can't in good conscience recommend this investigation firm to anyone and strongly suggest they seek assistance from some other source.

\# \# \#

As I'm putting the finishing touches to this story, I keep hearing a song on the radio. The song is by Bread and it's called, "Everything I Own." The lyrics that keep replaying in my head are:

> *The finest years I ever knew,*
> *Were all the years I had with you*
>
> *I'd give anything I own,*
> *Give up my life, my heart, my home.*
> *I'd give everything I own,*
> *Just to have you back again.*

The lyrics made me think. Would I give up everything to have Leslie back again? I wonder...

THE END